The mutie gator clamped its teeth around Ryan's ankles and jerked him into the river

The creature had incredible power, flailing him around like a toy in the hands of an excited child. The one-eyed man struggled to hold his breath, but it was impossible.

Twice he managed to get fingers on the butt of his SIG-Sauer blaster, but each time the gator twisted him around, dashing him facedown into the shingle, making him lose his grip. Ryan's third attempt was for his panga, and this time he was lucky.

But the cleaver, with its broad, heavy blade, was suited for slashing and hacking, rather than thrusting. Though Ryan tried to use it, the edge simply slid off the great knobbed scales of the giant reptile.

Battling against a shrinking supply of air, Ryan could feel his strength beginning to slip away.

And he was, slowly and surely, being dragged toward the deeper waters offshore....

**Other titles in the
Deathlands saga:**

JAMES AXLER

DEATH LANDS®

Dark Carnival

A GOLD EAGLE BOOK FROM

W❘RLDWIDE®

TORONTO • NEW YORK • LONDON
AMSTERDAM • PARIS • SYDNEY • HAMBURG
STOCKHOLM • ATHENS • TOKYO • MILAN
MADRID • WARSAW • BUDAPEST • AUCKLAND

After twenty-five years of magic and mystery,
wonder and love, this one is for Elizabeth

Second edition April 1999

ISBN 0-373-62552-9

DARK CARNIVAL

It is a profound mistake to underestimate the lure and attraction of a great evil. The highway of history is lined with the whitened bones of those who have fallen into that error.

—*The Abyss Within the Skull*
Thomas Wun

Chapter One

"It's time to go, son," Ryan Cawdor said, holding out a hand.

For several heartbeats the boy didn't move, only stood and stared at the one-eyed man.

"You're Dean?" Ryan asked.

"And your name's Ryan Cawdor?"

The child's voice was calm, his breath billowing in the cold, damp air. The noise of death and fighting was all around them.

Ryan knew that his friends, J. B. Dix, Doc Tanner, Krysty Wroth and Mildred Wyeth, would have reached the shingle beach of the Hudson River by now, near the ravaged ville of Newyork. They'd be waiting for him to join up with them so that they could escape in the recce wag.

"Time's one thing we don't have, son," he said. "Time for talk later. Now we gotta go."

"You my father?"

"Yeah, that's what they tell me."

"Truly?"

"Yeah."

Ryan had never been a man of limitless patience. Right now the boy was pushing things way beyond the limits.

"Don't suppose you got my knife? Green handle?"

"I got it." A short quarrel from a crossbow splintered against the stone wall just above Ryan's head, and he heard a guttural voice bellowing out commands. One of the scalies' leaders was trying to restore some order.

"Dean," he growled. "Now."

Finally the boy held out a hand, sticky with fresh-spilled blood, and grasped Ryan's fingers. Together father and son sprinted into the arched tunnel that wound its way toward the river.

THE BROKEN FRAGMENTS of fading moonlight had disappeared by the time J.B. emerged past the corpses of the scalie guards. A frail snow was falling, driven on a strong northeasterly wind. The shingle was dusted white, and the waves off the river tumbled and hissed on the gently sloping stretch of beach.

"Wag still there?" Mildred asked, panting.

"Can't see. You make it, Krysty?"

She held a hand above her eyes, trying to look a little to the side of where she thought their vehicle might be. It was a trick that Ryan had taught her, and it generally worked. But the sleeting flakes of snow pattered in her face, making it impossible to see anything.

"No. We wait here for Ryan?"

"Perhaps if we were to remove ourselves to the beginning of that broken pier, we might be better able to provide him with any covering fire he might require."

"Good thinking, Doc," J.B. said. "All of us trying to scramble up there in dark and ice, and something'd go wrong."

"I'll wait here," Krysty stated calmly. "Just reloaded my blaster. The rest of you go out there and keep watch for us."

They'd been together long enough to know better than to waste time arguing with the flame-haired woman when she used that tone of voice. With J.B. in the lead, they vanished into the stygian blackness.

Krysty held the silvered P-7A 13 Heckler & Koch in her frozen right hand, feeling all the better for the thirteen fresh rounds of 9 mm ammo in the mag.

She knew that the others would be reloading their own weapons, preparing for the charging pursuit that would inevitably come from the enraged scalies. Krysty had enough confidence in Ryan to believe that he'd come out of the tunnel ahead of any chasing muties.

She flattened herself against the wall of rock, pistol in hand, waiting. Something was nagging at her "seeing" sense, but too much of her mind was devoted to the immediate present. Still, a small part of her brain was whispering "Danger."

Amplified by the acoustically perfect shape of the tunnel, the dreadful sounds of dying were clearly audible. Screams, made high and thin, squeezed past the half-closed sec doors. Twice there was the noise of a gunshot, followed by what sounded like one of the scalies roaring orders.

Krysty put her head to one side, straining to hear

what was going on, imagining that she could hear the clattering of Ryan's steel-tipped combat boots striking sparks off the stones of the wide corridor.

"Gaia, help him," she whispered, her breath frosting the air in front of her face.

RYAN REALIZED how vulnerable they'd all be if a concerted attack from the scalies should hit them out in the open, on the crumbling, slippery jetty. Against his better judgment he stopped halfway to the steel doors, reaching for the spare caseless rounds for his assault rifle. He gestured for the boy to stand still and wait for him while he reloaded.

Dean hesitated, looking back toward the swelling babble of noise and raw menace, then ahead into the unknowable darkness.

"There's friends outside," Ryan told him as he bent over the blaster. "Best you go ahead and join them."

"No. Want to stay here." There was a long pause before he added, "With you. Here."

"When we're out of this, we'll talk about doing like you're told. Can't argue now."

Even as he readied the G-12 for action, a part of Ryan's mind strayed to the ten-year-old boy at his side—the son that he'd never been aware existed, had only known about for a couple of days, had only met ninety seconds ago.

"You chilled all those scalies. Rona said you were the meanest son of a bitch killer she ever saw in her life."

Ryan could hear feet advancing toward them from the main area of the scalies' base, shuffling along as though the muties were trying to move quietly.

"Dean, keep your mouth tight shut," he hissed, "and do exactly what I say."

"Sure." In the gloom Ryan caught a flicker of light from the deep-set eyes and a nod of the curly head.

"Pass that door. Go on. I'm with you." Both of them backed away, around the gentle curve of the passage, reaching the sec-steel exit and edging through it. Ryan considered the possibility of trying to lock it or wedge it against their pursuers.

A brace of feathered arrows thunked against the other side of the door as he hesitated, making his mind up.

He took the boy's skinny arm and heaved him across the open space, passing the bodies of the butchered sentries, out into the freezing air.

KRYSTY HAD HER FINGER on the trigger. The noise of the water breaking on the beach was louder, making it hard to hear whether anyone was coming out. And the darkness had become almost total.

She sensed movement behind her, between the tumbled rocks of the old wharf and the Hudson. She whirled, her right wrist braced in her left hand in the approved shootist's stance.

Whatever had caught her eye was gone. Or had never been there in the first place. Or had been a length of sodden driftwood, floating sullen and partly submerged in the shallows.

As she turned back, a figure emerged from the mouth of the tunnel.

Two figures.

"Ryan?"

"Yeah. Got the... Dean."

"The boy?"

"Sure."

"Scalies coming?"

"Reached the sec door. Where's the others? Everyone make it?"

"Yeah. Out toward the wag. Cover if we need it."

The snow was beginning to come down with a real vengeance, masking everything, dropping visibility to a couple of yards.

Ryan looked around and drew a deep, shuddering breath, realizing how much the past forty minutes or so had taken out of him—the tension of entering the strange, dreamlike headquarters of the scalies, picking his way between the sleeping muties and their chained prisoners, and the startling appearance of his lost son and the brief, bloody brawl.

There were a million questions that brimmed in Ryan's brain, questions about Sharona Carson, Dean's mother, about the whole ten years of the boy's life. And smaller questions, like how come the boy hadn't been chained? If he had been, then Ryan would already be cooling meat inside the cloistered caverns.

"Let's go," he said.

"Where?" The boy was staring out into the blackness, blurred by the whirling blizzard. "You got a boat out there?"

"Yeah. Come on."

Krysty led the way toward the jetty, picking cautious steps across the slippery, icy pebbles. Dean followed her, with Ryan bringing up the rear.

The woman skirted a drifting log, stumbled and nearly fell. Dean also stepped around the length of dark wood.

Ryan was passing the sodden hunk of driftwood when it opened its gaping jaws and made a hissing lunge.

Chapter Two

On dry, firm earth, Ryan's razor-honed reflexes would have carried him clear of the attacking mutie alligator. But the beach sloped, and the tiny stones shifted and slithered under his combat boots. As he started to fall, he threw the Heckler & Koch G-12 toward Krysty.

Then the gigantic saurian, well over twenty feet long, clamped its overlapping teeth around his ankles and jerked him off balance.

Fairly early in their relationship, Jak Lauren had told Ryan all about gators. The albino teenager had been born and raised in the festering bayous of Louisiana, spending much of his time hiding out or hunting among the gnarled roots of the mangroves, the demesne of the big crocodiles and alligators.

"They'll grab hold then roll you, try drag you underwater. Once got you in swamp, roll again and keep you under. Take and store you in tunnel. Like larder. Fight quick or finished."

There was a part of Ryan's brain that recalled that distant conversation, even while he was flailing in the freezing shingle, hands scrabbling for a grip among the whispering stones.

The huge gator was doing just as Jak Lauren had said it would.

Rolling.

If Ryan hadn't gone with it, the weight and pressure would have dislocated his knee and hip.

He heard Krysty scream his name and also a higher, younger voice. Then his head splashed into the shallows, and he was deafened by the crashing of the water.

Pressure pressed below both knees, but Ryan managed to kick one leg free. The alligator had incredible power, flailing him around like a toy in the hands of a maniac child. The one-eyed man struggled to hold his breath, but it was impossible. Some of the time his head was in the cold, snowy air. Much of the time it was beneath the freezing, bubbling river.

He could hear a raging, snarling sound filling his head, but he wasn't aware that it was his own voice making the noise.

Twice he managed to get his fingers on the butt of the SIG-Sauer blaster on his hip, but each time the gator twisted him around, dashing him facedown into the shingle, making him lose his grip again. Ryan's third attempt was for his panga, and this time he was lucky.

The hilt was in his fingers and he clung to it, literally, for the dearness of living.

But the cleaver, with its broad, heavy blade, was suited for slashing and hacking rather than thrusting. Though Ryan tried to use it, the edge simply slid off the great knobbed scales of the reptile.

Battling against a shrinking supply of air, Ryan could feel his strength beginning to slip away.

And he was, slowly and surely, being dragged toward the deeper waters offshore.

As SOON AS the gigantic creature erupted from the dark pebbles, Krysty had turned and drawn her pistol. She saw the futility of it and scrabbled for the Heckler & Koch rifle that Ryan had thrown away as he fell. But even with that in her hands, she realized she could do nothing with it. All she could see was a blurred, tangled shape, flailing and splashing in the bubbling whiteness at the edge of the water.

Dean was at her side, staring intently at the fight.

"It'll drag him under and drown him," he shouted to her.

"I know."

The boy at her side pulled a tiny knife from his belt, with a blade no longer than a man's forefinger.

"I'll do it," he said. "Save Ryan."

"No, you'll only—" But the child evaded her grab, ducking under her hand. He ran the few paces to the edge of the Hudson and jumped in.

"Oh, Gaia...!"

Simultaneously the gator gave a great swirling thrust with its tail and stubby hind legs, and dragged Ryan completely below the surface. There were a few bubbles, and then the dark, oily water became sullen and still.

As THE RIVER CLOSED over his head, Ryan managed a last, frantic, sucking breath, filling his lungs as he was drawn inexorably under. Holding the hilt of the panga in both his hands, he tried repeatedly to stab downward, toward the long, clutching snout that held him fast. But he was blinded, tossed and turned, unable to work out just where the gator's eyes were. The blade jarred as it struck bone and armored hide, but there was no hint of the creature being harmed.

A cold blackness began to crawl across the inside of Ryan's skull.

Another of the creatures began to attack him. Ryan tried to jab the cleaver at it, feeling its claws tangling in his hair, but he was too weakened. There was the illusion that the clamping jaws had released his leg and that he was being heaved upward toward the air.

Then his head broke the surface of the water, and a great surge of air whooshed into his strained lungs. But his hair was still locked by something that was pulling at him.

"Swim, Ryan!" commanded a small, thin voice.

"What?" he croaked.

"Swim! Before any others smell blood and come in after us."

"Yeah," he replied, beginning to kick feebly, hoping that Dean was leading them in the right direction. In the midnight blackness he had totally lost touch with where the shore was.

The boy still grabbed him by the shoulder, his skinny legs pumping at the water, driving them toward the band of deeper blackness behind them. Ryan suddenly felt his feet kick something, and for a moment he came close to losing control and screaming. Then he realized that it was a chunk of long-buried rubble and that he was now in less than four feet of water, able to stand and stagger out onto a sloping beach of sliding pebbles.

"Fireblast!" he panted. "Thanks for that, son. What'd you do?"

"Stabbed it in the eye. Lost that knife. Stuck in the socket. You still got my own knife?"

Ryan wiped the saltwater from his eye. "Sure. Give it you once we're safe in the wag. Which way do we go? That way?" He pointed north, guessing that the struggle would have carried them down the stream rather than against the flow.

"Yeah. Not far. You walk all right?"

"Sure." He turned and glanced back at the river, peering through the drifting snow. Something exploded into the air fifty yards out, a long, sinuous shape, twisting as it leaped clear out of the water. He heard a long, hissing exhalation of breath, rage and blinded agony.

As quickly as it had appeared, the wounded alligator splashed into the dark water and vanished.

THOUGH ETERNITIES SEEMED to have crawled by when he was under the surface of the Hudson, Ryan was surprised to find that they'd gone less than a hundred yards south, not even far enough to be beyond the second of the long jetties.

In between the snow flurries he could now see the yawning mouth of the tunnel that led into the scalies' headquarters. And, at the edge of the river, stood the figure of Krysty Wroth.

"Hey!" he shouted, but the wind carried his voice away.

The woman's mutie instinct reacted to his approach, and she turned to face him, seeing the slight figure of the boy at his side.

As they drew near, she ran and clasped Ryan to her, trying to draw Dean into her embrace. But the boy pulled away, uncomfortable.

"You did brilliantly, kid," she said.

"Don't call me that," he muttered. "Not a kid. Don't like it."

"Sure. You both all right?"

"Thanks to the boy," Ryan told her. "Got an ace on the line and stabbed that big mother in the eye and saved me. Did good."

"Better get out to the wag. J.B.'ll be worrying where we are."

Ryan nodded. He shivered as the wind began to penetrate the soaking clothes and was aware of the boy trembling at his side. "Sure. Don't want them coming back to look for us."

"How about the scalies?" Dean asked. "Bound to be after us real soon."

Ryan took the G-12 rifle from Krysty. "Let them come. We're ready." He turned to the woman. "Lead the way, lover. I'll watch our asses for the scalies."

But it seemed as though the decimating slaughter caused by the rapid triple bursts from the G-12 had been more than enough for the lizardlike muties. The tunnel opening gaped blank and empty.

Snow had covered most of the beach, stretching out

white and untouched. Nothing moved in the night, except the silently falling flakes and the ceaselessly rolling small waves of the Hudson.

The rocks and tumbled concrete of the jutting pier were also coated with snow and glazed with a layer of treacherous ice. Krysty picked her way along it, her silver-pointed boots slipping repeatedly.

Dean was far more surefooted, balancing with arms outstretched, dancing through the whirling blizzard like some elemental wraith, a part of the storm's soul. Ryan, shivering with cold, brought up the rear, glancing behind every now and again, unable to understand why the scalies were letting them escape so cheaply.

A shout erupted up ahead, and Ryan recognized the deep voice of Doc Tanner. Krysty called in reply, and then they were right by the recce wag, its metal flanks rattling as the swell on the water carried it against the rocks.

Mildred stood by the stern rope, Doc by the bow. J.B.'s head emerged from the driver's hatch, his gloved hand waving a greeting.

"Didn't want to risk starting her up until you made it. You got the kid?"

Dean was staring admiringly at the light-armored vehicle, dark eyes fixed on the powerful blaster on the turret. He didn't hear the Armorer call him "the kid."

"Get aboard, Dean, and hunker down. It was a tight fit before you came along."

"Sure, Ryan." He hopped on the slippery top of the wag and vanished down the open personnel hatch.

"Fire her up, J.B., and let's lay us some good safe space."

"I'll get on, lover?"

"Sure. Doc, you and Mildred cast off when the engine starts up and get on quick. Still don't trust those scalies. Could come after us out of the snow at the last minute."

The six-cylinder supercharged Detroit diesel rattled harshly as J.B. tried to get it going again. Considering that the recce wag was around a hundred years old, it was something of a miracle that it was still running at all.

"Give her another shot!" Ryan shouted, jumping cautiously on the top deck, clinging to the muzzle of the Bushmaster cannon.

The engine turned, coughing. Once. Twice. Then there was a full-throated roar, and the whole wag began to vibrate with the controlled power. Ryan beckoned to Mildred, who threw off the bowline and leaped on board, balancing effortlessly, following Krysty down the main entrance hatch.

"Come on, Doc!"

The old man fumbled at the loop of rope, while J.B. gunned the engine. The wag was now bouncing harder against the pier and its blunt nose was starting to swing out, making it harder for Doc to get aboard. Ryan thought he was going to have to help him, but the mooring line eventually jerked loose.

"Jump, quick!"

The northerly wind swooped down, pushing the twenty-five thousand pounds of armored steel away from the shelter of the dock. The gap was three feet and widening fast.

Doc hesitated, hands stretched out for balance. The top of the jetty was so rough there was no way of taking a run at it. Just when Ryan had decided the old man had left it too late, Doc jumped, a peculiar, straddle-legged convulsive leap, like a frog struck with an electric prod. He landed on the sloping side of the vehicle and reached up desperately for Ryan's hand.

"Gotcha!" His fingers tightened around the scrawny wrist, and he heaved Doc alongside him, using brute force.

"Thank you, my dear fellow. Much obliged for your assistance."

The gale and the snow, combined with the thunder of the engine, made conversation almost impossible.

"Get below!" Ryan shouted. "I'm staying here as lookout."

Doc nodded, pausing for a moment to gather his breath. Glancing behind them toward the open river, his body stiffened and he tapped Ryan on the shoulder, his bony forefinger pointing.

Ryan looked through the blizzard and saw what Doc had spotted.

"Fireblast!" he breathed.

Chapter Three

Ryan's fears had been confirmed. The scalies weren't intending to let them get away that easily.

The snowstorm had reduced visibility, but it didn't hide the three boats that were heading around the northern end of the jetty. Each one seemed to be packed to the gunwales with a whooping gang of scalies.

"Get below, Doc!"

"Whatever you say, Captain."

Ryan leaned down, putting his mouth close to the old man's ear. "And warn J.B. Tell him to watch that his ob slit isn't too far open. Just head straight west for about four hundred yards, then turn north. Should shake them off. Got that?"

Doc nodded, easing his way into the passenger compartment and disappearing. Ryan clung to the barrel of the blaster and watched the approaching boats. He felt confident that the scalies would have no weaponry that could do more than scratch the sides of the big wag.

From what he'd witnessed inside the subterranean lair of the muties, their armament didn't seem to run to much more than spears and arrows. And their boats were powered only by paddles, like long, clumsy canoes.

J.B. was maneuvering the LAV in a lumbering circle, bringing it close to the shore, then swinging back toward open water.

Ryan brought the G-12 to his shoulder, using the nightscope. He hesitated with his finger on the trigger. Since they were planning on leaving the ville, there was no profit in slaughtering more of the lizardlike muties. They'd just waste more bullets.

But the wag moved so slowly that the scalies' craft would be able to get alongside, and it might prove difficult to repel boarders. Reluctantly, knowing how incredibly cramped and uncomfortable it was below, Ryan moved to the main entry hatch.

An arrow whispered by his feet, rattling on the icy metal. Ryan half turned, raising the rifle, then checked himself. He stooped by the rectangular hatch and peered into the semidarkness.

"Coming in," he called.

There was general moaning and scuffling as everyone tried to shift to let him in. The interior was filled with equipment and was now packed with three adults and the boy.

While he waited, two more arrows hissed through the night air. Ryan heard the crack of a rifle, but on the pitching river there wasn't too much risk of being shot at medium range.

"Take your time," he called. "Got at least fifteen seconds before the scalies get alongside us. Don't hurry on my account."

"Come on down," Krysty called. "Just watch where you put your boots."

He wriggled in until only his head and shoulders were outside the hatch. Hands reached up to help him, as if trying to fit in the last piece of a difficult three-dimensional puzzle.

The trio of small boats was coming closer, handled with greater skill than he'd have expected from his experience with muties. They skimmed over the glistening ribbon of dark water, their paddles working in unison. Each boat had what seemed like a kind of officer in the stern, handling the tiller. And two or three scalies were armed with either bows or blasters.

J.B. had finally brought the wag around so that its bow was pointing toward the center of the Hudson, where the current flowed fastest.

One of the scalies in the nearest boat was shouting something to them. Despite his best intentions, Ryan couldn't resist the opportunity. He shifted the G-12 to single shot and put a bullet through the creature's throat.

Without waiting to check to see what effect the caseless round had, Ryan heaved his way down into the compartment and lowered the hatch, making sure that it was both sec locked and bolted.

J.B. sensed his movement and finally opened the throttle all the way. There was a surge of power, and they began to roar forward at something close to six miles an hour.

Ryan, squashed, cold and wet, was also totally blind in the confines of the wag.

"You see out, J.B.?" he bellowed.

"Got the ob slit nearly closed, so... One boat right ahead and other two splitting...one each side. Going to board us, Ryan."

"Can we stop them?" Mildred shouted somewhere underneath him and a little to his left.

"No. Go out on top and they'll pick us off. Just keep moving and hope not many get on."

"Sure they don't have grens?" J.B. called.

"Never saw any," came a squeaky, muffled reply.

"What?"

"Boy said he never saw any," Ryan repeated for the benefit of J.B.

"Might they not— My apologies for my elbow, Miss Wyeth. Might these villainous creatures not attempt to puncture our tires?"

"Not with what they got, Doc."

"Hang on. Dark night!"

There was a crash from the front of the vehicle, and for a few moments its forward momentum slowed. Then the impediment was gone, and they rolled steadily on.

"Sank one boat," J.B. reported. "Went right under us."

"Hope the bastards drown," Krysty muttered.

"Swim real good, like fucking fishes. Sorry, Rona told me not to use bad words."

Ryan wished he were closer to Dean, able to comfort the boy. But movement was impossible. They had to endure the cramped conditions for as long as it took.

All of them heard the clattering of nailed boots above their heads. Something bumped on the right side, and there were more feet.

J.B. swerved the wag, trying to deter any other boarders. Immediately next to Ryan there was a ferocious clanging on the hatch, but the locks were strong enough.

"See the other boats?" he shouted.

"No. Had to close the ob slit in front. Some triplebastard tried to push a spear through it. Definitely one sunk. Think one of the others got swamped. One on the left. But we got us around six extra passengers."

The little light in the compartment barely reached the panel of instruments, eighteen inches below Ryan's right hand.

"Which one did you hit that moved the turret, Doc?" he called.

"I'm not sure. Upon my soul, but I'm running a mite short of breath. I think it was the big round one, to the left."

Ryan stretched down, peering to try to read the label beneath the control. But it had long faded into illegibility. Still, it was worth a try. He got his fingers on it and turned it sharply to the right.

Even through the plated steel and above the thunder of the engine, they all heard the screams.

"What was that?" said Dean.

"Scalies going swimming," Krysty replied.

J.B.'s voice came crackling over the intercom. "Shifted some. Hear anything up top?"

It was difficult to make out anything above the

noise of the engine. Ryan was closest and he strained to hear, but there didn't seem to be any sound.

They now had a serious combat dilemma. Since there was no way of seeing out in the darkness, they had no means of knowing whether the swiveling gun had swept all their attackers into the Hudson.

Or just some of them.

"Can't tell," Ryan shouted. "You got your ob slit open again?"

"Yeah. Nothing either side. We're going against the stream and the wind. Bastards'll be pushed to keep up in the boats they got left. Reckon we've got clear of them."

Mildred spoke up. "How are we going to get back to the gateway?"

It was a fair question. In his desire to head away from the scalies' base, Ryan had automatically chosen to move north, along the western side of the ville. But he knew that the hidden redoubt was in the opposite direction. To turn back meant going past the muties again, and he had no idea how much fuel the wag carried or what its consumption might be.

"That river," he said, "the Harlem. Anyone know where it comes out?"

It was the boy who answered. "Comes out about twelve miles north of where we are. Into the big river. Then runs down into the other big river, clear through the ville."

"Sure?"

"Sure, Ryan."

"Hear that, J.B.?"

"No. Something about the Harlem River."

"Boy says if we keep north, about two hours, then we'll see it on our right. Follow it on down and we can get back."

EVENTUALLY RYAN TOOK a chance and cautiously unlocked the main hatch near his head. He lifted it a scant quarter inch and peered out into the cold air, fresh in his face after the stinking fug inside the wag.

He could see most of the deck of the vehicle, except what was directly behind him. Holding the drawn SIG-Sauer in his right hand, he took a further chance and heaved the hatch all the way back. When it struck the steel top with a resounding clang, Ryan heaved himself up, facing toward the rear, ready to shoot down a lurking scalie.

"Empty," he muttered.

THE REMAINDER OF THE TRIP northward was almost pleasant. The biting norther eased back, and J.B. was able to throttle down, chugging along at a steady three miles an hour.

Gradually the sky began to lighten toward the east.

Seen from the wide, powerful river, it was possible to appreciate the appalling devastation that New York had suffered more than a hundred long, long years earlier.

Ryan, J.B. and Krysty had seen pictures of occasional snatches of crackling vid that had given glimpses of prenuke life. But to Doc Tanner and Mildred Wyeth, the past was almost their present. Their concept of "then" was close to "now."

As the dawn rose gently to their right, all of the companions left the cramped compartment and stood on the cold deck of the recce wag.

J.B. had his ob slit thrown fully open, and he was actually humming quietly to himself, thoroughly contented with the goodness of life.

Mildred had managed to work her way forward and was now perched close by him, on the sloping bow of the vehicle as it thrust through the shallow swell. She constantly turned her head to the right, toward the shattered, silhouetted ruins of the ville. Krysty had been moving to join her when she saw that there were tears streaming down the black woman's cheeks. She turned away to join Ryan, sitting with Dean in the lee of the turret.

Doc was standing up, his gray hair streaming behind him, looking like some wild-eyed prophet seeking a promised land of golden spires.

Dean was looking toward the Jersey swamps, arms around his knees. Krysty noticed that Ryan had given him back the small knife with the Navaho turquoise hilt, and it was stuck in his belt. Seeing them huddled close together for warmth, her heart was wrenched by the similarity between the two. Whatever Ryan might pretend to himself, there was no doubt at all that they were son and father—they had the same sharp, stubborn profile, with the slightly hooked nose; deep-set serious eyes and tight black curls.

Feeling the cold wind about her, making her own

sentient hair cling closer to her skull, Krysty looked all around them, seeing the charred remnants of concrete buildings drifting by, with coils of cooking smoke rising farther inland. As far as she could see there was nothing else moving on the river.

Faintly she could hear the sound of Ryan and the boy talking, and she nearly went to join them, wondering what strange secrets they were telling each other.

For the first time since she'd met Ryan Cawdor, Krysty felt a violent pang of jealousy.

"Mind if I stand with you, Doc?" she asked.

They moved steadily onward, toward the beckoning mouth of the Harlem River.

Chapter Four

When the ten-year-old came and sat on the cold, damp stern of the recce wag, Ryan took several long, slow breaths. He could face a dozen ravening stickies without flinching, but knowing he was going to talk with his own son was inconceivably difficult.

"Warm enough?" he asked, conscious that his voice was tighter and higher than usual.

"Yeah."

"Shouldn't be too long before we get to the gateway and make the jump."

"What's a gateway?" The boy paused. "And what's a jump? Never heard of them."

Ryan tried to explain about the mat-trans units, mostly buried or hidden and long lost, about how none of them knew how they worked or how to control them.

"You get in this room, and then you're someplace somewhere else and you don't know where? Is that it, Ryan?"

"Sure. But it's not magic. Science. Lost science. Doc knows a bit about it." He wondered whether he should try to explain to the boy that Doc had been trawled forward from the nineteenth century, then pushed forward just before sky-dark ended the old world. No. Better to leave Doc for some other time.

"There's lots I don't know," the boy said, one hand playing nervously with the greeny blue hilt of the slim knife.

"Man I used to know, called Trader, used to say that he didn't mind a man admitting he didn't know something. But he couldn't stand someone pretending to know something he didn't."

"Rona told me about Trader. Said he was real triple-scary."

"Only to people who didn't know him. Best friend a man could have."

"Where is he?"

"Dead. I think, dead. Yeah, dead."

"Tell me about these people."

"Who?"

"Doc and the redhead and the black woman and the guy driving."

"Friends."

"Did they know my mother?"

"No. Well, J. B. Dix knew her. But only sort of casual, for a few days back in Towse. Ten years or so away."

"Rona said you..." The boy stopped. "Tell me about your friends."

"Sure. Redhead's called Krysty Wroth."

For the next fifteen minutes or so Ryan talked on, giving a potted biography of each of the quartet of companions.

The boy listened to him, only interrupting with an

occasional question. He was particularly interested in what kind of weaponry they each carried. Ryan's own Heckler & Koch G-12 caseless assault rifle fascinated him.

"I never saw anything like that in all Deathlands," he said.

"Might not be anything much like it left now."

Once Ryan's account was finished, they both sat silent, watching the bubbling wake of the wag. Occasionally a fish would break the surface, leaving a momentary ring on the water. Once something much bigger, long and coiled, followed them for a few minutes, a brutish, blunt head just visible.

It seemed as if the boy wanted to talk, as though he had something that was strung up inside him. But the cork was firmly jammed into the bottle, and Ryan couldn't see any way clear to help Dean lever it out.

"Ryan?"

"What?"

"Did you...?"

"What?"

"I mean, how did you find me? Did you come in after me or was it...sort of luck?"

"No such thing as luck, son. Everyone makes their own luck. We only just missed you in that stinking cellar."

"How come?"

"Scalies had lifted you."

"But what about Janya?"

"Woman who was looking after you? Chilled."

The young boy nodded, lifting a hand to brush a

strand of hair from his eyes. "Figured she must be. Stupid, isn't it?"

"What?"

"Spends all that time searching for you. One-eyed man in Deathlands. Must've found fifty of them since I can remember. Then she gets chilled when she finally tracks you down."

It was Ryan's turn to nod. "Nobody ever said anything to me about life being fair, Dean."

"But didn't..." Yet again his nerve failed him, and he abandoned the question.

Ryan let some time drift by. Now they were into the Harlem River, with its broken, jutting bridges and the rising buildings on either bank. Here the devastation was less severe than farther down the island. But the windowless shells stared down blankly on the empty streets.

"What happened to your mother?" It was one of the questions that had been brewing at the back of his mind, ever since he first heard of Dean's existence.

"Rona?"

"I knew her when she was called Sharona Carson. Out in the deserts by the Christ's Blood Mountains. Back then."

The boy shifted and, for the first time, stared directly into Ryan's face. "What she was like then? Was she beautiful?"

The aching need was painful to see and to hear. Ryan, moved on impulse, put an arm across the skinny shoulders and hugged the boy.

"Triple-lovely, son. Sharona was one of the most

beautiful women I ever saw in my whole life. Fair and rare.''

Dean smiled, showing a good set of white teeth. "I knew she must've been. Time I can remember her first, she'd...been hard times and..."

Ryan knew what he was saying. Deathlands was grindingly bleak for beautiful women, especially if they'd known wealth and power like Sharona Carson had. She'd been the wife of one of the most powerful barons in the whole Southwest. Then to become a wanderer, with a baby in tow... He closed off his mind to it.

"She dressed like an angel, Dean. Had a lot of strength and will. An amazing woman."

"Then why the fuck did you leave her? And me? Why d'you do that, Ryan?''

He shrugged the arm from his shoulders and shuffled a couple of feet away.

Now it was out in the open.

Between them.

Like Ryan knew it would be.

"What did she tell you, son?"

"Said that you left her."

"Really? That was what she told you? Tell me the truth, Dean.''

"Sort of."

"Fireblast! What's that mean?"

The boy hawked and spit, watching the white blob of spittle trailing away behind them.

"She sort of said that you left each other."

"Listen, and listen good, Dean. I'll tell you this

once. Your mother was a one-off. She and I had a sort of relationship for a few days, and then her husband, the baron, tried to coldcock Trader and all the men and women. He was a swift and evil son of a bitch. There was a lot of fighting, chilling. Last time I set eyes on Sharona she was astride a powerful two-wheel wag.''

"She used to speak about that. Like it was something she really loved.''

"Yeah. Well... Last time we saw each other we were ready to chill each other. She challenged me to back-shoot her. Knew I couldn't. Would've done with most people. Not Sharona.''

"You knew she was having me?''

"Course not. Only knew her less than a week. No time. I swear to you, Dean, that the first I ever heard I had a son was right here in this ville. Couple of days ago.''

"How do you know I'm your son? Couldn't the baron have fathered me?''

"Course he could. You're ten years old. Seen your face in enough pieces of glass and pools of water, haven't you?''

"Yeah.''

"I look at you and I see me. Know what I mean? No doubt about it.''

"I guess so. Always dreamed about meeting you. Never thought...'' His voice broke, and he lifted his hands to his face.

"Tell me about Sharona. What happened to her.

The woman, Janya, just said she was dead. Didn't give me any details.''

The boy battled for control, coughing and wiping his nose. Ryan had noticed earlier that they'd been following a great right-hand sweep of the river. Now he could see the huge tumbled ruins of a massive bridge not far ahead of them. To give Dean a little more time to recover his self-possession, he called forward.

"Doc?"

"What is it, my dear fellow?"

"That bridge?"

The wag dipped suddenly into the trough of a wave, and a great gout of freezing spray drifted over them all.

J.B. called out a vague, muffled apology from the driver's seat.

"The bridge? I think that it might have been the one named after our most honest of presidents."

"Who?"

"The one who chopped down the cherry tree and would not tell a lie, of course."

"Who, Doc?"

"Crossed the Delaware, wrapped proud and defiant in his cloak, the boat, not unlike our own study bark, tossed between the floes of ice."

"He means the Washington Bridge," Mildred shouted, unable to bear the old man's prevarication any longer.

"I was coming to that, madam. Coming to that."

The boy leaned closer to Ryan. "Why's he talk double-strange like that? He a mutie?"

"Not exactly, son. Have to find time to tell you a little more about Doc Tanner. You were going to tell me what happened to Sharona."

"Yeah."

"Well?"

"I was only a young kid."

Ryan suppressed a smile, sensing that it would upset his son. "How long ago?"

"It was when I was about seven. Around then. Three years ago. Been on the road all my time, traveling. Remember places with snow and places with hot sand. Floods and droughts. Mountains and valleys. Been all over, looking for you, Ryan."

The man risked the arm around the shoulder again, and the boy didn't pull away. "I wish I'd known, Dean."

"Yeah. Been good if we could've got together before Rona went into the long quiet."

"How did she die?"

"Think it was a sort of rad sick. Jack was scarce, and she went with lots of men."

"How d'you...?"

The boy looked up at him, his eyes brimming with unshed tears. "Don't be a stupe, Ryan. Rona worked at fucking in gaudies in pesthole villes. Left me with Janya for weeks. Out west. Bad place for rad sickness. Came back with it."

Ryan had seen plenty of cases of the lingering nuke-bred disease. He didn't want to think about the tall and beautiful blonde, riddled with the sickness, but his imagination was too powerful, too insistent. Images of pain filled his mind: Sharona's strong teeth falling out of bleeding gums; the sweep of hair, like summer wheat, coming away in rotting clumps; her violet eyes turning pink and sinking into hollowed sockets; her thighs streaked with the crimson flux as control over bodily functions disappeared; her smooth skin pitted and cratered with septic scabs and bone-deep ulcers.

That was how it would have been for the lady who had once been Sharona Carson.

"Don't talk about that part of it, Dean."

"She went away before the last of it. Left that picture with Janya, kissed me and walked away into the night. Out of the hut we lived in. Told me she was going to go outside and she might not be back for a while. I knew, Ryan. I was only a kid, but I knew where she was going. Knew I wouldn't ever see her again."

The little body fretted and shuddered, and Ryan held him as close as he could, aware of the brittle bones beneath the taut skin, the heart beating against his own chest.

He knew that he could never, *never* tell his son that his mother had been a feral, rutting, murderous slut, immensely desirable and giving Ryan a sexual experience he'd never forget. But the woman had lacked any concept of morality that anyone might understand.

The engine spluttered suddenly. The wag slowed, then picked up again.

"Stay here, Dean," Ryan said, glad to get away from the welling spring of emotion that he'd released, knowing how difficult this new relationship was going to be.

Mildred called back to him as he stood. "John says the fuel gauge is into the red."

Ryan stared ahead. "Seem to recognize the stretch ahead. Tell him to steer to the left shore."

Dean was at his elbow. "Can I ask you one more question?"

"Sure. Many as you like, son."

"Did you love Rona?"

Ryan hated lies. He looked down into the young boy's face, meeting his eyes. "Yes. Course I did."

Chapter Five

Krysty had read old books as a child, where amazing coincidences seemed to happen to all the heroines and their handsome paramours. So when they seemed to be running out of fuel at almost precisely the spot they were seeking, she wasn't that surprised.

In some way she was more surprised when J.B. reported that the gauge was defective and they actually had enough diesel to keep going for several more hours.

"Least Harry Stanton'll be pleased if he gets his wag back in one piece. Find he can still drive it," J.B. said as he clambered stiffly out of the front hatch.

Dean stared intently at the Armorer. During the journey he'd met and spoken with Doc, Mildred and Krysty, but here was the other person in the team who'd actually met his mother.

"You're not very tall, are you?" he said.

"Next time I'll wear my stilts. And you're not very old, are you?"

Dean grinned. "How d'you get that big scar on your face?"

"He disagreed with something and it bit him," Mildred said.

"No, something he disagreed with ate him," Doc insisted.

"That's wrong, you dogmatic old fart. Comes from an old James Bond vid."

"I know that. Felix the CIA agent. Think there's something awry with my memory, you doxologizing old windbag!"

J.B. held up a hand to stop the argument. "Insect bite that turned bad."

"Daylight's wasting," Ryan observed. "Let's get on to the gateway. Usual skirmish line. Dean, you stick with Krysty in the center."

"I'll come with you."

Ryan turned and bent down, grabbing the boy by the front of his ragged jacket and lifting him up onto his toes.

"One rule, boy!" The man's voice grated and was tight with anger. "Do like I tell you. Argue afterward, not before. Remember that, and we all stay alive. Forget it, and you can get us all chilled. You understand me?"

"Yeah. I understand. Sorry, Ryan. Won't do it again. I swear."

"Good. Let's go. Everyone got their rope?"

The coils of strong cord that they'd acquired in the ville were about to prove their worth.

THE STREETS WERE deserted. A watery sun had broken through a band of high, pink-streaked cloud, bringing little warmth to the snow-dappled ville.

"Don't know this part," Dean said to Krysty. "Never got this far north. This place close?"

"Not too far. Listen, when we're in a skirmish line like we are now, it means everyone on maximum concentration, watching and listening."

"And not talking, Krysty?"

"You got it."

Ryan led the way past the various signs of the street gangs' turfs, looking for the distinctive bird of prey—daubed in red paint, with yellow hooked beak and oversize claws—that marked off the Hawks' own part of the South Bronx.

He began to spot them as he neared the ruined hulk of the old Yankee Stadium. But many of them had been covered with a white fist, showing where another gang had moved in on the territory of the leaderless Hawks.

Someone shouted and a stone was thrown, skittering along the ice-covered pavement. Ryan swung the muzzle of the G-12 toward the call, but the avenue was deserted.

"Keep moving," he ordered over his shoulder.

For a moment he had an awful nagging doubt that he might not recognize the mansion that concealed the buried gateway.

It was an odd fact that Ryan Cawdor could find his way through a featureless wilderness with unerring accuracy. Yet in these urban ruins he was uncomfortable. Every street seemed the same, every pile of twisted, scorched rubble like another.

He was tempted to ask Krysty or one of the others

for guidance, but that was to show doubt. And the leader who showed doubt wasn't really a leader. Yet another of the Trader's little homilies.

There was a long street with a tumbled wall on one side and some stunted, diseased shrubs flanking the wreckage of the houses. Down to their left he could see the colossal shape of what had been Yankee Stadium.

They were getting closer.

"Ryan!" Mildred called.

"What?" He lifted a hand to halt them.

"Isn't that…?" She started to point to a building that Ryan had already marked as a probable.

"Sure it is. Just keep close."

He knew that if he turned and caught Krysty's eye, she'd know that he hadn't been really sure. Some things a man liked to keep close.

J.B. STAYED TOPSIDE while the rest of them picked their way slowly and carefully toward the entrance to the long-hidden elevator shaft.

The huge sec doors, bent and twisted, remained slightly ajar, just as they'd left them. The large empty room didn't look any different. Ryan pushed his head through the gap, peering down into the cold, sighing darkness.

"Don't think anyone's been here."

From behind and above they all heard a faint whistle.

"Stay here," Ryan snapped, running up toward the pale light of day.

The Armorer was crouched, peering between the jagged ends of a broken pillar. He pointed to his right. "Company. Four."

"Scalies?"

J.B. shook his head. "Street gang. They must've been trailing us. The shaft open?"

"Yeah. Doesn't look touched."

The Armorer flashed him a rare smile. "Be a great place to get ambushed. Halfway down there, swinging on bits of rope."

Ryan risked a glance out onto the street. At first he saw nothing, then his eye caught a flicker of movement across the way—a pale, feral face, with a headband of ragged white cloth. As soon as Ryan was spotted, the head bobbed down out of sight.

"Better get to it. No profit trying to take them out. Bring more down on us."

J.B. considered the options. "Guess so. Want me to stay here or come help?"

"Need you with the ropes. I'll send the boy to watch."

"Dark night, Ryan! You sure?"

"Sure."

"Kid of ten."

"I know. Way he's lived, he should be fine."

J.B. wasn't an arguing sort of a man. "Fine by me."

DEAN WAS DELIGHTED to be trusted with such an important mission.

"Give me a blaster, Ryan."

"No. I don't want chilling. I want to know if the stupes up there make a move. You shout and tell us, then you get your ass down here."

"Sure." He reached out a skinny hand and slapped Ryan on the palm. "On my way, José!"

His feet pattered up the filthy staircase.

"I am inclined to the opinion that the young man might prove to be rather a handful, would you not agree, my dear Cawdor?"

"I agree, Doc."

"THREE HUNDRED FEET." J.B. had dropped a small, rough pebble down the shaft. Head to one side, he counted to himself, all of them silent as they waited. When the sound came, it was very small and far-off, swallowed by the shaft.

Ryan nodded. "Yeah. I make it around three hundred. How much rope we got?"

Everyone had uncoiled the loops of thin, strong cord from around their waists. J.B. ran them through his hands, measuring them against his own arms' span. "Each one's close to twenty feet. Call it a hundred feet, give or take a few."

"Two hundred feet short," said Mildred. "Longish sort of a jump, John."

"We aren't jumping," he replied, his voice showing his preoccupation.

"It was a joke, John. Just a small joke."

Doc laughed quietly. "A *very* small joke, if I may make so bold."

She ignored him.

"In stages," Ryan mused. "Need anchoring points on the way. Difficult."

"Not impossible. Trouble is…" J.B. paused. "Trouble is, if it can't be done, we'll only find out when it's too late and we can't climb back up to the top again."

Krysty patted Ryan on the arm. "Kind of trip I like, lover. Only one way and all downhill."

WHILE THE OTHERS STARTED knotting the lengths of rope together, Ryan went back up the staircase again, calling to his son.

"Anything, Dean?"

"Double-creep street kids. I made around eight or nine. More joining up with them all the time."

"Think they're going to come at us?"

The boy considered the question. "Yeah. But they're all chicken-shit, and they probably seen the blasters we got."

"Fine. We're nearly ready. Soon as I shout for you, come straight down."

"Sure."

The boy looked out again through a gap he'd made between two fallen piles of bricks. Ryan watched him for a moment, seeing the excited set of the shoulders, noticing the boy's hand was resting on the turquoise hilt of his slim knife.

"Dean," he said.

"What is it, Ryan?"

"Just…take care."

The boy smiled. "I will, Dad."

"TROUBLE IS, IT'S BLACKER than a stickie's soul down there." J.B. was on hands and knees. He looked around as Ryan rejoined them.

"Clear up top, but the gang's gathering. We'd better move."

"I don't want to make the first tie-off out here. Too bastard vulnerable. One knife cut, and we'll have us about four and a half seconds to think about eternity."

"And kiss our asses goodbye," Mildred muttered. "Christ, friends, but I surely wish that this was over and I in my bed again."

"I'd like that very much," J.B. said quietly.

"Better move before we get company down here." Ryan glanced behind them, listening for any threatening noise. Nothing.

Doc had also been staring into the void. "Is there no other way to get at the gateway? I fear that the journey thither seems beyond the realms of possibility."

"You can always stay here, Doc," Krysty said, patting him on the arm. "You'll be fine. Be over before you know it."

"Yes," he replied, drawing out the syllable. "That is what concerns me, my dear."

"How we doing this if it's much longer than the rope?" The boy had gone to the brink of the shaft, looking fearlessly into it.

J.B. finished knotting the cords. "Long as we can find something partway down to tether to we're fine. Use a release knot up here. All get down and wait.

Then tie off and do it again. Three times should do it.''

''Yeah…but…''

''What, kid?''

''Don't call me 'kid,' please. What if there's nowhere on the way down to rest?''

Ryan smiled at his son. ''Then we fight our way out of here and find some other place.''

Above them they all heard a muffled shout and stones clattering. J.B. looked around at his friends. ''Time to go, people.''

Chapter Six

Dean plucked at Ryan's sleeve.

"What?"

"How about him?"

"Who?"

"The old man."

"Doc? What about him?"

"He won't get down a rope."

"Why not?"

"Too old. I never seen anyone old as him. How come he's not dead?"

Doc had good hearing, and he caught the end of the exchange. "I often ask myself the same question, young friend. But worry not. One day I shall explain to you all the facts about my true age. I'll get down the rope as well as you."

Dean sniffed, not bothering to conceal his considerable disbelief.

"Right." The voice of the Armorer was muted, reaching them from inside the top of the shaft.

"Got it tied?"

"Yeah. Plenty of shit around here to use. Old winding gear. Might not be so easy farther down. I'll go first. Rest of you follow when I call. Not before."

"Mildred first?" Ryan looked at her.

She nodded. "Sure. Used to wow them in gym classes with my rope climbs. Going down should be easier."

"Brace it between your feet. Hand over hand. Don't slide. Whatever you do, don't slide."

She grinned at him. "See you down there."

"Wait for the word," Ryan said. "Doc, you next. Then you, Dean. Krysty and then me last."

"I confess that I've never really been all that good at heights, my dear Cawdor."

"Fastest you can go is about a hundred and twenty-five miles an hour, Doc. What they call terminal velocity," Mildred whispered. "And in three hundred feet you won't get anywhere near that speed."

"Your so-called sense of humor, madam, is about as funny as undergoing an urgent appendectomy at the hands of a blindfolded, drunken gorilla."

Mildred paused in the damaged doorway and blew him a kiss. "Wish me luck as you wave me good-bye," she said.

Dean tugged at Ryan's sleeve. "I can hear them up top. Be here soon."

"Yeah. Better give them something to think about, huh?"

The boy grinned.

J.B.'s voice came from the echoing shaft. "Ready in here."

"You get moving," Ryan said. "I'll just wait awhile."

The Heckler & Koch G-12 caseless rifle was set on

triple-burst. Single shot would be less effective, and full-auto a waste of precious ammo.

Ryan moved, light-footed, to the bottom of the flight of stairs, picking a position to the right, under an alcove. Hidden in a block of dark shadows, he watched as the others pushed their way past the elevator sec doors and reached for the dangling lengths of rope.

Krysty was last.

She gently shepherded the young boy in front of her, patting him on the shoulder to encourage him into the freezing chasm. Her eyes, glittering emerald in the dim light, turned toward Ryan's hiding place.

"Don't take too long, lover," she called quietly. Then she eased herself past the dull metal of the doors and out of his sight.

Ryan was only too aware of how intensely vulnerable their position was. If any of the gang in the street above came down from the ice-shrouded rubble while they were still climbing on the thin cords, then life would become very brief and bloody.

The one-eyed man waited.

A tiny pebble, hardly larger than a grain of dust, came skittering down the flight of steps, reaching the bottom and rolling from sight.

They were on their way.

The tip of Ryan's tongue flicked out and ran across his dry lips. Now he could hear whispering, the shuffle of boots on concrete, the rasp of clothes, once the dry sound of a blaster being cocked. Even a muffled cough.

Ryan's finger tightened, putting a couple more ounces of pressure on the release mechanism.

The shadow of the first of the invaders was edging along the steps, sliding down toward the floor, then was joined by a second. The whispering voices carried clearly to Ryan.

"Fuck gone."

"Look, sec doors."

"Hey…blown fuckin' open. Must have good blasters for that."

"More stairs?"

"Gotta be."

"Follow 'em."

"Yeah." The shadows moved quickly toward the warped sec doors to the elevator shaft.

"No," Ryan Cawdor snarled.

As a firefight, it never even got close to first base.

Ryan drew a bead on the shoulders of the leader of the gang, aiming at the center of the clenched white fist daubed on the back of the tattered jacket.

He squeezed the trigger and felt rather than heard the triple concussion, the three rounds so close together they sounded like a single shot.

He wasn't even watching as the teenager was flung forward by the hammering impact of the caseless bullets, his chest exploding with gobbets of flesh and shards of white, splintered bone.

Ryan shifted his aim, his finger tightening repeatedly on the trigger.

Twelve rounds were spit out in less than four seconds, and the first quartet of the white-fist gang was clinically dead in the dirt at the bottom of the stairs.

Only now did Ryan move from his hiding place, darting to one side so that he could see up the old staircase.

There were four or five more of the skinny youths, only one holding a blaster. Ryan shot him through the throat, the bullets also killing the lad behind him.

The others dropped their knives and ran screaming up and out into the street beyond.

Ryan considered going after them, but he mastered the killing urge. Slinging the rifle across his shoulders and moving past the jumble of bodies, he squeezed through the narrow gap in the doors and reached for the knotted rope.

WHEN THE ELEVATOR CAGE had tumbled down the shaft, trailing its snapped cables behind, it had done considerable damage to the interior of the shaft. Some of the rusted supports had come away from the sides, leaving a number of places where they could all rest in comparative safety before pulling down the rope from its release knot above. It would then be retied and the procedure repeated.

"Going to have to get through the remains of the elevator," J.B. said. "Must be wrecked down at the bottom."

"Shouldn't be that difficult." Ryan tried to see into the stygian pit. "Face it when we get there."

The only serious problem that confronted them was the ice. During the time that they'd been in the ville of Newyork there'd been a lot of snow and rain. It had seeped through and run down the inside of the shaft, coating everything in a hard, glassy layer.

It was difficult to fix the ropes, and Ryan had to use the eighteen-inch blade of his panga to chip away at the ice, sending hundreds of tiny diamond splinters cascading to the bottom of the shaft.

Despite the problems, they eventually made it safely down. There'd been some alarms and diversions on the way, the worst of them being Doc Tanner's boots slipping as he abseiled down. For some unaccountable reason this left him dangling upside down, swinging slowly and majestically like an antiquated pendulum.

It was Dean who shinned down the narrow cord to help the old man, hanging on by one hand while he tugged him the right way up. He allowed Doc time to recover his equilibrium, then carried on to the next tethering point with him.

When Ryan came down last, Doc still had his arm around the ten-year-old. It was hard to tell who was pretending to comfort whom.

THE THREE-HUNDRED-FOOT fall had smashed apart the passenger compartment of the elevator like a matchstick box. The roof had split back like a peeled orange, and the sides had impacted and fragmented. The whole cage was less than three feet high, giving them all a chilling glimpse of what their fate would have been if they'd failed to escape the drop.

One by one they picked their way through the devastated heap of twisted metal and plastic into the passage beyond.

Ryan was the last one out of the shaft, and he paused for a moment as he heard faint echoing shouts above them. He strained his head back and peered toward the tiny pinprick of silver light, but he couldn't see anything.

As he joined the others, they all heard a series of rumbling crashes as lumps of masonry were heaved down the shaft.

"Close, lover," Krysty commented.

"Not close enough," Ryan replied, grinning.

THE COMPANIONS WALKED down a staircase and then along a curving passage, its walls hewn from living rock. Bare quartz glittered in the darkness.

The overhead lights seemed even more faint than they'd been a few days ago. J.B. led the way through the control area and into the anteroom next to the gateway entrance.

Dean hung back, his face turned up to his father's. "We have to go in there?"

"Only way out of here."

"You sure I'll be safe?"

Ryan knelt by his son. "It's unpleasant and it can be dangerous. I won't lie to you about that. But it'll get us someplace else. And whatever happens, happens to all of us."

The boy smiled, reaching out to take Ryan's hand. "Then let's go."

Chapter Seven

"How's it—"

"Just sit down here, back against the wall, like the others."

The boy looked around. Doc was squatting to his left, cross-legged, knees cracking like muskets. Krysty was making herself comfortable beyond Ryan. Next was Mildred, leaning back, an expression of unease on her face. J.B. was last around, taking off his spectacles and folding them carefully before tucking them into one of the pockets of his capacious coat. He caught Dean's eye and winked at him.

"Doesn't take long," he said.

"Sure," Mildred agreed. "It's like banging your skull against a wall, Dean. Terrific when you finally stop."

Ryan patted the boy on the head. "Ignore them. You'll feel a bit dizzy and maybe a bit sick. You black out. We all do. Nothing to worry about."

"How does it work?"

Krysty laughed. "Work that one out for us, Dean, and you'll get the biggest ace on the line ever. Last person who knew the answer to that probably died off around a hundred years ago."

Ryan moved to the heavy door, hesitating with his

hand on it. "All we know is that we shut this and there's a kind of humming noise and a sort of mist. And then we're someplace else."

"Could we be someplace…dead?"

Ryan shook his head. "Never happened yet. Everyone ready? Here we go."

He tugged the door shut, hearing the familiar solid click of the locking mechanism. He moved into the space beside his son and sat down, stretching his legs out ahead of him, pressing back against the cold, golden armaglass.

The metal disks in the floor and ceiling began to shimmer, and tendrils of pale fog came ghosting out of the empty air. A distant humming sound, like a thousand hives of bees in a far-off valley, began to filter into the chamber.

"My head hurts, Ryan," Dean said, pressing his hands over his ears.

"Soon be over."

He could feel the whole thing vibrating against his spine, more strongly than he remembered, quivering like War Wag One tackling a deep incline. The humming grew louder.

On one side Krysty was reaching for his hand, shouting something he couldn't hear. On the other side Dean was screaming, high and shrill. Ryan glanced down and saw that a thin caterpillar of dark venous blood was trickling from the boy's nostrils.

Doc was halfway across the polished floor, hands out toward Ryan like claws. The old man's pale rheumy eyes were staring blindly, almost as though someone were behind them, trying to press them out of the sockets. Blood seeped from the corners of Doc's open, mutely screaming mouth.

Mildred had fallen sideways, her face as gray as parched soil, her knees drawn up to her chest in an agonized fetal curl.

J.B. was trying to get to his feet, reaching toward the locked door, but the wraiths of cloud were now so thick inside the chamber that he'd become almost invisible.

The vibration was getting worse and worse, and Ryan could feel a jolting within his spine, as though a steel rod were being rotated in the core of each individual vertebra.

There was a voice inside his head, a harsh, slow voice, with a grating Louisiana accent. "Does the controlling control need control?"

Ryan knew that something had gone appallingly wrong.

And he knew that it was too late to do anything about it. His final sentient thought was to reach out with both hands—one toward Krysty and the other toward his son.

Then came blackness.

Then light.

Chapter Eight

Krysty stood on tiptoe, the rock warm and rough beneath her bare feet, the sun hot across her shoulders, glowing over her bare breasts, rousing her taut nipples. She flexed the muscles that tightened along the back of her thighs, into the firm buttocks. Lifting her arms slowly, she looked out across the lake of azure water toward the snow-tipped peaks in the distance.

She breathed in slowly, filling her lungs with the cold thin air of the high country, tasting sagebrush and the sharp scent of balsam from the ocean of dark pines on the mountains around. She didn't look down.

The drop to the water was more than fifty feet, a gasping exhilaration as you sprang out, a second and a half of freedom before your arms sliced the icy water apart and the shock of plunging beneath the surface.

The lake was several miles from Harmony ville, and few ever bothered to take the long, winding trail. The area was known to harbor a number of savage mutie grizzlies and her uncle, Tyas McCann, had warned her to take the greatest care.

But she refused to carry a blaster, relying instead on her own power of "seeing" to warn her of the proximity of any harmful creature.

Mother Sonja had told her how to behave if she encountered one of the forest behemoths—try to make oneself small and back slowly away; don't make any challenging eye contact with the beast. The chances were very good that it wouldn't go after someone unless it felt threatened.

That thought came to Krysty as she readied herself for the dive. And freedom.

This time was different. There was no sensation of the swooping plunge into the lake.

Krysty had closed her eyes in an almost sexual anticipation of the moment. Now she opened them, blinking in disbelief, almost blinded by the platinum sheen of the sun dazzling into her face.

She hung there, maybe eight feet out from the cliff top. Stasis, a stillness.

Finally she looked down.

To where the mirrored surface of the lake should have been. Instead there were jagged rocks, like red-orange spears and daggers, gathered beneath her, waiting to accept her fragile skin, flesh and bone and crush and tear them to bloodied flags.

Motionless in space, not daring to try to move so much as a finger, Krysty Wroth began to scream.

And scream.

DOC TANNER FELT the familiar, sickening sensation as the gateway began to function. It seemed as though the inside of his skull were being fluffed and folded, his brain being sucked and scraped out of the familiar creases and wrinkles of moist bone.

He'd been five years old, still living in South Strafford, a tiny hamlet in the wilds of Vermont. During the harvest a traveling medicine show had come through, a poor, threadbare group, selling quack curealls from the back of a rickety Conestoga wagon. The outfit was led by an old man with a patch over one eye and his younger wife, a handsome black woman with plaited hair. Their daughter had danced for money thrown by the local rubes. She'd been a tall girl, with a mane of scarlet hair that whirled about her brocaded shoulders as her bare feet skimmed the mown grass.

There'd been another child, Doc remembered, hiding in the shadowy depths of the rig, peeking out now and again through eyes like molten rubies. The boy had been an albino with milky skin and hair like the finest sierra snows.

And there'd been a merry-go-round, operated by a small, wiry man who had a pince-nez with golden frames. It was simply a circle of seats surrounding a central pillar, garishly painted with designs that seemed to have their origins in the Mexican celebrations for the dead—yellow skulls and gibbering skeletons; fleshless fingers that beckoned to the excited children as the carousel whirled them around and around.

The little man spun it by hand, slowly at first.

So that little Theo Tanner and the others could see their watching mothers' faces going by, could take in the long straight street of the village with its sharp bend at the northernmost point and all around the endless undulating carpet of trees.

Faster.

Now the faces were blurred as they hissed by, and your eyes betrayed you so that you couldn't quite focus on anything anymore.

Faster.

Theo realized that he was on his own on the smooth polished seat. The other children—his laughing chums—had vanished.

So much faster.

Now there was nothing to be seen, except a swirling, endless smear of colors, the only sound a high whining from the friction of the central pillar, a sound that rose until it passed beyond human hearing, sending farm dogs into hysterical, barking rages.

Doc was aware that he was crying, tears flooding his eyes, running down over the grizzled stubble on his cheeks. His fingers gripped at the bar along the rear of the seats, his lips moving in a silent, pattering prayer.

A rope of saliva dangled from his chin onto his waistcoat. His swordstick, with its silver lion's head hilt, spun away from his feet and disappeared.

It wasn't humanly possible to rotate at such a speed. He was pushed back in the chair, feeling the skin on his face tightened by the whirling force.

Doc began to weep.

And weep.

J. B. DIX SAT crouched over in the dead end of a long, narrow tunnel, holding an empty .25-caliber Bauer automatic. With a neutral satin stainless finish and American walnut grips, the little gun looked much like the Baby Browning.

"Know everything about it," he whispered, holding the cold metal against his cheek. "Made in Fraser, Michigan. Bauer Firearms Corporation. Says so, right here on the side of the barrel in this pretty, incised writing."

The walls of the tunnel were bare earth, running with brackish water. It was two feet and four inches wide and less than three feet from muddy floor to dripping roof.

J.B. tightened his finger on the trigger, knowing what would happen if he squeezed it. There'd be the cold click of the dry-fire, the noise carrying through the lingering stillness far beneath the earth. Bringing them to him.

"Empty," he said.

There was nowhere left.

He couldn't quite recall why he was in the tunnel, or whom he'd been with. There was the memory of a woman. Funny. He knew her name but couldn't remember what she'd looked like.

"Mildred."

The darkness was pressing in on him, suffocating his mind so that it seemed to be melting within his skull. Everything was falling apart, and he knew that he couldn't put it back together again.

"Finished," J.B. whispered laconically.

Now he could hear them.

Soft sounds, far away, like a finger being rubbed over rotting silk, moved toward him.

"Enough." He lifted the delicate metal shell of the Bauer to his face. It was empty, not even a spent cartridge remaining.

J.B. opened his mouth, jumping for a moment as some tiny creature wriggled over his skin, and parted his lips just wide enough to slip the barrel inside.

"Better this way," he mumbled, hearing the sounds drawing closer.

He bit hard on the metal to hold it steady, then pulled the trigger.

The dry click.

"Bang," he said.

J.B. sat alone in the circling blackness and waited. And waited.

MILDRED WYETH WALKED along empty streets, the heels of her shoes tapping on the dusty concrete. The sound traveled around her, before and behind, like the ripples from a pool-tossed pebble spreading outward.

It was a city that she sort of recognized. Parts of it were familiar, but parts were different—hills where the highway should have been flat; squares instead of shopping malls; office towers where she remembered tree-lined suburban streets.

And all empty.

There was a child's small yellow ball resting in the gutter, and she paused and stared down at it, certain that it must mean something. She stooped to pick it up, then a worm came from the heart of the golden apple. Mildred was conscious of a prickling warmth between her thighs and she wondered where John had gone.

"John?" she called, trying to focus on a face to go with the name, seeing only the glittering blankness of sunlight reflecting off the lenses of metal-rimmed spectacles.

Standing still, she was aware of the silence.

"I don't feel myself," she said.

"A young girl who begins to feel herself will come to a bad end," said a deep, menacing preacher's voice from somewhere above her.

"But if nothing is true than everything is permitted," she replied.

"Nobody loves a smart-ass."

This voice was different, older and creaky.

Without her being aware of change, the city was gone and she was sitting on a porch in an old rocking chair. It was a hot summer evening, with the cicadas chittering away from the trees that fringed the garden. A pitcher of homemade lemonade stood on a round table, its sides misted with cool dew beads of condensation.

A little boy was standing beside her, holding a swatch of cloth, a dry, crackling, ivory material that smelled strongly of pitch and cinnamon.

Mildred smiled at him, but the boy didn't respond. He began to wind the cloth around her head and face, masking her eyes, muffling her hearing, choking her with its oppressive heat and scent. She opened her mouth, and the material flooded in, pressing down on her tongue like the shed skin of a serpent.

Her arms and legs felt paralyzed.

Suffocating in darkness, helpless, Mildred sat very still.

DEAN CAWDOR HAD been born into fear. There'd been scarcely a single day in his ten years of life where fear hadn't squatted grinning in his shadow.

Fear had come in so many different shapes, lurking behind myriad changing masks. Some pretended to smile, and some offered true friendship. But you looked into the eyes that lay beneath the sockets of the masks and you saw the cold flames of Hell itself burning there.

Some found no need of masks. Their pride, power and pomp was out in the open, naked and lustful.

Dean was more afraid of the smilers with the knives beneath the cloaks.

But all his life he had been taught to live with fear, to conquer it and keep it under control. His mother had always told him that. "A man who lets fear beat him isn't a proper man. He's a cringing, cowering corpse on two legs."

Dean remembered that. As he remembered everything that Rona had taught him.

But she hadn't told him anything about small rooms with walls of thick, golden glass, rooms that filled with humming sounds and whirling, blinding mists, rooms where your head began to slowly turn itself inside out.

The young boy felt sick. His stomach churned, and the taste of bile rose in his throat, making him gag at its seething bitterness.

He was out in the desert, with mesas scarring the horizon. A two-lane blacktop stretched ahead of him, narrowing into a penciled line. Turning his head, he saw the same thing in the opposite direction. The road ran the whole length of a vast, flat valley, farther than the eye could see, both ends disappearing into a blur of heat haze.

Far above him Dean could see a hawk soaring effortlessly on a thermal, its eyes covering the dusty, baked land, watching for the flicker of frightened movement that would mean food.

The boy was waiting.

Waiting where his mother had left him, waiting for the man with one eye to come riding on a gold-and-silver two-wheel wag, a handsome man, tall and straight astride a roaring machine that would take them both off like the hot wind. Dean could imagine locking his arms around his father's waist as they soared effortlessly across the dusty, baked land.

There was something in the boy's pocket, and he took it out to look at it. The object was a shaped prism of crystal, pure and clear, reflecting every color of the rainbow within itself.

Dean held it up to his face, seeing a thousand shimmering images of the red-orange world around him.

But the crystal began to melt, turning warm in his fingers and soft, like the wax of a candle left too near a camp fire. The brightness disappeared as did the sun and the highway.

The wind came up, the wind from the farthest edge of Bible-black, raven's wing beyond, the wind that carries the ice breath from between the stars.

And it entered the boy, sliding like a knife of molten snow into his eyes, ears, nose and mouth. In through the tiny eye of his penis, freezing his groin and his heart.

Dean began to die.

RYAN CAWDOR FELT the familiar symptoms—the queasiness and the cold sweat that gathered at the forehead, dry lips and damp palms. The mist grew more dense from the metal disks, and the humming noise was like a drill probing at the core of his bones.

It was as it had been before.

"Worse," he mumbled.

He experienced the same sucking and whirling of the brain within the skull, making all of the normal functions shut down. He closed his eye, fingers clenching against the nausea.

Something was going wrong. He could hear it and feel it, taste it like iron in his mouth.

With the most enormous effort of will, Ryan fought off the unconscious dreams that had possessed everyone else in the chamber, clawing himself back from the darkness.

Slowly, painfully, he managed to open his good eye again.

Chapter Nine

Darkness. A cold, paralyzing darkness.

Ryan could feel his bile rising in his throat, and he swallowed hard to try to fight it back. The freezing air smelled of fresh-spilled blood.

He closed his eye again, leaning against the chill wall of armaglass, listening, hearing rasping breath and a faint moaning sound—and the distant whirring of a giant turbine running itself down.

The second time he opened his right eye, Ryan realized that the mat-trans chamber wasn't totally jet dark. There was a faint glimmering of light from the metal disks in the ceiling, and a purple glow seemed to shimmer through the main door.

He could just make out the sprawled figures of his four friends and his son.

Grunting with the effort, Ryan managed to get to his knees, then pull himself to his feet. His body felt oddly light, as though someone had tampered with normal forces of gravity. The sickness came flooding back, and he doubled over, retching noisily.

Even that failed to disturb any of the others.

It crossed Ryan's mind that the jump might have been so appalling in its malfunctional effects that it could have brought death.

"Open door," he muttered, wiping his mouth on the sleeve of his coat. He propped the G-12 against the wall and took cautious, unsteady steps across the floor. The feeling of unnatural lightness was worse when he was up and moving.

The hand on the steel latch didn't seem to belong to him, and he could just see it in the strange sepulchral light that filtered in from outside. He tightened his fingers, aware of the movements of tendons and ligaments within his wrist and arm.

"Coming out. Get ready."

He stopped, his forehead wrinkling with bewilderment. It hadn't sounded like anyone's voice that he recognized. A man, so that ruled out Krysty and Mildred. Too deep for a boy, so it wasn't Dean. Not the right pitch for Doc, and it hadn't sounded quite clipped enough to be J.B.

Maybe he'd said it himself.

"Coming out. Get ready." Why would he have said that, even in his present confused and brainfucked mode?

"Outside," he breathed, seeing his breath frosting the cold air in front of him.

In all the jumps they'd made in Deathlands, and the one or two beyond, they'd never come across a gateway with people in it, though a couple of times there'd been the odd feeling of a complex that had been in recent use.

Ryan's fighting mind was beginning to find itself a working level, recovering from the scrambling it had taken.

If there were people beyond the armored door, then they might not be friendly. He remembered one of the Trader's favorite sayings: "Put a hundred strangers in a room and guess how many are friendly. If you're real, *real* lucky you might find one."

Ryan looked over his shoulders, wondering whether to pick up the Heckler & Koch automatic rifle, deciding it would be too clumsy while he opened the heavy door. His hand went to his belt and drew the piece of metal it found there.

A wave of nausea came clawing up from his guts, churning his brain to oatmeal. Ryan blinked and peered at what he held in his right hand, struggling to make sense of its size and shape.

"Blaster," he whispered.

He slowed his breathing, concentrating on the gun, remembering all the details.

Schweizerische Industrie-Gesellschaft was the SIG part of the name engraved on the side of the pistol. Sauer, J. P. Sauer & Sohn of Eckenforde; the P-226 model; nine millimeter; length was 7.72 inches with the barrel being 4.41 inches; weighed in at 25.52 ounces; fifteen rounds with a push-button mag-release; built-in baffle silencer.

Ryan nodded. That was good. His mind was clear again, and he was ready for whatever lay behind the door. He pressed his ear against the icy armaglass, but it was tomb silent.

A small part of his brain nagged at him, whispering insistently that he'd imagined the words, heard them only through a distorted mind. There wasn't anyone out there.

There was *never* anyone out there.

Gripping the blaster in his right hand, Ryan slowly eased open the catch with his left hand, hearing the soft, hydraulic kiss of the lock. The light grew a little brighter.

Behind him in the chamber someone stirred and moaned softly.

Very slowly the door inched open. Ryan put his eye to the crack and squinted. There was the usual small room outside, with a second door that stood ajar beyond that, showing him a corner of the main control room with its banks of consoles.

The air still felt light and it tasted stale, as though it had been recirculated too many times. Ryan took in a deep breath—and caught the faint scent of human sweat.

He swallowed, finger tightening on the trigger of the SIG-Sauer.

The door opened a hand breadth more.

"Yo! Out there!" he called. Since they obviously knew the chamber was occupied, there was no point in continuing the standoff. "Want to show yourselves, whoever you are?"

He heard the crackle of an intercom being used, but it was too muffled for him to catch any of the conversation. His keen hearing caught the shuffle of boots, and then the unmistakable click of a blaster being cocked.

Suddenly a blaze of magnesium-bright light exploded around him. An amplified voice boomed through the complex.

"Throw down your blasters and surrender, or you'll all be instant-chilled."

Ryan didn't hesitate. He heaved the sec door closed, knowing that this would be enough to trigger the mat-trans operating function. In the nanosecond before it slammed shut, he saw an odd sight. Out in the control room three or four men leaped into view, all holding silvered blasters, all wearing some sort of uniform with a black stripe down maroon pants and a cream top. Each had some kind of goggled mask concealing his face.

The door was closed and Ryan heard a burst of gunfire, ricocheting off the purple armaglass. The whirring started and the mist began to flood the gateway, but he heard the noise of someone shouting a command to stop blasting.

He turned, grabbed the G-12 and threw himself on the floor, glimpsing the ghostly figure of J.B. standing opposite him. He leaned against the wall, his face as white as ivory, blood trickling from nose, mouth and ears.

"Not again," the Armorer croaked.

But it was way too late for that.

THE FOG SWIRLED through the chamber, penetrating into the depths of Ryan Cawdor's mind, clouding out all of the present and most of the past, taking him into an unknowable future.

He huddled up, loosening his grip on the SIG-

Sauer. It fell on the steel floor by his head, with a resonant clanging chord that stretched endlessly on and on. It was the last sound that Ryan carried with him into the painful blackness.

When he began to recover consciousness, he could still hear it ringing inside his head.

Chapter Ten

"Fireblast!"

As he lay sprawled on the floor, Ryan realized to his infinite surprise that he didn't actually feel any worse than he had after the first, abortive jump.

His stomach still ached as though a mule had kicked it, and the inside of his skull was aching as though a stickie had been trying to rip it loose from its moorings.

He'd bitten his tongue, and a little blood trickled from a corner of his mouth.

Krysty groaned and rolled over onto her back. Her green eyes were unfocused, and her sentient red hair was curled tightly over her scalp. "That was the triple-pits, lover," she said, her voice sounding unusually hoarse.

"Worse than you know," he said. "And weird. There was an intermediate stop along the line."

J.B. came around next and wiped the blood from his face as he sat up. He took out his spectacles and perched them carefully on the bridge of his narrow nose. "I had this dream that I was in a tunnel under the earth and then I stood up and you were there, Ryan, slamming the door. Purple walls and a bright light. What was real and what wasn't?"

Ryan noticed two things. The armaglass had changed color, from purple to a delicate shade of blue-green, and the cold had gone. The air was much warmer and humid.

"We stopped when the first jump went wrong, and we finished up someplace else."

"What's that mean? In Deathlands?"

Ryan shook his head, immediately regretting the movement, and pressed his fingers to his throbbing temples. "Sorry, lover... No, I don't think it was in Deathlands at all."

"Back in Russkie territory?"

"No, J.B., not there, either. Just somewhere odd. There were people there, like sec guards. Uniform and masks. Tried to chill us."

Mildred was back with them. "Tried to chill us? Why? Who were they?"

Ryan chose to keep to himself the strange feeling that gravity had been lighter than usual, even though it fitted in with a theory that he'd been wondering about for several months.

"Don't know. Probably we'll never know. But this second jump was better. How d'you feel?"

The doctor grinned. "Felt better. Then again, I've felt worse. That first one was a real son of a bitch. How's Doc? And the kid?"

Ryan felt an instant pang of guilt that he hadn't checked out his son. The boy looked as though he were asleep, both hands thrust between his thighs, mouth open. Like most of them, Dean had been bleeding from the mouth and nose.

Doc looked less than well.

The old man had an arm thrown across his face, and his mouth was working as if he were trying to rid himself of something unpleasant. Both hands were trembling, and his legs were twitching. He'd been sick, and threads of bloodied spittle dangled from his parted lips.

Dean moved first. He uttered a little cry, then his eyes flicked open and looked around, revealing the blind fear of someone who didn't know where he was.

"It's all right, son," Ryan soothed, managing to kneel beside the boy and put an arm around his narrow shoulders. He smoothed the child's dark matted hair.

At first Dean pulled away, then recognition flooded in and his face cleared.

"Hi, Dad," he said, coughing. "We there?"

"Yeah."

"Where's here?"

"Don't know yet, Dean. You feel all right?"

The boy hopped to his feet. "Sure. Bit sick. Can we go?"

"Got to wait for Doc."

"He don't look good."

"Doesn't," Krysty corrected.

The boy looked at her. "What?"

"He *doesn't* look good. Not *don't* look good. You should try to speak properly, Dean."

"Yeah, sure."

But it was true. Doc didn't look good at all.

Mildred got down on her knees by the old man,

gripping his wrist between finger and thumb. She put her head on one side to listen to his breathing.

"Fast and shallow," she commented. "Pulse and respiration both."

"What's the matter with him?" Ryan asked, realizing that it was unusually warm inside the chamber. He wiped sweat from his forehead.

"That first jump was a real bitch," she said as she stood looking down at the old man. "Maybe we should cover him and try and keep him warm. He's gone into a kind of shock."

J.B. looked at Ryan. "Hope it hasn't turned his brain again."

Ryan picked up the G-12 and slung it over his shoulder. The worry over Doc's mental balance was a constant running sore. The time-trawling that he'd undergone had certainly done permanent damage to the old man, and he sometimes seemed to find it hard to hang on to exactly "when" it was. Was it the late 1890s? Or the end of the twentieth century? Or was it closing in on the year 2100, the real present?

If the jump had been too terrifying for Doc, then it might have leaped on the fingernails that clawed at the edge of reality and plunged him deep into some abyss of confusion.

One that might hold him for whatever remained of his life.

"What if he's lost it, lover?" Krysty asked.

"Have to leave him."

"Wait a minute, Ryan..." Mildred began, her eyes narrowed in anger.

"Let's see," he interrupted. "Depends. But we can't split up for long. Maybe he'll be fine. Maybe not. We've seen Doc when he didn't know which way was up." He shook his head. "Get into a double-red situation with someone like that, and you all go off on the last train west. But let's see."

"He's coming around, Dad," Dean said. "Saw his eyes flicker."

"Should we get him on his feet, Mildred?" J.B. asked.

"Not yet, John. Lift his head and prop him up against the wall."

Ryan helped the Armorer ease the old man into a sitting position. Doc gave a long, breathy sigh, his lids clicking up like blinds. His eyes looked out vaguely, a faded blue, like a shirt that'd been left too long in the sun.

"Lushington," he said, pronouncing the word very carefully.

"How's that, Doc?" Ryan asked.

"I'm a famous lushington, my dear fellow. Too much of the major's best port."

Dean nudged Ryan. "What's he saying?"

"He's a bit confused about where he is right now. He'll be fine soon." But in his heart Ryan felt a feather touch of fear.

The old man gazed down, seeing the pool of vomit on the floor. "That looks sadly like the remnants of one of Mother Payne's delicious veal-and-pork pies. Such a waste. That bowwow sauce quite snapped at the end of a fellow's tongue." He gave the watching circle of faces a lopsided smile. "And the plum duff with cloves... All gone. Finished. Left. Departed with the captains and the kings."

Mildred wiped blood from under his hawklike nose. "There," she said. "Feel like getting up on your feet, Doc?"

He looked at her, shaking his head in confusion. "You are not one of those quadroon women working in that sporting house on Vine, are you?"

"No, Doc, I'm not."

"I thought that you were not what I thought that... I fear I have lost my thread of words."

J.B. leaned in and patted the old man on the arm. "Don't worry about it, Doc."

"Did you call me 'Doc,' my good man?"

"Sure."

"Never eat at any places called 'Mom's' or play cards with anyone called 'Doc.' Is that not what they say? Is that my name?"

"Dr. Theophilus Algernon Tanner," Krysty told him. "Remember?"

"What truly wonderful hair, you have, child." He stroked it with his right hand. "Like sparks from the very chariot of Phoebus. But beware the sad fate of Icarus who flirted with the sun and melted his wings of wax." He closed his eyes and swayed a little on his feet. "More water with it," he whispered.

Ryan looked at the others, seeing his own concern mirrored in their faces.

"Let's move out of here," he said quietly. "See how he is in a while."

J.B. and Mildred helped Doc between them, supporting him while Ryan eased open the lock on the gateway door.

"I'm tired and I want to go to... Go where?" A note of panic had crept into the old man's voice. "Where is Emily? And where are my dear children? Oh, Jolyon, Rachel, come to Papa! Where are all the snows of my yesteryears? Gone to graveyards every one."

Tears had overflowed the corner of his left eye and coursed through the stubble on his cheeks, touched the edge of his lips and rolled off his chin to plop onto the floor.

"Bad one, lover," Krysty whispered.

"Yeah. Been like it before and he's snapped out of it."

He pushed the door open a little farther, his SIG-Sauer cocked and ready in his right hand. A slow wave of moist warmth coiled out, making him take a deep breath.

"Feels like swamp country," he observed.

The small room beyond was much like the others in previously visited redoubts.

This one was about fifteen feet square with a table upended in one corner. A double row of shelves was empty. On the floor was a layer of smeared mud and a baseball cap with a torn fastener.

The second door was closed.

"I have nothing to say, Officer. I shall plead the Fifth Amendment. But spare the gray hairs of my poor old mother."

"Shut up, Doc," Ryan hissed.

The old man succeeded in making a bow toward him, despite the efforts of Mildred and J.B. to hold him steady.

Ryan eased the door open a quarter inch and pressed his right eye to the narrow crack. He opened it a touch farther, then pushed it wide.

The control area of the mat-trans gateway was much like the others. Row upon row of desks, each with a comp console, with a constant flow of information dancing across each screen. Run by timeless nuke-gens, these sections would carry on for eternity, relaying and sifting information as they'd been programmed a century before.

"I believe that I was once the proud owner of a malacca cane with a hidden blade of steel and the carved head of a silver lion," Doc said. "Perhaps one of you servants would be good enough to find it for me? I shall reward you with a union card and a wedding coat."

"His swordstick," Ryan said. "I'll get it. Sit him down then recce the place. Check the sec doors."

He went back into antechamber, seeing the long black weapon lying on the floor of the main chamber. As he picked it up and walked out again, his eye was caught by a crumpled scrap of paper almost buried in the dust. It looked as if it had been hidden by the discarded baseball cap.

Ryan's insatiable curiosity couldn't let him just walk by it. He holstered his blaster and stooped, picking it up in his right hand. The swordstick got in the way, and he tucked it under his arm, carefully unfolding the fragile, dust-dry piece of paper.

It had been torn out of a ring-bound notebook, and the writing on it was faded to the point of illegibility. Ryan angled the paper toward the light to try to make out the words. It crackled between his fingers as though it were about to disintegrate. He could see that there were a few words, each with some numbers alongside them. The sheet had been torn raggedly across the middle and obviously dropped by accident.

Ryan screwed up his eye, but the writing was too faint.

"Come on, lover," Krysty called. "You all right in there?"

He'd been about to throw the shred of paper onto the floor again, but he stuffed it into one of the pockets of his coat.

"Here's your swordstick, Doc," he said, walking into the control room.

"I am most grateful. One needs some sort of protection against the sturdy rogues, buggers and muggers, thugs and punks that infect the gutters of our fair city."

A faint smile puckered the corners of the old man's lips as he took the cane from Ryan, but his pale eyes still seemed to be focusing a thousand mornings away.

"At least he's up and walking good," Mildred said quietly.

"We going to all try outside?" J.B. asked from

where he stood by the main entrance doors to the gateway complex.

Ryan thought about the question for a few moments. If they left Doc here, then someone had to stay with him. Mildred didn't have the combat skills if there was serious trouble. They needed Krysty's "seeing" for any exploration, which meant either Ryan or J.B. had to remain behind. And now there was the added complication of the young boy.

"Let's stick together. Mildred, you and J.B. keep an eye on Doc. If..." He hesitated. "If things look condition-red, then get him out. Fast as you can."

"Want me to open the sec doors?"

Ryan nodded. "Yeah."

The green lever that was present in almost all of the gateways was in the down position, showing the doors were locked shut. The Armorer paused, lifting a hand to the barely healed wound on his neck, looking at his fingers for signs of blood.

"Nothing," he said. "Thought it hurt some. Must've been the jump."

He grabbed the lever and began to heave it upward. There was the familiar sound of hydraulics, and the door began to open.

"No!" Doc shouted.

Chapter Eleven

The old man jerked back from Mildred's helping hand, throwing himself flat on the floor, hands spread, legs wide apart.

"Close the door again, J.B., quickly," Ryan ordered.

There was the hissing of the locking mechanism as the green lever was pulled down.

"What is it, Doc?" Krysty asked, kneeling by the weeping man.

"Speeding away."

"What?"

"Such speed, my friends."

Dean tapped his forehead, grinning at Ryan. "Old man got a spent round in the chamber."

"Shut up." Ryan turned to Doc. "Tell us the problem, so we can help."

The tearstained face looked up at him. The tendons in the back of Doc's hands were straining like bowstrings with the effort of hanging on to the floor. "We'll all be thrown off. Earth moves. It does. Oh, it does. One thousand and fifty miles an hour in rotation and sixty-two thousand miles an hour around Father Sun. By the three Kennedys! My burning feet of fire! Save me."

Ryan could feel his own anger starting to smolder along its short fuse. Unless Doc snapped out of his present dementia—at least enough to function—then it might be better to tie him up and leave him safe. That way he wouldn't endanger anyone else's life. Or his own.

Mildred and J.B. pulled Doc to his feet, stopping him from slumping back to the floor.

"Can't you help him, Krysty?" Mildred asked urgently. "You have the power. Use it for him. Or he'll sink."

"I am not waving, my dear companions, but I fear me that I'm drowning." There was a shuddering void of horror in Doc's melodious voice. "I shall grow not old, as you who are left will grow old. I shall not turn to the path that was not taken."

Krysty stood in front of him, lifting her hands to touch him on either cheek. The old man cringed from her fingers. "I won't hurt you, Doc. Want to try and help."

"Where we live is the end of the long, winding road. Deathlands... Truly the lands of death. I once met a very old and wise man who told me what the American dream had become."

"What?" J.B. asked. "I always wondered about that."

"Old Bull Lee, he was sometimes called. Said that the American dream had become to vulgarize and falsify until the bare lie shines through."

Doc said it very slowly, his voice becoming grating

and harsh. Nobody spoke, the only sound the whirring
and clicking of all the control consoles around them.

Krysty closed her hands, holding him tightly. She
shut her eyes and put her face closer to Doc. "May
the force of Gaia cleanse you of this darkness and
make you whole again."

He blinked, eyes rolling upward until only the
bloodshot whites showed.

"Hang on to him," Krysty whispered. J.B. and
Mildred tightened their grip.

"Why does...?" Dean began, stopping as his father's angry face glowered at him.

"Come on back to us, Doc. Back to your friends
who care for you and love you. Come back and walk
again in the shining of the sun and the turning of the
tides. Come back, Doc."

His head rolled, and he seemed suddenly to become
weightless. Words started to pour from him like yards
of cheesecloth being regurgitated by a phony medium.
Doc's hands opened and the swordstick clattered on
the floor.

"My yesterdays are ever-present, tomorrow is another now. We all know that our life must end, but
no one can know how. I was once lost in a rainstorm
in Juárez, Eastertime it was. All I had to sustain me
in that dire fog was my pearls and my amphetamines.
Speeding away like James Dean. I see a young man,
sorely wounded, hiding among row upon row of
snowy sheets, his blood crimsoning them. My head,
it pains me, my dear Emily. A physic might...sucked
forward, like a cork from a temporal bottle."

The words were coming more slowly, and his head had straightened, his eyes opening and looking at the faces all around him.

"It's getting better, Doc," Krysty said, still holding his face in her palms.

"It's getting better all the while," he said, half smiling. "A friend once blew his mind out while sitting in a car, waiting for a set of lights to change. Better, all the time. I think that I know you. The horror, yes, the horror recedes."

"Do you know us, Doc?" Ryan asked.

"You are my trusty friend, Ryan of Cawdor, in whom I am well pleased. In the land of death, it is said, the one-eyed man is king."

"How about me?" Krysty asked, letting go of him.

"Beware the wrath of Wroth. Krysty Wroth. A lady who is perfect and gentle, yet fiery and armed against the lords of chaos. Thank you for your laying on of healing hands, my dear."

"You're welcome, Doc. Think you can stand without any help? Yeah?" She nodded to J.B. and Mildred. "Try him out."

Doc looked at his two supporters as they moved away from him. "The young lovers. And they said it wouldn't last. John Barrymore Dix, weapons expert extraordinaire and man of few words. A chevalier without fear and without reproach. A man could not choose better company to die in. And Mildred Winonia Wyeth." He smiled broadly at her, showing his oddly perfect teeth.

"You go taking a flying fuck at a rolling doughnut,

you doped-up old bastard,'' she said, tempering her words with a grin.

"Yes, I remember you, Mildred. But this young man here…?''

"My name's—''

"No, pray don't tell me. No clues, my dear young man. Let us see if this poor befuddled old brain of mine can string together a fact or two and deduce from it. Now, what did the dog do in the night? Nothing. Precisely.''

"What's a dog got to do with who I am, Doc?'' Dean asked.

"One day, as we travel through this vale of tears, this valley of darkness, this land that once was Avalon, I shall explain all. Now, you have a determined chin. Black curling hair. Blue eyes that speak of courage. Broad shoulders and a deep chest. A knife on your hip that tells me that you are a person not unacquainted with the lists of combat.''

"Doc, why not just—'' Ryan began, but the old man waved a dismissive hand at him.

"I am nearly there. A boy who is the son of his father. And there I see the man who is undoubtedly the father to that son. You are the son of Ryan Cawdor and your name is Dean.''

"You're right,'' the boy replied with a grin. "You remembered.''

Doc patted him on the head. "I once was lost, but now I'm found. We are together again, my friends. Doc Tanner is himself once more.''

"Fine,'' Ryan said. "Now let's get that bitching sec door open again.''

Chapter Twelve

"Corridor's clear," J.B. reported.

Ryan and the others joined him, finding themselves in a wide, curving passage with an arched roof. It was about twenty feet across, and the ceiling was about fifteen feet at its highest. There was concealed strip lighting that cast a steady glow on the dusty floor. Ryan noticed several sec cameras dotted along the roof, but none seemed to be activated.

To their left the corridor terminated in a blank wall of solid rock. They couldn't see much because of the long bend, but there were no side doorways or passages in sight.

Ryan looked at Krysty. "Feel anything? Apart from hot and wet?"

She grinned. "Certainly warmer than Newyork was. Considering this is recirculated air, it must be rad-blast hot outside. But no, I don't feel anyone around here."

"The control area looked like it had been cleared out carefully," J.B. said.

Ryan nodded. "Right. Seemed to have been a planned withdrawal."

"What is this?" Dean asked cautiously. "We still in the ville?"

"No. Feels like we're a long ways off, but you never can tell. Believe half of what you see, son, and nothing of what you hear."

"Skirmish line," Ryan ordered. "Me first this time. Then Krysty, Dean, Doc, Mildred and J.B. last."

For a second he thought his son was going to argue with him, but Doc stepped in quickly, putting his arm on the boy's shoulders. "They need steadiness and men of iron resolve in the heart of the patrol, Dean. So, that's you and me."

They set off, and in less than two minutes they found themselves facing a huge pair of sec doors. Painted a bilious shade of pale green, they stretched from floor to ceiling. At the side was a small control panel of letters and numbers.

"This is it." Ryan looked behind them. There'd been no other options; the way out was either back through the gateway or past these vanadium-steel doors.

"Try the usual code?" J.B. suggested. "Worked before."

"Three-five-two," Krysty said.

Ryan keyed in the numbers while the rest of them spread out, blasters ready.

For several stretched heartbeats there was simply a great stillness. Ryan was about to try the control panel again when they all heard a distant hissing, like the heavy sigh of some massive monster wakened from a reluctant sleep. Weights and counterweights moved into grudging life, and the doors began to slide upward.

Dean had thrown himself down on his stomach so that he could be the first to peer out beyond the ponderous wall of sec steel.

"Nobody there," he said, his voice cracking with his excitement.

"Get back, son," Ryan said quietly. "Keep out of our fire line."

"Can't I have a blaster, huh?"

"Maybe… Now keep your lips tight-shut and your eyes wide open."

The double doors finally stopped moving.

Beyond it an identical passage carried on, the walls painted a mat magnolia color. Ryan saw immediately that the sec vids were working. A tiny ruby eye glowed beneath each of them, and they moved slowly from side to side, like the heads of world-weary eels.

J.B. had also seen them. "Could be on auto. Triggered by body heat, movement, sound, anything."

Mildred stared up at them. "Maybe I should give them a wave and a smile. Show them we're friendly. What do you think, John?"

The Armorer shook his head. "Chances are that there's nobody watching their screens, Mildred. Probably hasn't been anyone there for a hundred years."

"Shouldn't you shoot them out?" Dean asked. "Stop them spying."

"Fireblast! I've never known anyone ask so many damned questions. I wonder how you managed to live to be ten years old."

The boy shuffled his feet. "Real sorry, Dad. Just that there never seem enough answers to go around, so I ask more questions."

Ryan laughed. "All right, Dean. But learn to pick the right moment for the right question. Now let's move on."

Once again the passage came quickly to a dead end. They retraced their steps, past the opening that led toward the gateway. Ryan paused by the familiar sign: Entry Is Absolutely Forbidden To All Except Personnel Cleared To Level B-14 Or Higher.

"Might be worth closing the doors again," he said. "Just in case anyone wanders down here."

The reverse number code of 253 sent the heavy doors sliding remorselessly down, settling into place with a faint crunching sound.

Punching in the digits made Ryan wonder for a passing moment about the crumpled piece of paper he'd shoved into his pocket. But a call from Dean made him forget about it again.

"Stairs and an elevator here," the boy shouted. "Shall I press the call button?"

Krysty saw the expression on Ryan's face, and she quickly put her hand on his arm. "Slowly, lover," she warned.

"But he's—"

"You were ten once."

He nodded grimly. "Yeah, and I knew the value of checking the safety before squeezing the trigger. The boy must learn silence, lover."

"He will."

Outside, Dean was waiting patiently for them, finger hovering over the recessed black button by the door of the elevator. Ryan remembered the problems in Newyork and waved a hand.

"No. If there's stairs, we take them. Not so much risk of getting trapped."

Krysty wiped sweat from her forehead. "Gaia, but it's sticky in here! This air feels like it's been going around and around and getting wetter and hotter all the time."

"I am beginning to have some passing appreciation of what it must be like to spend one's life as a hothouse orchid," Doc said.

"We going up?" Dean asked, craning his neck so that he could see to the top of the wide spiral staircase. "Not too far."

Ryan joined his son, looking more cautiously up the steps. There was a flat landing area about fifty feet above them, with what looked like another door beyond it.

"I'll go first," he said. "Rest of you stay down here until I've cleared the way."

The blaster in his right hand, he began to pick his way carefully up the steps, his boots ringing softly on the slatted metal. Occasionally it came to him how odd it was that he might be the first human being to tread this way for the best part of a hundred years. The last set of feet probably belonged to a senior sec officer, making a final check that the complex had been properly cleared in those terrifying final days

before the skies grew dark and nuke-black night came
to the United States.

Around the door he saw a wide wooden frame. But
the damp had ravaged it, leaving it soft and covered
in a fibrous brown mold.

The door itself was made of steel, but it hung loose
on its hinges. Ryan pushed at it, and it slumped open
at his touch.

"Come on up," he called. "Looks like an abandoned redoubt."

A COUPLE OF HOURS LATER they were sitting around
a folding table, the remains of their meal scattered
across the top.

Dean belched noisily and grinned at the others for
approbation. "I never seen any place like this...like
this redoubt." He pronounced the new word with extra care. "Rona told me about them, but she said
she'd never actually seen one herself. I never met
anyone who had. Plenty of big-lip liars pretended."

J.B. nodded. "Always find people eager to pretend,
Dean. Make them seem more important. We don't
know how many of these redoubts there are in Deathlands. All we know is that they were built in the very
end of the 1990s, and mostly hidden. A part of what
they called the Totality Concept."

"What was that?"

Ryan answered him. "It was a war plan. Like most
war plans, it never worked. The nukes won."

"Any more of that juice-sub?" The boy licked his
lips. "Real good." A thought struck him. "Hey, why

can't we live here forever? Nobody can get in, and there's food and blasters.''

"We maybe could," Krysty said gently, "but there's more to life than hiding in a safe cave. We just stock up here on fresh clothes and what we need. Then we move on.'' She looked across at Ryan, and a note of bitterness entered her voice. "I sometimes think that I'll be always moving on.''

COMPARED TO SOME of the huge labyrinths that they'd found in the past, this redoubt was relatively compact. There was sleeping accommodation for only fifty people, in four dormitories; a central dining area and kitchens; a dozen identically empty cubes that must have been admin offices; some sealed storage areas holding food, clothes and some weaponry.

It was odd.

The place looked as if it had been partly evacuated. Some of it was totally stripped, but sheets and blankets had been left on the bunks. All of which had rotted away in the moist air. There were no personal effects left anywhere. Yet the warehousing facilities were amazingly well stocked.

Predictably the boy had wanted to go explore this treasure trove from the past, but Ryan had insisted that they took the usual precautions.

"We check out the whole complex. Make sure it's secure. That means we're going to be secure, Dean. Next comes food. Then we explore.''

It hadn't taken them long to go through the redoubt, finding that there appeared to be only one exit. That was a surprisingly small sec door tucked away in a corner beyond the sleeping quarters. There was a sec vid unit that had been built to show a view of the world outside.

But when Ryan tried the controls, it was locked onto a mass of thick foliage. A solid wedge of green filled the screen, barely moving, making it absolutely impossible to work out where in the world they might be.

"Hawaii?" Mildred suggested.

Doc snorted. "Don't think so small, my dear woman."

"Don't 'dear woman' me, you sententious old fart! What's wrong with Hawaii?"

"I would hazard a guess that we have terminated our journey a little farther away than that."

Ryan shook his head. "You mean outside Death-lands, Doc? I doubt that. The place in Moscow was a one-off freak. There for a reason. No, I figure we've hit the ace on the line for some local hot spot. But it looks like it's getting dark out there. We'll check it out tomorrow."

Then they ate.

The redoubt, like most of the others, was still self-sufficient, running off its own nuke-powered generator. The light and the power still functioned properly.

Apart from one section where lines had gone down and whole containers of food had rotted to a dark, odorless liquid, the larders were full.

Ryan was surprised at the degree of the boy's literacy. Considering the traveling life he'd led, he was good with letters. Even bright, barefoot ten-year-old boys in frontier villes had to take their pants down to count to twenty-one.

But Dean had walked along the lines of steel shelving in the cool storage rooms, rattling off what he could see.

"Chicken curry and chili and beans and tofu bake and fried prawns and trout and beans and more beans and breakfast fry-up and pork chops and burgers and burgers and veg burgers and salmon and oatmeal and green jelly and orange jelly and red jelly and green beans and ham and chicken dumplings and beef slices and lamb cutlets and nut cutlets and—"

Doc had stopped him. "If you carry on without pausing to draw a breath, my dear young fellow, then you will turn white and fade away. Just take your pick and we can set to cooking it."

Other sections of the facility held clothing and weapons, but that was also for after the meal.

DOC AND J.B. CLEARED away the table, dumping everything into a garbage compactor. Mildred had calculated that they could use fresh plates and cutlery every day for a month and simply throw them out.

"Want to check the rest of the complex, Dean?" Ryan asked.

The boy was leaning forward at the table, head on his arms. He didn't react at all.

"Kid's bushed," Krysty said. "Best get him off to bed."

Ryan looked across at her. "Maybe we could do the same, lover."

She smiled. "Why not?"

Chapter Thirteen

Doc had picked one of the dormitory cubicles for himself. Bundled under a pile of fresh blankets, he'd quickly fallen asleep.

Mildred had stood from the table, looking across at J.B., who, as taciturn as always, had simply nodded to her. They'd gone off hand in hand to another section of the redoubt.

Ryan had tried to pick up the boy, hoping to get him to bed without waking him. But the moment he was touched, Dean had reacted violently, kicking and yelling, but stopping as soon as he came to and realized what he'd been doing.

"Sorry, Dad," he muttered.

"Don't worry about it, son. Been a long, long, hard day for all of us."

Krysty had collected some blankets for the boy. She followed Ryan into the room, quickly making up a bed for Dean.

"You can take off your boots and pants," Ryan told his son. "Not many places you can. But this is about as safe as it gets."

Dean looked at him dozily. "Can't I sleep in the same room as you?"

"No. Most nights of our lives we all have to sleep

in together. Either for security or warmth. Or both. This is somewhere we can close a door on the world. Doc's that side of you. Me and Krysty'll be this side. And Mildred and J.B. are one room along. You know where the can is?''

''Yeah. End of the passage on the right.''

Ryan and Krysty stood and waited for the boy to get into bed, but he didn't move.

''I'll be fine, Dad. Good night, Krysty.'' He paused. ''You can leave me now. I'm fine.''

Krysty tugged Ryan away, giving the despondent little figure a smile and a half wave. ''Sleep well, Dean.''

She closed the door and pulled Ryan with her into the next room, closing the door behind them. ''Kid wants some privacy, lover. Doesn't want me watching him get undressed.''

''Guess so. You mind watching me?''

Krysty grinned. ''Wait and see.''

They pushed two of the metal-framed bunks together and laid mattresses sideways across them. The blankets and sheets were all single, so it needed some skill to contrive a comfortable arrangement. Fortunately the complex was warm enough for it not to be too big a problem.

Ryan took off his clothes and stacked his weapons on the floor near the head of the bed. Krysty kicked off her dark blue cowboy boots, the overhead light glinting off the chiseled silver points on the toes. The rest of her clothes followed until she stood by the bed wearing only a pale turquoise pair of bikini panties.

"Light off or on, lover?" she asked.

Ryan had already climbed carefully into the nest of bedclothes and he looked up at her. "Part of me says 'on' and part says 'off.' I guess off. Save one of us having to get up afterward."

She nodded and walked to the main light switch, conscious of his gaze on her. She deliberately sashayed her hips as she moved, turning and placing one arm coyly across her breasts, blowing him a kiss as she plunged the room into total darkness.

Ryan heard her bare feet, then felt the mattresses dip as she climbed quickly in beside him. For a moment there was a stretched stillness, then Krysty shifted closer, her knee brushing against his thigh.

"Hi, lover," she whispered. "Been a long time since we had this sort of luxury."

"Can't remember when." He eased his body against hers, his hand reaching for her.

"Too long." Her fingers found him, feathering across the flat wall of his stomach, grasping him with a gentle firmness.

He rolled on his side, closer, lips brushing the skin of her throat, kissing her softly. Krysty moaned as his right hand delved between her thighs, bringing her to instant arousal.

"Love you so much," she whispered, her breath quickening, brushing the short hairs on the side of Ryan's neck.

"Me you, too," he said.

"Let's do it, lover."

RYAN ROSE FIRST. He climbed silently into his clothes, carrying his heavy-duty combat boots outside so he wouldn't disturb Krysty.

The air in the corridor still held the scents of last night's supper, confirming his suspicion that the conditioning was on the blink. He walked into the kitchen and switched on a pan of water, intending to use it to brew up a hot drink and to shave.

A sound behind him made him whirl, to see J.B. grinning at him. The Armorer was wiping his glasses on the sleeve of his shirt.

"Getting jumpy, friend?"

"Better to be jumpy—"

"Than asleep," finished the slight figure. It had been one of the Trader's favorite sayings.

"Want some coffee-sub?"

"Sure. Krysty asleep?"

Ryan nodded. "Yeah. Mildred?"

"Was when I left her. How about the boy? Didn't hear him in the night."

Steam billowed as Ryan poured out the boiling water, the harsh smell of the drink filling the kitchen. He passed one of the mugs to J.B.

"Didn't hear a sound. Oh, yeah, I heard Doc coughing his way to the pisser. Once or twice." He took a great gulp from the hot, brown liquid. "Fireblast! This is *damned* good coffee-sub!"

"What're your plans for the boy, Ryan?"

The one-eyed man sighed. "Only knew about him a couple of days ago. Spend all my life thinking one thing, then I'm a father. Boy of ten. By a woman I knew for less than a week. Haven't seen for over ten years. Thought was dead. Is dead. Now..." He shook his head. "I don't know, J.B., and that's the honest truth. What do you think?"

"Trader used to say you never went out on the highway with either animals or young children."

Ryan sipped at his coffee-sub. "Sure. One thing I was wondering..."

"Jak Lauren?"

"That's right." He was startled at the way the Armorer had thought along the same lines. "If we can get him down there. Long way. But he'd be safe."

"*Safe*, Ryan?"

The kitchen was silent. Ryan was trying to run some alternative plays through his mind. From what he'd already seen of Dean, there didn't seem any doubt that he was an amazingly tough and self-sufficient ten-year-old boy.

But he *was* a ten-year-old boy.

"NEW CLOTHES!" Mildred exclaimed. "I can't fucking believe it. Oh, pardon my French! But I'd forgotten that such things existed."

"Be a good idea if everyone got fixed up, best as they can." Ryan looked along the shelves at the shrink-wrapped, sealed packs of equipment. The stores were controlled for temperature and humidity, and everything looked to be in fine shape.

"Changing rooms out back here," J.B. called. "Must've known we were coming. There's six of them."

Ryan beckoned to Dean, ticking items off on his fingers. "Combat boots. Tight but not too tight. All-weather combat top and pants. T-shirt and underclothes. Good socks. Put those on before you try the boots. Shirt. Cotton, with pockets. Nothing in bright colors. Some kind of hat."

"Don't like hats."

"Get something, anyway. When you've got everything ready, come show me. All right?"

"What about a blaster?"

"Clothes first."

"All right, Dad."

Everyone eventually managed to make some changes to their wardrobes.

Some things altered, some things remained the same.

Doc agreed to get fresh underclothes and a new white shirt, but he clung to the old-fashioned frock coat and antiquated breeches, as well as the cracked and worn knee boots.

J.B. kept his leather jacket with its infinity of infinitely deep pockets, but he found a new pair of dark brown boots with steel toes and heels. He also outfitted himself with a pair of pants and a matching light brown shirt. Mildred tried to sneak away his beloved old fedora, but he caught her at it.

"Wasn't there a pre-dark song about knocking a man down and stepping on his face?"

"But whatever you do, don't steal his blue suede fedora," she said.

Mildred had gone for a completely new look, toe

to toe. A black beret covered her plaited dreadlocks. She'd chosen a crisp white cotton shirt, a denim jacket with a quilted lining and reinforced military jeans tucked into calf-length boots in black proofed leather.

"I'm greased and ready to kick ass," she proclaimed. "And you hippy bastards should know that rock and roll is here to stay." She caught Doc's eye and got her retaliation in first. "Brings out the thespian in me."

Dean tugged at Ryan's sleeve. "Isn't that the name for a woman who sort of...you know...with another woman?"

"Nearly, son, but not quite. Let's look at what you picked out for yourself."

Dean hunched his shoulders shyly, uneasy at being the sudden center of attention from five grown-ups. He turned around slowly.

"That's good," J.B. observed. "Shown a lot of sense there, Dean."

"Like the jacket," Mildred added.

"I'm almost tempted to obtain one of those fetching caps for myself," Doc commented.

"Yeah." Krysty nodded. "Makes you look a whole lot better. And older."

"Dad?"

Ryan looked at him, feeling an unaccustomed swell of emotion. Dean was so eager to secure his approval that it was painful.

"Let's see. Lined cap. Good dark blue color. Sensible peak to it. Keep the sun and the rain out of your eyes.''

"How about the rest of the stuff? I can always go change it if you—''

"No. Looks fine. Dark blue shirt. Matching pants. I'd cut some of the metal loops and stuff out of the black denim jacket. Could snag on things. Belt's good, and the knife looks about right there on the hip. Boots comfortable?''

"Sure. Smallest size they got. Didn't get them too tight 'cause my feet are still growing.''

"Right. No. You look a new man, Dean. I'm proud of you.''

"Honest?''

"Honest.''

Krysty patted the boy on the arm. ''Now let's look at just what Dad's picked out for himself.''

Ryan had chosen some new underclothes, adding a new shirt of blue denim. He also changed his pants, picking some heavy-duty, dark blue cloth. His combat boots were wearing a little, but they fitted his feet like sprayed plastic and he decided to keep them rather than face the hassle of having to break in a fresh pair. He kept his trusty long coat. The white silk scarf with the weighted ends remained around his neck.

"Look almost the same,'' Dean said.

"Way I like it, son.'' Ryan looked at Krysty. "Don't see much alteration with you, either.''

"I've got clean clothes on from top to bottom, and it feels real good. I'm going to try and get a hot bath later to go with the gear.''

She looked crisp and fresh, her dazzlingly red hair curling over her shoulders. Krysty had gotten a white shirt and a pair of the dark blue pants, with a matching jacket. She'd retained her trusty Western boots with the embroidered silver falcons.

J.B. leaned against the wall. "We look like a load of sec men," he said wryly.

Dean caught his father's eye, and Ryan nodded, unable to hold back the smile. "Yeah," he said. "*Now* we go look at the blasters."

Chapter Fourteen

J.B. was in the nearest thing he knew to heaven on earth. The state of the weapons section of the redoubt's stores seemed initially to confirm the feeling that the evacuation of the whole complex had, for some unguessable reason, been abandoned halfway through. Otherwise, it was unthinkable that the armament section wouldn't have been stripped clean.

As soon as they entered the area, with its printed warnings about sec-clearance ratings, J.B. stopped and closed his eyes, taking in several deep breaths.

"Oil, grease and perfectly machined metal," he said quietly.

"The holy of holies, John?" Mildred asked, smiling at him.

But he didn't respond to her. He was busy looking along the ordered rows and shelves. "Enough here to equip an army and rule all of Deathlands," he said.

That eventually proved to be something of an exaggeration.

As they examined the section, it became clear that an attempt *had* been made to evacuate some of the weapons. The areas of the storage complex where grens, machine guns, mortars and heavy armament had been stored were stripped bare.

Also, a lot of the crates held only spare mags, sights and replacement parts.

Even so, there was still a fair array of infantry blasters and ammo.

Dean turned to his father, who shrugged and pointed to J.B. "He's the man for blasters. If there's anyone in Deathlands who knows more about weapons than the Armorer here, then I haven't met him yet."

"I want a Magnum. Bit .357. Blow a hole in a wall."

J.B. shook his head. "First thing you learn, Dean, is to pick your weapons to fit yourself. You fire a Magnum, and there's an even chance someone your age and size'll snap his wrist. And the bullet's wasted, straight up in the ceiling."

"Then I want—"

"Not a question of what you want. Question of what's the best weapon for you."

"Why can't—"

The Armorer lifted his right hand, touching the boy gently on the lips with his index finger. "Quieter," he said. "That's better. Remember that we're all a team. Might be a time your life depends on me. Might be a time my life's on the line, and you're the way out for me. You need the best blaster there is, for what you need."

"A .38?"

J.B. smiled. "No. A good .22."

Dean looked like someone had just placed a dead

slug on his tongue. "A .22? Give me a fuckin' break, you—"

His sentence got cut off by a round-arm blow from Ryan. Halfway between a slap and a punch, it knocked the boy flying, flat on his back, sliding against the wall. He lay there, dazed, one hand touching his mouth where a thread of blood was worming down over his chin.

"What d'you—"

Ryan knelt by his son, the crimson anger still glittering in his good eye, his mouth a razored line. "You listen, and you listen good! I warned you and warned you, and you still don't take any notice of me."

"You still didn't—"

"Oh, yes, I did. Fireblast, but I did, Dean! You spent most of your life running, dodging and hiding. I understand that. You come with us, and you'll see a different life. A life where you don't take shit from anyone. A life of standing and fighting. Together. You got that?"

"Sure." He sat up. "But—"

Ryan helped the boy to his feet. "No 'buts' about it, Dean. What J.B. said was right. We each carry the lives of the others right here in the palm of our hand. And that means you, too."

"I'm sorry, Dad." He turned to the Armorer. "And I'm sorry, J.B., as well."

"A .22," J.B. said, as though Ryan's flaring anger had never erupted. "But a good one. Not a Saturday-night special that falls apart on you. Most of the chilling gets done at a range of less than fifteen feet. I've found you a blaster that you can work with. Then you can put a man down with it, eyes open at the sky, ten times from ten.''

"And it'll be light enough for you to heft without any problem," Ryan added.

"Thought about a Ruger Mark II," J.B. said, looking through a stock inventory list he'd found hanging on a nail. "But it's stainless steel and more of a target gun. Looks nice, like the Luger parabellum, but this is better."

"What is it?" Dean asked eagerly.

"Smith & Wesson Model 425. Lightweight alloy frame. Rimfire, holding ten rounds. Here..."

The boy took the blued gun from the Armorer's hands. "Light," he said.

"Sure. Look, it's got edging and fluting to cut down on reflections. Walnut grips. Adjustable sights. Chamber's over the trigger. Nice design, based on the 422. Enclosed hammer."

"What's this? Safety?"

"No. That's above the left grip. By the slide-release catch. That's the mag-release catch on the front grip strap."

Ryan caught Krysty's eye, both of them struck by the look of wonderment on the boy's face.

"Can I try it out?"

The Armorer shook his head. "I'll give you a box of a hundred rounds, and you and me'll go to the range I saw at the end of the passage. So wait. While we're all looking around, get yourself a decent holster."

"Sure, J.B., and thanks."

Neither Doc nor Mildred could be persuaded to change their firearms.

The old man stuck with his bizarre Le Mat, the nineteenth-century revolver with its scattergun barrel. J.B. tried to persuade him to take a modern automatic.

"I'm really most awfully grateful, my dear chap. But I shall carry on with this until I finally run out of ammunition for it."

"As long as I can get Smith & Wesson .38s, I'll keep with my ZKR 55," Mildred said. "If there's a better target pistol around, I haven't found it yet."

"How about you, Krysty?" the Armorer said. "That old Heckler & Koch is a bit past its best now, isn't it?"

"I'm used to it. You got a better idea?"

"Sure." He unpacked a shrink-wrapped weapon. "Here, stainless and smooth. No snags on it. Smith & Wesson double-action. Six-forty model. Only five shot, but it's real compact. Close combat. Two-inch barrel. Weighs around twenty ounces. Why not bring it to the range and try her out?"

"Sure," she agreed, hefting the little blaster.

"Ryan, that Heckler & Koch G-12 caseless is a real fine weapon. But you know the problems we've been having in getting ammo for it. There's none listed for it in this redoubt."

"Oh, come on. I've learned to love this baby."

"Once the baby runs dry, she's a piece of scrap metal, Ryan."

"Best I had for what we want."

J.B. rubbed a thumb thoughtfully along the angle of his jaw. "Reckon we should think this through. We got blasters. All of us. What we need now is a really fine long gun. You're the best shot, Ryan."

"Sniper's rifle?"

The Armorer nodded. "They got a case of Steyr SSG-70s. Bolt action, 10-round with a neat little nightscope and laser image enhancer. All we need, really."

"What's it fire? The 7.62 mm round?"

"Right. Pick them up anywhere."

Doc coughed. "Far be it for me to interrupt this highfalutin and exceedingly expert conversation, but Mildred and I are becoming a little bored. We shall return and brew up some more of that execrable coffee-sub."

"Sure," Ryan agreed, barely listening to the old man. All his thoughts were concentrated on the blaster needs of the group. He grudgingly agreed with J.B. that the G-12 had finally had its day for him.

"Then we need something as a real close stopper and some sort of machine pistol," he said.

"How about your handgun?"

"I'll stick with the SIG-Sauer. No reason to change. Nine mill ammo's all over the place. What about you? Ditch the Steyr and get an Uzi? Something like that, J.B.?"

"They got six of the Uzi pistols. Not the mini-Uzis. Twenty rounds of nine mill. Looks about as pretty as a drowned stickie. Give us instant saturation fire when we want that."

Ryan looked at the snub little blaster approvingly. "Leaves you shy a long gun. What's it to be? Big pump-action stopper?"

"Better."

"Better, J.B. Do tell."

The Armorer was smiling. "Come look." He walked along the avenue of shelving, ticking off numbers from the inventory listing. "Here it is," he announced.

"Smith & Wesson. The M-4000," Ryan said. "Seen them before. Twelve gauge, holds eight rounds. Pistol grip and a folding butt. What's so special about that?"

J.B. beckoned to him, pointing to some boxes of ammo. "Haven't seen these before, have you, old buddy?"

"Fléchettes," read the one-eyed man. "What the fuck's a fléchette?"

"Nail with fins," the Armorer replied. "Here. I'll show you."

There were two different kinds of boxes of shotgun rounds, all marked 12G Fléchette.

Some were manufactured by Remington, and others carried the name of Winchester-Olin. J.B. broke open a box of each, showing them to Ryan, Krysty and Dean. He tore a red Winchester round in half, picking out a number of tiny nails from the white plastic packing. Each was about an inch in length, very thin, with little flights at the blunt end.

"Get twenty of these little bastards in a single round," J.B. said, offering them to the other three.

"Very sharp," the boy said, looking at a pearl of blood on the ball of his thumb where he'd tested one of the fléchettes.

"How about accuracy?" Ryan asked.

Krysty was looking at the contents of one of the green Remington cartridges. The slender miniarrows were packed into black granules of plastic.

"Vicious," she said quietly.

J.B. answered Ryan's question. "First off they found, back in the days of the Nam War, that they tended to tumble when they were fired. That brought the effective accurate range to over a hundred feet. By then they'd straightened out and were lethal. Other thing is, they aren't too great in undergrowth. No penetration."

"Which rounds you going to take?" asked Dean.

"Read someplace that the Remington had better penetration and tighter grouping. So, I'll take their spare ammo."

"You boys go and play with your new toys," Krysty said. "I'll join Mildred and Doc."

In fresh clothes and newly armed, Ryan, J.B. and Dean went to the range to do some test firing.

Chapter Fifteen

The range was at the farthest end of the redoubt and was obviously only the thickness of one wall away from the outside. It was extremely warm. The concrete was filmed with moisture and covered in a coating of iridescent lichen.

There were also a number of holes at floor level, particularly in the corners of the shooting range, some of them more than a foot in diameter.

Dean noticed them and asked what they were. "Look like rat holes to me," he said, "but they're double-big."

Ryan bent and tried to peer into one, wrinkling his nose. "Stinks seriously evil inside. Can't see anything."

"The internal door's sec steel," J.B. said. "If they get in here, they can't get anywhere else. Whatever they are."

Dean had quickly gotten used to his new possession, firing under the Armorer's instruction. The range was only forty yards long, and all of the targets had rotted years ago. But J.B. ripped up some old veneer boards to use, propping them against the damp sand at the far end.

"Slow and easy. Sight and squeeze. Don't jerk at the trigger."

At first the boy squinted, closing his left eye as he sighted along the barrel of the weapon, and managed to get most of the bullets inside a two-foot circle.

"How's that?" he asked proudly.

"Good," J.B. replied, bringing a smile to Dean's lips—and removing it immediately. "But a country mile shy of good enough."

"Why?"

"Your father here shoots one-eyed. The gods didn't give him much choice. He's been like that since he was young. Got used to it. Become a better than adequate shot. Specially with a long gun."

"I thought you had to close one eye."

J.B. shook his head. "No. Certainly not with a handgun. Some think it's better with a rifle. I don't, myself. Like I say, it's a matter of opinion. But with a blaster like this, you keep them both open. You got that? Then try it."

Dean fired the small pistol, the ten rounds running into each other like a continuous explosion of sound. J.B. waited until he heard the hammer fall on an empty chamber, then started to walk up to check the target.

Ryan turned to his son. "Small point, Dean. Try and count shots so it gets to be a habit. You got an enemy in a firefight and he hears that dry click, he knows you're empty. And he comes looking for you."

"Oh, yeah."

"And try standing side-on. Smaller target. While we're here, with plenty of ammo, practice a lot. You won't get a better chance."

"How many men have you killed, Ryan?" the boy asked, reloading the blaster.

"Do that with your eyes shut."

"What?"

"Reload. In the dark. On your belly. On your back. One-handed. Other-handed."

"Yeah."

J.B. was walking back with the piece of plywood in his fist.

"Better. Not much more than a foot spread this time. Better."

The boy grinned at him. "But still not good enough...by a country mile."

"It's not bad. But you gotta remember this is calm and friendly, and you and me and Ryan. Warm and dry and well lit, and a target that sits there and smiles at you."

"Sure." Dean looked at his father. "Didn't answer my question."

"What?"

"My question."

J.B. took the Smith & Wesson from the boy. He worked the action a couple of times, head on one side to listen to it. "Nice. Keep it oiled, Dean. You stop looking after your weapons, and you fill six of cold wet dirt. Right?"

"Sure."

"What was his question, Ryan?" the Armorer asked, handing back the blaster.

"How many?"

J.B. turned to look at the boy, his eyes invisible behind the polished lenses of his spectacles, his sallow face curiously blank. "You want to know how many your father's chilled?"

"Yeah."

"No, you don't."

"Why?"

"Chilling's a craft, like any other. You learn it. Learn it hard. Ryan hasn't kept score of the men. The women. The children. Oh, yeah, Dean…there's been plenty of kids sent off on that last train to the coast."

Ryan held his son by the shoulders and stooped to look directly into his face. "You don't count the eyes. The spilled guts. The severed fingers. The blood boiling from the groin. The screams. The open mouths and the white lips. Splintered teeth and ripped flesh. You don't count any of that. The best—the very best—you can hope for is to forget some of it."

"But you do that…because you have to. Yeah? So, doesn't that make it right?"

J.B. answered him. "There's no such thing as a good war, Dean. But there's sometimes such a thing as a right war. Same with chilling."

"Talk's cheap and time's passing," Ryan said. "Let's try out the other new blasters."

"Not worth bothering with your Steyr rifle," the Armorer stated.

"Guess not. Need a lot more distance to try and sight it in."

"How about that machine pistol, J.B.?"

The boy's question went unanswered by the Armorer who simply cocked the snub automatic and pumped all twenty rounds at a ragged sheet of wood.

There was a single, continuous ripple of sound, like a sheet of taut calico being torn in half. The piece of plywood danced and bounced, almost disintegrating into shreds of white splinters.

"Evil," Dean said admiringly.

J.B. laid the empty gun down. "Not bad," he said.

"Going to try out the scattergun?" Ryan asked.

"Waste it on dirt. Want a different sort of target to test it."

At that precise moment, almost as if it had been sent special delivery, a giant mutie rat appeared in the shooting range.

Ryan spotted it first, with J.B. a shard of a second behind. The boy didn't see it until he picked up on the men's reactions.

The creature was the size of a small pig. Its body was over two feet long, with its reptilian tail adding another eighteen inches, and it stood over a foot tall at the shoulder.

Its head was broad above the eyes, narrowing to a feral muzzle, and its jaws were open, revealing a double row of yellow, needled teeth. The rodent stared unblinkingly at the intruders to its domain, its red eyes gleaming with a manic fire.

"Shit," Dean whispered.

Ryan's hand fell to the butt of the SIG-Sauer, ready to blast the nightmare creature. The boy also started to level his own blaster, but both of them stopped at a word from J.B.

"Mine," the Armorer said.

The stock on the Smith & Wesson M-4000 was folded forward. J.B. kept one eye on the crouched rat, while he clicked the stock back, bringing the blaster up to his shoulder.

The mutie rodent was hissing between its teeth, a thin string of spittle trailing from its lips to the concrete floor. Its powerful hind legs were flexed, ready to propel it in a leap.

Either for the safety of its hole, or toward the trio of invaders.

Nothing moved.

"Go on," Ryan said very quietly.

The claws of the rat were scratching at the stone in a sound that grated on the nerves.

"Better test of the shotgun if it started to move." J.B. stood braced, ready.

"I'll make it move," Dean offered taking three steps forward, hawking and spitting. The ball of saliva struck the creature between its left ear and eye.

For a moment it didn't react, then they heard a weird sound, halfway between a squeal and a snarl, starting deep in the creature's gray-furred chest, breaking from the scummed lips.

"Watch..." Ryan began, seeing the tail flick and the muscular hindquarters quiver.

But his warning would have been way too late.

The giant rodent was already powering itself toward the slight figure of the boy, less than twenty feet away from it. Its mouth was open, and its bucked teeth were ready to rake and tear.

The boom of the Smith & Wesson filled the low-ceilinged bunker. For the first time in his life Ryan heard the noise of fléchettes in lethal flight, a brief hissing sound, like a sharp exhalation of air or a stiff brush against a sheet of honed steel. His eye caught the glitter of movement as the twenty miniature arrows burst from the barrel of the 12-gauge.

The rat was in midflight when it was struck by the fléchettes. The range was short for the effective use of the weapon, but the result was still totally devastating.

The tiny nails hit the leaping animal in the side of the chest, every one of the twenty finding its target. The power of the impact sent the rat toppling to its left side, a high thin cry bubbling from its throat. It landed heavily, making one attempt to rise, then lay still, only its legs scrabbling with a residual memory of what living had been.

Most of the fléchettes had ripped clear through, taking flesh, muscle, bone and tatters of torn lung with them. Some tinkled against the far wall, dropping spent and bloody.

J. B. Dix grinned delightedly. "Hey," he said, "it works!"

Chapter Sixteen

They stayed in the redoubt for another day, using the time to rest their bodies and minds, to get used to the uncomfortable stiffness of new clothes and to acclimate to their change of weaponry.

Dean spent most of his waking hours down in the range, though Ryan and J.B. made sure that there was always at least one other person with him.

Mutie rats of that size didn't hunt alone. The danger was emphasized by the disappearance of the corpse of the slaughtered rodent. But there was no sign of any fresh threat. However, everyone made extrasure that the sec doors to the range were kept firmly shut and locked.

Krysty shared Ryan's interest in the past, and she spent much of the spare day going around the complex, hoping to find something left behind from the far-off days.

But it had been well cleared.

That second night she was lying pressed close to Ryan, like two spoons, cradled together. They'd just made love for the third time.

"Ryan?" she whispered.

He groaned. "Not yet, lover. Give me a couple of minutes to recover from that last one."

She slapped him on the naked shoulder. "Just watch that mouth of yours."

"Wasn't what you said ten minutes ago."

"Listen, I'm being serious."

"Sure. Go ahead."

"Know what I dream about?"

"Yeah. Finding someplace where there's green grass, clean water and good air. A safe place away from the chilling and rad sickness, where we can settle down together. Right?"

There was a long pause after he'd spoken.

"That wasn't what I was going to say, Ryan, my love, but you got the best ace on the line with it. Sure, that's what I want most in the world. Some nights, around two in the morning—blood flowing slowest and the time when the soul is at its darkest—I think we'll never do it. Stupid dream, that's all. Other times I still hope and...and dream."

"You don't have any dreams, then there's no way they can come true," Ryan whispered, reaching out and taking her hand in his.

"Yeah, I know that. I guess we keep on walking and looking." She paused again. "That wasn't what I was thinking about. I always hope that we'll find a redoubt that's still got the letters and stuff from the last men and women there. Diaries. You know. But there never is anything."

Ryan remembered the piece of paper he'd picked up under the discarded cap, near the entrance to the gateway.

He slid out of bed, padding barefoot across the

floor, touching the light button. "Cover your eyes," he warned.

"Why?"

"Wanna show you something. Found it yesterday after the jump."

The light clicked on, filling the bare room with a harsh glare. Ryan reached into the pockets of his coat, finding the crumpled bit of paper.

He sat down on the bed, unfolding it with a careful delicacy. Krysty sat up in the nest of blankets and leaned forward.

"What is it, lover?"

"Words and numbers. But triple-faded. Can't read them properly."

"Let me look."

She bowed her head over the paper, her hair uncoiling across her shoulders like a cascade of fire. "Can't see the… Some kind of a code?"

"Could be."

"Places?"

Ryan squinted at it, angling the surface to try to catch all of the available light. "Looks like…like 'San Isidro,' or something like that. Then eight numbers and letters."

"Gateway code?" Krysty looked at him, her face excited. "If only we could control the jumps, lover…"

Ryan shook his head. "No good. Still can't read it properly. Anyway, there's only a few places listed here. Must've been loads of gateways built."

He took the paper and replaced it in the pocket of

his coat, switched off the light and clambered back into bed.

"Feeling better, lover?" she whispered, fingers creeping over his chest and stomach.

"Hell, why not?"

DAWN WAS ALWAYS the best time of day to move on.

They ate together, everyone making a hearty breakfast. All of them, including Dean, knew from bitter experience how long it might be between meals. There was tinned ham and recon eggs; beans with five different sorts of spice; some self-heat loaves of bread that weren't voted flavor of the day.

"Like chewing a pair of old socks," Mildred commented.

"I bow to your superior experience in the field of sock chewing," Doc said, smiling. "I prefer the simile of laundered cotton wool."

Oddly some blueberry muffins, with the same brand name on the cans, were universally declared a great success.

Ryan found some tinned herrings, but remembered his appalling and near-fatal experience the last time he'd tried something like that. He went for the ham and beans with four muffins, swilling it all down with three mugs of the coffee-sub.

Dean barely smothered a belch. "Can we go outside now? I checked that vid-pic lots of times, and there was never anything there. Just a fu— Just a big mess of green."

Ryan stood. "Sure. Everyone finished? Let's go."

THEY STOOD TOGETHER in front of the small sec door that was tucked away behind the sleeping area of the compact redoubt.

Ryan had checked the screen, which still showed the same picture of unrelieved vegetation, moving under a light breeze, illuminated by the dawn's early glow. There wasn't a hint of any sort of life, human or animal.

"Everyone got everything?"

"Is that question directed at me, by any chance?" Doc asked.

"Everyone. We can't come back here for anything forgotten. Blasters and spare ammo? Bit of emergency food and water?"

Dean's hand went to his belt, checking that the slim knife with its turquoise hilt was still there. Ryan had tried to persuade him to take a longer, thicker blade, more like the Armorer's Tekna, but the boy had insisted on sticking with what he'd already got. The fact that he'd been given it by Sharona Carson, his mother, was obviously a factor in his choice.

"Skirmish line," Ryan said. "Me at point and J.B. at the back. Krysty second, then Doc, Dean and Mildred. All right? Then let's move."

The sec door had a simple Open and Close control set into a discolored Plexiglas panel. Ryan pressed the top button.

They heard the familiar hissing, and the sec lock clicked open. Ryan reached for the main handle to pull it toward him when Dean coughed, the sort of cough that was used to draw people's attention to the fact that someone had something to say.

"What?" Ryan probed.

The boy shuffled his feet, thighs squeezed together, eyes down. He didn't reply to the question.

"I asked you—" Then Dean's body language communicated itself to Ryan. "Oh, I get it. You should've gone sooner. Go on. Quick. We'll wait for you."

They heard the tipped boots clattering away through the dormitory region, fading along the corridor.

J.B. glanced at Ryan. "Have to teach him. Everything, all the time."

Ryan nodded. "Yeah. I know it. Here he comes. We all had to learn it all, one time."

"Sorry, Dad," the boy muttered, resuming his place in the line.

Ryan took the handle and pulled it slowly open.

The wave of hot, damp air took everyone's breath away.

"Upon my soul!" Doc exclaimed. "There used to be a Turkish bath somewhere around Fortieth and Third in New York. Tiles and Biblical paintings. Had to watch out for the shirt lifters, I recall. But it felt remarkably like this place does."

"Louisiana," Mildred said.

J.B. fumbled in his pockets for his location-comp, took it out and tried a sighting at the sun. "Difficult to tell from here. Could be Louisiana. Could be Florida. Someplace in the south and east."

"Not Hawaii?" Doc said.

"No. Definitely not Hawaii, Doc. Sorry about that."

All they could see from the doorway was a waving wall of dense, luxurious bushes. There was the rich scent of some heavily perfumed flowers, like orchids, filling the morning breeze.

Ryan glanced over his shoulder at Krysty. "Anything?" he asked.

"Not close, but there's a definite feel of people not far away."

"Can I take some clothes off?" Dean asked. "I'll melt."

"No, you can't, son. We travel light, and we carry everything. Once you leave something behind, you find you need it the next day. Put up with it."

The grass was thick and long, rising around Ryan's ankles as he stepped from the doorway. The earth was moist and spongy, sucking at his boots, moisture springing from the soil. There were bushes and trees all around, the higher branches meeting above their heads, cutting out all but a filtered section of palest blue sky.

After less than a dozen paces forward, the undergrowth had closed in around the companions, making it impossible for them to see the entrance to the concealed redoubt.

Ryan stopped, beckoning the Armorer to join him. "What do you reckon about this? Could get ourselves double-lost in a quarter mile."

J.B. sniffed and pushed his glasses back up his

nose. He reached into his pocket and pulled out a small silver disk. "Homer," he said.

"Got a receiver for it?"

"Nope."

"Great."

"Just have to watch our directions triple-careful, won't we?"

Ryan wiped sweat from his forehead. "Yeah. Thanks a lot, J.B. Plenty of help."

Ahead of him he suddenly glimpsed the silvery reflection of light off water. Cautiously he moved on, entering a small clearing. His foot pressed down into the turf and he felt rather than heard a faint mechanical click.

"Mine!" he yelled, hurling himself flat, the pistol already in his right hand.

Behind him, everyone threw themselves down into the wet grass.

There was a muffled whirring sound and the rustling of movement in the bushes. Only a couple of yards ahead of Ryan the leaves parted and the gray, wrinkled head of a gigantic horned animal loomed through, eyes glittering at the sprawled man.

To Ryan's right there was more movement, and he saw a black man, a good seven feet tall, naked apart from a loincloth and a feathered headdress, heading toward him with a vicious stabbing-spear in his hand.

"No!" Ryan shouted.

But he was too late.

Chapter Seventeen

The view of the others had been slightly obstructed by the bushes, and they hadn't had that extra fraction of a drawn second to see what Ryan had been able to see. So they all opened fire at both the menacing creature and the man with the spear before Ryan could yell his warning to them.

All of them except Doc Tanner, who dropped his heavy Le Mat in the long grass as he dived forward.

Dean put three bullets into the head and neck of the horned animal. Krysty saw the man as the biggest danger and planted two .38s from her new Smith & Wesson double-action into his chest. Mildred didn't like shooting from the prone position, but her target ZKR 551 was as lethally accurate as ever, one round striking the threatening native between his staring eyes.

And J.B.'s Uzi did its stuff. A 6-round burst opened up the skull of the animal.

The results of all that firepower were completely devastating.

And surprising.

The head of the creature, including the long horn, was blown apart, into a mass of tangled wires, small wheels and torn fiberglass.

The native with the spear toppled forward, revealing that he had no legs, but was balanced on two short metal struts. His chest and head exploded into optic threads, multicolored cables and comp panels.

The electronic carnage shorted out some of the relays in a shower of fizzing sparks and triggered a hidden loop tape.

"Oh-oh! Looks like we better steer clear of shore. That rhino's got a mean horn waiting for us, and the Zulu warrior could spear us with his *assegai* before you say 'Jungle Adventures.' Watch it, folks!"

The voice was calm and slightly weary, as though the speaker had overdosed on tranks.

Everyone stood up, looking at the two destroyed mechanical creatures. The cogs still whirred around in the stump of the animal's skull, and the tumbled native was trying to wield his short spear, the point digging a furrow in the grass.

The tape continued, slower and more slurred, sometimes sticking or speeding up. The voice finally faded away into a strange, self-centered muttering, then drifted to silence.

The burst of gunfire didn't seem to have attracted anyone's attention. The trees and bushes were still and quiet, the water beyond drifting by on its own tranquil way.

Ryan looked at the others. "Tried to warn you not to open fire."

"You see they were some kind of droid?" J.B. asked, reloading his Uzi.

"Yeah. Paint's peeling off the black guy, and one

eye was falling out of the rhino's head. That what a rhino looks like? Read about them. Never seen one. Big mother, I guess.''

"What is this?" Dean asked.

"You replaced the shots fired, son?" J.B. asked. "If not, do it."

"Sure, sure. But—"

Mildred answered him. "I think we might have finished up in something called a theme park, Dean."

Ryan looked around. "Should move. Don't know who might have heard all that."

"Trees'll muffle it." J.B. sniffed the air. "No wind to carry it."

"What's a theme park, Mildred?"

"Sort of funfair, with white-knucklers. Disney was one of the first. And best. This doesn't—"

"White knuckles? What are they?"

"Later," Ryan told him.

THE OVERGROWN REMAINS of a winding path ran alongside the water, which turned out to be a shallow river, no more than fifteen feet wide, its surface rainbowed and oily.

They passed rotting blocks of lightweight plastic that looked as if they had once been some sort of Oriental temple. They spotted more droids that Ryan recognized as being elephants, and there was a dried-up waterfall with some kind of heavy machinery behind it.

"Look!" Doc exclaimed. "What a fearsome saurian!"

"If a saurian's a gator, Doc, then it isn't. Another of those models."

The trail wound on, leading them past other unlikely combinations of wild animals frozen for eternity—lions with giraffes watching them, empty eyed. Birds had pecked all the fake fur off the pride, and the weather had faded the patches on the coats of the giraffes to a muted gray.

It was swelteringly hot.

Ryan waved for a halt, wiping the streams of sweat off his cheeks, lifting the eye patch where the salt was irritating the raw socket.

A tiger was lying on its side a few yards ahead of them, its legs stiff and helpless, little metal wheels rusting in each paw. Beyond it was a line of ducks, caught in midwaddle, in decreasing sizes.

"People pay to come see this, Mildred?" he asked. "Double-dull."

"Wasn't just like you see now. There'd be noises, movements and stuff, and this'd be only a small part of the place. Probably lots of other rides and entertainment. My father brought me to Magic Mountain when I was only..." The memory was suddenly so strong that she almost choked on it. Tears flooded her eyes, and her voice swallowed into silence. "Popcorn and piñon pine..." she said almost to herself.

Dean had finally reloaded his Smith & Wesson and tucked it into its holster. He left the others and walked a few paces around the next bend, calling back to them.

"Hey, there's a shit-evil snake here. Looks as real

as life and has bright colors. Big as a subway tunnel back in the ville.''

"Wait for the rest of us," Ryan said.

"Sure, Dad, but it's—''

The sentence stopped dead, as though someone had swung a huge machete and sliced the boy into a fourth dimension.

"Dean!" Ryan called.

"Oh, Gaia! Quick!" Krysty gasped, starting to move.

But the one-eyed man was a clear two yards ahead of anyone. He sprinted around the corner, nearly stumbling into the river, where a part of the bank had subsided. His blaster was cocked and ready.

Ryan came to a sliding halt, holding up his hand to stop the others.

"Wait," he ordered, his voice so harsh and grating that it was hardly recognizable. He holstered the SIG-Sauer. This wasn't one for a pistol.

Unlike the rhino, the lions and the rest of the creatures, the snake wasn't an electronic android creation of the workshop.

This snake was real.

Its overlapping scales shone with a coppery, iridescent gleam. It was impossible to guess at its true length, as much of it was coiled out of sight, around a massive baobab tree. But there was enough to see that it was a mutated giant.

The head was blunt, like a great chisel, and tapered to the narrow lipless mouth, which was half-open to reveal the scarlet forked tongue. It flicked in and out, tasting the air currents around it, the creature's small reptilian brain interpreting the messages and judging safety or the threat of danger.

The body just behind the head was the thickness of a muscular man's forearm, widening until it was bigger than a weight lifter's chest. And held within the twining coils, his feet a yard from the ground, was Dean Cawdor.

The boy wasn't struggling, realizing the utter futility of trying to pit his puny strength against the monster python. One coil was around his ankles, another about his upper chest, pinning his arms down to his sides. Ryan noticed the .22 blaster lying in the grass, showing that the boy had come close to saving himself.

Dean's face was suffused with blood, eyes protruding with the pressure around his body. His mouth was open and he was trying to call out, but the snake was slowly suffocating him.

The only sound in the clearing was the faint rustling of the reptile's dry skin moving against the branches of the tree, and the venomous hissing of its warning breath.

"Poisonous?" J.B. whispered, answering his own question. "Don't think so."

Doc identified the creature. "Must've escaped from a zoo or park or something," he said quietly. "It's a boa constrictor. South American. Indian. Can't tell. Kills its prey by crushing it. Then it devours it slowly and—"

"Enough, Doc," Ryan said.

The snake's head was weaving hypnotically, backward and forward, close by his son's face, making any attempt at a shot incredibly hazardous.

And to put bullets into its body wasn't likely to kill it outright. The odds were that any wound like that would enrage the mutie reptile and make it tighten its enormous length in a convulsive reaction, instantly squeezing the life from the helpless, dangling boy.

Ryan reached for the taped hilt of his panga, the eighteen-inch butcher's knife with the razored steel blade that ended in a sharp point.

The weapon slid from its sheath in a whisper of sound.

"Lover," Krysty cautioned.

Ryan nodded. "I know."

Dean was dying. The python was tightening its grip with an effortless, indifferent ease, paying its victim no more attention than a man crushing a worm under his heel. Ryan could see that his son was sliding into unconsciousness, head lolling. Blood was trickling from beneath the boy's fingernails.

"Right, you son of a fucking bitch," Ryan grated through clenched teeth, fist tight around the hilt of the long knife.

The snake ignored him, its shovel-shaped head moving from side to side, as though it could hear the distant beat of a different drum. Its eyes looked once at the approaching man, then through him and past him, dismissing him as no sort of menace.

Ryan slapped his left hand against the blade of the

panga, making the steel ring, attracting the attention of the snake.

"Come on, come on, come on," he chanted to it, shuffling in closer, pushing one foot forward, keeping his balance, his own eye fixed on the reptile's head.

Ryan waved the panga around his head until the honed metal rang, the filtered sunlight dancing off the steel.

Now he was within less than three good paces of the mutie python.

"Come on, come on..."

The tongue darted out faster and the head swayed more quickly, giving the first clue that the monster was becoming concerned at the possibility of a threat to itself. It seemed for a moment that it had also relaxed its crushing hold on Dean. The lad's face was no longer purple, and his tongue no longer protruded from his swollen lips.

It was difficult to judge the right fraction of a second to strike. The snake was above him, in the foliage, but it was lowering its head, bringing Dean down with it, until the boy's feet actually scraped the wet grass.

Ryan started to move his own head from side to side, copying every sinuous sway of the reptile, slowly at first, then faster and faster.

The tiny eyes were fixed now on his face, the jaws open, the hissing louder. He could taste the python's breath on his skin, warm and sour, like rotted flesh.

It had to be the moment when the head of the mutie snake was far enough away from Dean.

"Now!"

Ryan's reflexes had been whetted by an infinity of firefights.

But the snake was quicker.

Dark Carnival 141

"Nooo!"
Ryan's scream he froze wracked by an infinity of troughs
But there...

Chapter Eighteen

The attack was nearly successful. The edge of the panga nicked the skin at the side of the snake's head, drawing a tiny worm of dark blood. But the reptile was dazzlingly fast. It dodged the singing steel and struck at Ryan's head. If it had been accurate, the power of the blow would probably have killed the man.

But the effort of evading the cutting blow took away part of the effect of the python's counterattack.

Its head struck Ryan a glancing blow on the side of the skull, forcing him to take a couple of staggering steps backward. It made him blink, but he didn't fall, and he didn't drop the panga.

The energy of the thrust took the giant snake farther forward than it had intended, and it dropped a loop of coils onto a lower branch. That, in turn, made it relax its hold on the unconscious boy. Dean slumped on the grass, only one single coil around his chest preventing him from falling free.

The reptile's long head weaved back, eyes turning to look down at its victim. Just for a moment the creature's attention wandered from Ryan.

"No shooting!" he called, forcing his muddled brain into action.

He powered his way in, ducking under the reptile's neck, swinging the panga upward, hacking at the pale, soft skin of the exposed throat.

Cold spots of blood pattered onto his face, nearly blinding him, and he was aware of the piercing hiss of pain and rage from the wounded beast.

"Again!" shouted a voice that he dimly recognized as J.B.'s.

Something hit him on the left shoulder, numbing the muscle, nearly knocking him to the earth. But he kept his balance, hastily wiping his face on his sleeve, clearing away the snake's blood, seeing the black shadow of the head driving toward him for a third time. He managed to half duck, half parry the blow, bringing the eighteen-inch blade around and down, putting all of his strength into it.

Ryan felt the edge bite, drawing it through the muscle behind the creature's head. The steel grated on something that he knew must be bone. He tugged it free, dodging away to his left in anticipation of another deadly thrust from the snake.

But it didn't happen.

"You got it! One more time!"

This time the excited voice was Krysty's, urging him on.

He blinked away the sticky mix of blood and sweat from his good eye, seeing that the python was seriously wounded. A dark ichor was flowing from the gaping lips of the wound in its neck.

This time Ryan had leisure to measure his attack, take his time, step in with the cautious shuffle of the great knife fighters. He dodged the swinging head and brought the panga up and around.

And *down*.

The long skull was severed from the trunk, falling to the dirt with a dull, wet, thudding sound.

There was a second, fainter noise as Dean dropped free, landing at his father's feet, his eyes closed, his face like ivory.

The vast length of the giant snake's body began to thrash and flail among the branches of the baobab. Leaves fell, and part of the main bole of the tree split in half. Blood jetted everywhere, and the air seemed filled with an insensate maelstrom of thunderous noise and movement.

Ryan dropped the blood-slick weapon and scooped up his son, carrying him away to safety on the near side of the clearing.

He stooped and laid him on the grass among the friends. The boy seemed no weight at all, and his arms and legs dangled limply.

"Mildred?" Ryan said questioningly.

"Move away. Probably shock." She knelt and felt for Dean's pulse, nodding. "Steady and firm. He'll be fine."

On the farther edge of the glade the headless trunk of the giant boa constrictor still moved in the tree, but more slowly, the coils gradually sliding off, finishing in an untidy mountain of muscle on the trampled, bloodied turf. It seemed that the bright hues of the scales were already fading, the bronze gleam becoming dulled.

By the time that Dean's eyes twitched open, the dead snake was completely still.

"How do you feel?" Mildred asked, gently wiping his forehead.

"Throat's dry. Chest hurts a lot."

The woman unbuttoned his dark blue shirt and pulled it open, whistling softly at the livid bruises that blotched the white skin around the ribs.

"You can see the actual scale marks on his flesh," she said.

"Broken bones?" Doc asked.

"Can't tell yet. Feel like standing up, Dean? Check you out."

"Might want to be sick," he said, his voice sounding hoarse and strained.

"Let me help you, son," Ryan offered.

"You killed that motherfucking snake?" The boy looked up at his father. "Thanks, Dad."

"Sure. Want a lift?"

"Dad?"

"What?"

A trembly hand beckoned him lower so that the others wouldn't hear.

"Something, Dad."

"Injury?"

"No."

"So, what?"

The boy's pale cheeks flushed. "I think I've pissed my pants."

FATHER AND SON WASHED in the turgid waters of the slow-moving river.

It was good to wash off the stinking blood of the snake and to try to cool off a little, though the water was only a little less warm than body heat.

Dean didn't seem to have suffered too much damage from his ordeal. The bruising would soon begin to turn yellow and fade, and Mildred was certain there were no fractures.

"He'll be stiff and sore for a few days" was her only comment.

The boy found his fingers were tender and his neck hurt when he tried to turn his head too quickly to the left.

He swam easily, but Ryan noticed that the boy was careful not to move any distance from him. The experience had taught him a degree of caution, which was no bad thing to learn when you were moving through Deathlands.

"Best get out and put your clothes on."

They'd both stripped out of their top layers, and the boy had also removed his underclothes, washing them hastily in the river before pulling them on again over his pale loins.

The others were all sitting on a fallen log, talking quietly together, and looked up as father and son rejoined them.

"Mildred and Doc reckon this must've been a sort of park. But there might be other parts to it. Could've been a zoo. It'd explain the giant snake."

Ryan nodded at Krysty's words. "Makes sense. Best be careful. Everyone ready now? Then let's go."

A BRIDGE STRETCHED across the river, with the rusted remnants of an iron chain dangling from it. A rotted sign still carried the message: Please Keep Out. Service Personnel Only.

"Looks like the end of the attraction," Mildred commented.

"There appear to be the poor stranded hulks of some pleasure craft lying over yonder," Doc said, pointing with the silver ferrule of his swordstick. "I imagine they carried the seekers of joy around this strange jungle environ."

The boats had been plastic and looked as if they'd once had some sort of awning over them. It was still possible to see that they had all borne numbers on their blunt bows.

"Can still make out names on them," J.B. said, head on one side as he figured them out. "One called *Queen of the South.* That's *Old Man River.*"

"Listen," Dean said, his voice squeaking upward in excitement.

"Sounded like a shot," Krysty suggested. "Way off, though."

"Could've been an M-16 carbine." J.B. looked around. "Can't tell distance or direction in thick undergrowth like this."

The path wound on.

Ryan was leading, and he was the first to see the huge fallen tree ahead of them. It had been some kind of ornamental redwood, with a massive girth. By its condition it could easily have toppled over during the brief days of nuke-fall.

The path vanished under it, and it was possible to make out a dense growth of trees and bushes on the far side of the great hulk.

It was an effort to scramble over the tree, and Dean had to be helped on both sides. His sore ribs made any kind of physical exertion difficult, though he resented not being able to cope on his own.

"Could jump this, easy," he said. "Fucking snake did me in a bit. That's all."

Ryan caught a warning glance from Krysty. "Try and keep the swearing down, son. Keep using a word like 'fuck' and after a while it doesn't mean anything. All right?"

"Sure, Dad." He looked at the redhead. "Sorry, Krysty," he added.

The traveling became infinitely harder on the far side of the tree. In among the droids it seemed as if the paths had been kept open by animals. Here there was just unbroken undergrowth.

"Botanist's paradise," Mildred murmured, ducking under some overhanging branches dappled with sweet-smelling pink flowers.

"Walker's purgatory," Doc sneered, raising an arm to prevent himself being slapped in the face by tendrils from a thorny bush.

"Hold it."

Ryan had seen light ahead. The bushes and trees seemed to be growing thinner, and he'd spotted what looked like some sort of wider path. The others stopped and waited in silence. He glanced back and beckoned to Krysty.

"Feel anything, lover?"

She closed her eyes and concentrated. Sweat was beading her forehead, but she ignored it. "Yeah. There's something around here. Confused sort of feeling, but I'm sure of it. People. Lot of them. Muddled signal coming through. Sorry I can't tell you any more than that, lover."

"It'll do." He waved the others to join them, and they all squatted in a closed circle on the damp earth under a gigantic bougainvillea.

"Seems like we're close to civilization. Now, we know that most villes are fairly safe. Outlanders get regarded with suspicion, but we should be okay if we stick together." He looked around. "Or we can go back to the redoubt and try another jump someplace else."

"Anywhere's the same as anywhere, isn't it?" Mildred said.

"By the three Kennedys! On the scale of all-time facile remarks, madam, yours would stand remarkably near the top."

She pulled a face at him. "What's that mean, you double-stupe old goat?"

"It means that I have personally encountered a number of 'anywheres' that were profoundly wonderful. I have also inhabited some 'anywheres' that would have made the scuppers of a Victorian slaving ship seem like the gates of heaven."

"Doc's right," J.B. agreed. "But there's only one way to find out, and that's to go take a look. Man can get awful tired of always turning his back on the future.''

Mildred laid a hand on his arm. "I'll drink to that, John."

Ryan waited. "So it looks like some votes for going on and breaking some ice. Any objections? No? So we'll move on."

IF THEY WERE SOMEWHERE on the outskirts of a frontier ville, it was one of the trimmest and neatest that Ryan had ever seen.

The wide paths were swept and lined with rectangular stones, each painted a shimmering white. Beds of flowers were set out in geometric patterns, and small streams meandered over delicate pebbles. In the first hundred yards they passed four small fountains. In one a little boy held a conch shell. In another a girl danced with a flower. A third had a prancing horse and the last, a warrior on one knee. All were skillfully sculpted and preserved.

"Some place," Dean said, walking at his father's side.

The slopes were gentle, the surface of the interlinked paths smooth. The banks of flowers rose to high walls of yew hedges that blocked off any distant perspectives.

"Someone's watching us, lover," Krysty informed Ryan in a quiet, conversational voice.

"Yeah. I can feel it, as well. Everyone on alert-red. And keep—"

He was interrupted by a strident, amplified voice roaring from the bushes all around them.

"You outlanders lay down the blasters right now, or you get a bad case of lead-shred. Do it now, people. Now!"

"Do it now," Ryan said.

He was interrupted by a sudden, amplified voice, roaring from the bushes all around them.

"You outlanders lay down the blasters right now or you get triple-chilled. Land-blasters, now, you piss-poor crew of feebs. Any man or woman or mutie don't drop it away, they get chilled."

Chapter Nineteen

For several heartbeats nothing happened at all.

Ryan laid his new Steyr rifle by his feet, letting his pistol remain in its holster. Both Krysty and Mildred put down their blasters, and Doc, snuffling with anger, drew the Le Mat and placed it carefully on the raked gravel. J.B. put the shotgun down.

Dean had remained frozen in place, the .22 Smith & Wesson gripped in his right hand.

"Kid puts down his little toy. One-eyed man and the runt with the glasses better dig out those automatics and get them in the dirt. Fast, people!"

Ryan sighed and took the P-226 from its holster and placed it on the path, butt towards him, ready for a last despairing grab. J.B. also put down his new Uzi.

Dean didn't move.

"Don't wanna chill a kid, but he gets powdered in five secs from now if he hangs on to his blaster. Five and countin', people."

Ryan turned to his son, seeing the tightness of the boy's jaw and the blank stare in his eyes. All around them the amplified count was down to three.

"Two."

He took the couple of steps and gripped his son by

the wrist, feeling the fragile strength in the boy's bones and muscles.

"Give it me, Dean," he demanded. "Or we all go down in a river of blood."

His son's face looked up at him. "Rona said never give in," he whispered.

Ryan took the Smith & Wesson from the unresisting fingers and put it carefully down. "Your mother was part right. But Trader used to say that he who doesn't fight but runs away, lives to run away another day. Get it?"

"Yeah." He cracked the shadow of a smile. "Yeah, I get it."

There were a few moments of almost total silence, broken only by the hissing of the concealed speakers. Then the voice came back, softer.

"Done good, one-eyed man. Now just stand a few paces off from the blasters, and me and some of my men'll come out from cover and take you all to have a talk with Boss Larry."

Ryan looked round at J.B., standing almost at his elbow. "Boss Larry?" he mouthed.

"No." The Armorer shook his head. "Must be the local baron, I guess."

From behind the tall screen of trimmed yew trees, the first of the hidden sec men made his appearance. He was holding an 8-shot, Government Model Colt .45. His uniform was a camouflage jacket and pants in a variety of shades of green and brown, and he wore polished combat boots. There was a dark green beret on his head. He looked around thirty and had a casual professionalism that hinted at some efficient training somewhere up the line.

He had four silver stripes on his left sleeve.

"Best of the day to you, people. Welcome to the ville of Greenglades. Home of the Baron Boss Larry. I'm called Kelly, and I'm in charge of the squad of general layabouts and vagabonds you see emerging from the bushes around you."

There were ten in the patrol, all armed with identical Colt blasters, all in the same uniform and showing the same sort of alertness as the noncom, Kelly. They kept a careful distance from the six friends, making sure each one was covered.

Any kind of move against the sec men would have been instant suicide. Seeing they had only handguns, Ryan had considered risking a firefight. But that would almost certainly have left some of them down and dying.

So far, everyone was still alive.

So far.

"Not very talkative bunch of outlanders, are you?"

Ryan looked at the stocky figure. "Haven't had much chance to get a word in."

Kelly laughed. "Right. Right, my one-eyed friend."

"You taking us to the baron?" J.B. asked.

"Course. Any objection?"

"No. Getting bored with waiting."

"You I like also. Maybe we'd better just run some names by me. So I can introduce you properly to Boss Larry."

"I'm Ryan Cawdor. Boy here's my son, Dean."

"And where do y'all come from, Ryan Cawdor and your son, Dean?"

Ryan waved a hand vaguely toward the trees. "Around," he said.

"Sure. Rest of your names? Ladies?"

"Krysty Wroth."

"Dr. Mildred Wyeth."

"Doctor? Like you heal people? Cure them of croup, mumps, measles, the pox, the flux, the wasting sickness and—"

Mildred held up a hand. "Yeah, but not all of them at once."

Kelly laughed. "Sense of humor. Like that. My best point is my sense of humor. So they tell me." He looked at Doc Tanner. "How about you, old-timer? You got a name?"

"Of course I have a name, you pumped-up little parakeet! My name is Dr. Theophilus Tanner and before you ask me, I will not be curing any pox or flux. Or any other illness, if it comes to that. My doctorate is in science and not in medicine."

The muzzle of the big Colt moved a little to center on the old man's belt buckle. "I like a sense of humor, but don't like lippy pricks that think they're better than the rest of the baron's creatures. You reading me, Dr. Tanner?"

Doc nodded. "I accept the rebuke, Mr. Kelly. A touch of verbal dysentery has always been one of my vanities."

"Vanities? What the sucking death are they?"

"Weaknesses. I have many vanities, my dear fellow. So many that I sometimes think that I should consign them all to a large bonfire."

Kelly looked him slowly up and down. "You I might like. Again, I might not. How about you? Little guy with the punch-packing blaster. Incidentally, people, I never seen any outlanders traveling with such an interesting mess of hardware. Where d'you—" He stopped as if a thought had just struck him. "Yeah, that's for the Boss. Just your name for now."

"Name's J. B. Dix. Can we pick up our blasters?"

Kelly laughed, head back, eyes wrinkling with amusement. Ryan thought the man was probably one of the most coldhearted killers he'd ever seen. Then again, a man could always be wrong.

One baron he'd met, up on the edge of the Darks, had a woman sec chief who'd looked like everyone's favorite granny. But Ryan had personally seen the apple-cheeked old lady hack open a prisoner's chest and tear out his lungs.

You never could tell.

"We'll carry your blasters for you, Mr. Dix. You, and all your outlander companions. Maybe the baron'll let you have them back." He added after a calculated pause, "And maybe he won't."

"I'd like to see you walking in a nice line. Keep a couple of yards gap. Mr. Cawdor first, then the ladies and the funny old man. Mr. Dix comes last of all."

"What about me?" Dean asked, the first words he'd spoken since they'd been taken prisoner.

Kelly narrowed his eyes. "Your name was...? What was it?"

"Dean."

"You walk along with me, son. So if your daddy or any of them get foolish ideas, then I get to blow the side of your head all over the path. What a mess, what a mess!" He put on a silly, squeaky little voice. "Blood and brains and itsy-teeny sharp bits of bone all everywhere."

Ryan caught his eye. "We going to stay here and hear you jerking off all day, or do we get to meet the baron?"

The smile vanished like late frost off a sun-warmed roof. "Sure," Kelly said. "Yeah, sure."

THE PATROL OF SEC MEN had been well trained. They kept a safe distance from their prisoners, some walking ahead and some behind. Kelly strolled amiably at the front, occasionally pointing something out to the young boy, who mostly kept silent.

It was an amazing ville.

Ryan had seen pix in old mags and vids of the theme parks that sprang up toward the end of the twentieth century. There were wild rides through tottering webs of steel while everyone screamed. He knew there were also different kinds of attractions, most of them aimed at children.

"What was this place called, pre-dark?" he shouted to Kelly.

The noncom glanced over his shoulder. "Nowhere

else like this in all Deathlands. Used to be called Greenglades Theme Park. Best in Florida.''

At last they knew for certain where the jump had landed them. It wasn't all that far from one of their earlier adventures in the heart of the bayous. Home of young Jak Lauren.

"What's it called now?"

Kelly laughed. "Still the same. Greenglades ville. Like it?''

Ryan nodded. "Like you say. I never seen nothing like it before.''

Krysty whispered at his shoulder. "Anything. Not nothing. Anything.''

A HUGE AMOUNT OF JACK had been expended on bringing the old park up to its present state, and an impressive quality of technical expertise.

Even the old signs had been repainted, telling what the attractions were named.

They walked past several. Some were what Mildred told them had been called roller-coaster rides, where people were strapped into little cars and sent hurtling at speeds that defied gravity and death.

"They took you over, under and around. Up and down and through. Backward, forward and inside and out.''

"I recall a visit to Coney Island," Doc said, "where I ate some hideous pink confection like sugared mist. I threw baseballs at coconuts and tried to win a Kewpie doll with a missighted Winchester. And I rode a Swirly-Whirly.''

"Like it, Doc?"

"I fear not, my dear Mildred. I went with my friend, Brutus Featherstonehaugh. Brutus was sick in an omnibus, and I was sick in my hat."

Kelly looked around. "Keep the noise down, people. Not far from Centerpoint."

They'd gone by the Undersea Cruise and the Pharaoh's Curse, past what had once been some kind of fast-food eatery but was now a sec base. Paraglide Paradise was a huge tower with chutes clipped on to steel cables. A massive ship hung from a sort of pendulum; the name on the sign was Billy Bones' Brain-Basher.

"Hey, Kelly?" J.B. called.

"Yo?"

"Who goes on all these rides?"

"Boss Larry."

"Nobody else?"

"Sure. Friends and helpers."

Doctor Phibe's House of Mystery and Illusion was a cavelike attraction, with its entrance designed to look like the rot-tooth jaws of a scabrous skull. Next to it was Mehitabel's Carousel. A sign near a low gate read If You Are Too Tall To Go Through Here Without Stooping, Then You Don't Get To Ride The Ride. Sorry.

Ryan noticed that his son was, despite his natural reserve, becoming entranced by the wonders he saw offered on every side. He was now talking animatedly to the sec man, tugging at his sleeve to attract his attention.

Kelly turned around once and saw Ryan watching him speaking to Dean. The sec man's lips curled into something like a merry smile, but his eyes remained as cold as sierra meltwater.

"How much farther to meet the baron?" Mildred called.

"That's Centerpoint up ahead. Step it out, people."

Now they could see their destination.

It was a tower about two hundred feet high, with a wider part on its top. Which, Ryan noticed, appeared to be revolving slowly in a clockwise direction. It was filled with windows.

It was an amazing structure, and it seemed to be in perfect condition.

Kelly held up a hand, and the patrol stopped smartly. The prisoners shuffled to a less formal halt.

"How come all this stuff from before the long winters is still standing?" Krysty asked.

"Lot of questions, little lady. Better save them for Boss Larry. But I can tell you the answer is neutron bombs. Not that a pretty filly like you'll have heard of those beauties."

"Don't be a double-stupe," she said. "Bombs that kill life and leave buildings."

"Well, yeah."

There were two light machine-gun emplacements on either side of the entrance. Inside, Ryan could make out at least a dozen more sec men standing around. He glanced behind, seeing the oddly deserted paths winding among the greenery. The sky was an almost colorless blue, and the intense humidity of the early morning had abated.

"Ready, people. Boss Larry's up top this time of day, watching his world go by him. So, we'll all go to him."

Dean rejoined his father. "Kelly says we can mebbe go on some of the rides. Wouldn't that be a hot pipe?"

"Yeah," said Ryan, who hadn't the least idea what a "hot pipe" was, but got the general drift.

THERE WAS A BANK of six elevators.

Kelly took Dean into one of them, his blaster drawn and resting, so casually, against the side of the boy's head. The others went separately, each with two of the sec men. It was a fine chance for Ryan to chill the guards with him, but it would have been a pointless exercise.

The numerals above the sliding doors clicked all the way to Roof.

There were more of the guards on the top floor, each dressed in the same camouflage gear, each holding a Colt that was in immaculate condition.

The entire tower top was a large, circular room with a number of chairs and sofas scattered about it. A few of the windows had draperies of deep purple, but most were uncovered. Ryan noticed some antique vid games on one side, most with screens alight with flickering colors and shapes.

An oval table was covered with the remains of a gargantuan breakfast. Polished metal dishes held a few shreds of scrambled egg or a dried rasher of bacon. Another one, shaped like a tureen, held the scummy dregs of some sort of fish chowder. A pile of pancakes had tumbled wearily in on itself, soaked in a spilled pool of syrup.

The air was dusty and filled with the pungent, acrid odor of good grass.

Dimly visible, across the far side of the room, was a very large chair, almost as big as a throne in a kids' storybook. It swiveled, but the sunlight left the occupant in darkness.

"Outlanders, Boss Larry," Kelly said. "Let me introduce them to you."

The voice was obscenely rich and thick, like bubbles through whipped cream. "Two of them I know already from a long time back. John Dix and Ryan Cawdor. I swore when last we met that I'd kill them when I saw them next. And now I will."

The only sound in the stillness of the slowly revolving room was a click as a machine pistol was cocked.

Chapter Twenty

"My knife'd be in your eye before either of them hit the floor."

There was a long stillness that seemed to stretch beyond belief. Ryan heard Kelly whisper a curse under his breath. Out of the corner of his good eye, he could see that his son had slithered away to the right, drawing the turquoise-hilted knife. To hit the man who sat veiled in black shadow would have tested the edges of even Jak's skill, and the albino boy had been the best with a throwing knife that Ryan had ever seen.

Then again, Boss Larry wasn't to know that.

"Is that a dwarf or a child, Kelly?"

"Kid. Cawdor's son."

"Have you allowed them all to keep their knives, Kelly?"

"Yeah, Boss. Sorry."

The figure moved slightly. "I know the one-eyed man and the small one with the glasses. Put them in a room with six of your best. Them just with knives, and ours with their Colts. I wouldn't give you odds, Kelly, about who would walk from the room. They're two of the most dangerous men in all the length and breadth of Deathlands."

Then Ryan knew him.

"Larry Zapp," he said. "Least, that was what you called yourself back then. Fireblast, it must be at least ten, twelve years."

J.B. remembered him, too. "Up on the west side of the Big Lakes. Ran a traveling gaudy. Dozen girls and a couple of wags. Sure."

They heard a throaty laugh. The figure shifted slightly, and Ryan saw light dancing off the man's hands. "Same old people. Trader taught you boys well. Never thought you'd both still be living. Deathlands is hard on men like us."

Larry Zapp. The memory came cautiously forward, like a child entering an adults' party, uncertain of its welcome.

They'd been up near where Duluth would have been if it hadn't been wiped off the map by a massive earth shift that had sent parts of the lakes flooding southward and westward. The Trader had been checking out reports of a baron who'd discovered a huge store of gasoline and was ready to do some business.

In the end the story had been, as most were, grossly exaggerated.

But Larry Zapp had been up there with two wags, converted from Winnebagos, the insides stretched and cut around to provide cubicles for six women in each of the brightly painted vehicles. He had three hired guns who did nothing but sit around drinking cheap liquor and taking some of their wages out in jolt. Every now and again they'd get to kick the shit out of a dissatisfied customer who wanted his jack back.

But Zapp ran a good, tight gaudy, and trouble didn't come very often.

But, Ryan remembered, the big man had been greedy.

Way back then, Larry had been around two-fifty pounds, with a shoulder-length mane of greasy hair, the selling line had been Cold Beer And Hot Women. And in most frontier pestholes that had been all it took.

But Larry Zapp had gotten greedy.

Who had it been? Was it Henn, the tall, black guy with a lacerating sense of humor? Or was it Cohn, their radio operator? Ryan couldn't remember, and it didn't much matter. It had been one of the male crew members of War Wag One. That was certain.

One of the whores... Bernice, that was her name! Tall, skinny part-Indian with one ear missing. Larry had used her to try to bribe the crewman to betray the Trader and his wags to the local baron.

The Trader had found out about it and sent Ryan and J.B., as his head honchos, to talk to the foolish and greedy Mr. Zapp.

"I could've died, you sons of bitches," Zapp said, his voice breaking into Ryan's threads of distant memory.

"You threw the dice," J.B. replied. "You get snakes' eyes and you don't whimper for your mommy. You didn't die, because we didn't chill you. Simple as that."

"And now it's my turn to cast the dice again, John Dix."

"Yeah."

Ryan recalled that Larry Zapp had carried a cut-throat razor up his sleeve. He wasn't a man you turned your back on.

After they'd called on the brothel keeper, both his vans had been burned-out wrecks, the column of oily smoke rising in an unbroken pillar into the chill fall sky. His girls had fled, accepting the suggestion from Ryan that their health depended on their traveling at least two hundred miles in any direction.

Two of his watchmen were on their backs with rain falling in their eyes. The third one had vanished.

And Larry Zapp was still alive.

He was hurting some, but he was still breathing. Both his elbows were broken, the result of having been kicked by steel-tipped combat boots; both his knees had gone the same way; one shoulder was dislocated; both the collarbones had been snapped; several fingers were bent back and swollen; five ribs had given into the kicking.

"Not my face!" he'd screamed as they came in after him.

So they hadn't touched his face.

They'd walked away and left him lying crooked and puking in his own blood and piss.

But alive.

And, in the manner of things, the wheel had gone rolling slowly and soundlessly around. Now he was sitting with all his pomp and his blasters, and Ryan and J.B. were stuck at the wrong end of the table.

So it goes.

"Tell your boy to put his knife away, Ryan."

"You tell him."

The chair shifted a little more. "Don't know how well your daddy taught you, son, but you get to throw your little blade. After that you got nothing. How's that seem?"

"It seems fine to me. Sure, your sec men chill us all. But you don't get to see it, because you're dead on the floor."

Ryan nodded approvingly. "Right, boy," he said quietly.

Boss Larry laughed. "You taught him well. It occurs to me that you had no knowledge that I was baron here in Greenglades ville. True?"

Ryan nodded again. "True. We were sort of passing through when we ran into your boys."

There was a silence.

The room continued to revolve slowly. Ryan was barely aware of it until he looked out of the side windows and watched the movement of the surrounding country. Then he felt a sudden wave of nausea.

The shadowed figure in the big chair clapped his hands, a soft, moist sound. Two dark shapes rose at the signal, moving into sight from behind one of the tables. They were both short and muscular, wearing the same camouflage gear. But both were bareheaded, showing shaven skulls.

One moved to each side of the chair, and there was a controlled, violent struggle. After much panting and heaving, Boss Larry spoke again.

"I'm up, sod your fumbling! I'm up!" The companions heard the sound of a hard slap on bare flesh.

Supported by the two young men, Boss Larry Zapp finally lumbered slowly out into the light, where they could all see him.

"Been eating well, Larry?" J.B. asked sarcastically.

A rough guess would have put the baron of Greenglades at the four-hundred-pound mark, give or take fifty pounds.

His hair was uncombed, shoulder length and mainly silver. He wore a loose caftan of dark maroon silk, with bare feet showing beneath it. His eyes had almost vanished in waves of fat, and his small mouth rode triumphantly over several layers of jowls. The baron's hands were small and feminine, and his short fingers each sported a different ring.

Unusual among barons, he didn't appear to be carrying any sort of weapon.

"You didn't come to pursue me," he said. "If I thought you had, then you'd be chilled, like that!" He attempted to snap his fingers, but they were too plump. "You may live. To err is human and to forgive is divine. You erred, Ryan and John, and now I forgive you. I spare you. I let you live. You may go free. But..."

"We get the message, Larry," Ryan said. "Give us our blasters back, and we'll go right now."

"The boy's knife?"

"Sheathe it, Dean."

Though they were still surrounded by the blasters

of the sec force, the tension of the moment had passed and Ryan no longer felt threatened.

"Don't rush off, people. There are old times to mull over. Good and bad times to remember. Years to discuss. But I see I have failed to notice your three other friends."

Kelly coughed. "Can I tell you who they all are, Boss?"

The baron was panting with the effort of being vertical. "Yes, you... One small point, Ryan."

"Yeah?"

"'Boss Larry' will do nicely. Or 'Baron Larry.' 'Baron Zapp' is adequate. But 'Larry' alone isn't the sort of respect for someone of my wealth and power. Remember it, won't you? Now, Kelly, their names."

The noncom rattled them off, ending with Doc Tanner, who bowed the the shuddering figure of the baron.

"I am delighted to make your acquaintance. Positively delighted."

Boss Larry stared at him, no sign of any emotion on the great slabs of flesh that made up his face.

Ryan asked the question that was most intriguing him. "How did you get all this?"

"This? The ville?"

"We left you up by the lakes, and you didn't even have a pot to piss in."

There was a readjustment of the face that was a sort of a smile. "There are those who can do it, Ryan, and those who can't. Trader was one of those gifted individuals who could do it. I'm another." He paused as a thought struck him. "You heard, of course, that Trader is still alive?"

"What?" The exclamation came simultaneously from J.B. and Ryan.

"Surprised?"

"He died months ago. Who told you he was still living?"

With an effort Boss Larry managed to raise a ringed finger and tap the side of his nose. "Aha. Now, there's a thing, isn't there? You saw his corpse, did you?"

"No. Nobody did. Went off alone."

Zapp laughed, his whole body vibrating in a series of seismic shudders. "Alone. And so the fable started of his passing."

It was a bombshell to Ryan. The Trader had been suffering for months from a cancer that was chewing up his guts. He *had* to be dead.

"I don't believe it. The story's a lie," he said flatly.

"Now, you may say that, my dear Ryan, but you couldn't possibly expect me to agree with you."

"Boss?" Kelly said questioningly. "What do we do with them? Give them back their blasters? They got some real good weapons."

"Of course they have. Of course they have. Ryan and John wouldn't have lived this long unless... I never answered your question, did I, Ryan? Got sidetracked with that tale of the Trader."

"Yeah. How did you get here?"

"Women. *Cherchez les femmes,* as the French used to say." As he spoke, he stared at Krysty and licked

his lips in an unmistakable gesture. "After I healed—
you did a good job, people. Afterward I found some
more women. Gaudy sluts are five for a meat stew in
those pestholes. Changed them for a quantity of gas.
Traded some of that for some horses and a few old
carbines. More blasters and more gas. Moved into
food." He giggled. "One of my real favorites. Then
I found this place, and now I rule it all and everyone
calls me baron and boss."

A voice came from behind them, from by the elevators, "Everyone but me, Lard Ass. Everyone but
me."

Chapter Twenty-One

"And who the sweet sunlight is this miserable bunch of raggedy bastards?"

Ryan deliberately didn't turn around quickly, as everyone else did. His main interest was in watching the face of Boss Larry Zapp. A secondary interest was in seeing the reaction of Kelly, the noncom sec man.

Larry started to blink very fast, and his hands clasped so suddenly that his rings clashed like temple bells.

Kelly's reaction was more fascinating. Despite the gross insult to his baron, the stocky guard showed no reaction whatsoever.

Then, and only then, did Ryan turn around.

He'd rarely seen anyone that he'd so disliked at first glance. Cort Strasser was one name that came to mind.

But the man standing by the entrance to the slowly revolving tower room was up there with the very best. Or the very worst.

He was only about five feet six inches tall, and skinny, weighing around one-twenty-five. He had long black hair that curled over his narrow shoulders, and his mustache spilled down both sides of his full, almost feminine lips. His eyes were dark brown, with long lashes.

The man's clothes were a mix of the functional and the overdecorative. His jeans were stained and torn, patched around both knees in darker material. His shirt had ruffles down the front and around both wrists. Over it he wore a black leather jacket with long fringes, and small patches of broken mirror sewn all over it. He wore a pair of silver sunglasses with blue lenses, hung on a yellow braid around his neck.

Ryan spotted a small, pearl-handled, silvered pistol tucked into the man's belt. It wasn't possible to give a positive identification, but it could have been a Beretta Model 95.

The stranger returned Ryan's once-over stare.

"See Lard Ass is collecting some more outlander waifs and shit," he said in a drawling voice.

Ryan didn't respond to him, looking instead at Larry Zapp. "Do you get to introduce your friend to us, Boss?"

"I'll introduce myself, thanks very much, Mr. One-Eyed Jack. My name's Traven. Adam Traven. Adam, like the son of man. That's me, isn't it, Lard Ass? Man's son. I'm a close friend of the baron, here, Jack One-Eye. Real close. Me and my posse."

"Posse?" Ryan repeated.

Boss Larry answered with an uncomfortable eagerness. "Means the group of friends that Adam's got here. Adam's posse. Couple of young men and about six young women. Very lovely young women, if I might say so, Adam."

"You may, Larry, baby."

Ryan realized something was weirdly wrong in Greenglades ville. A baron like Larry Zapp, with a well-organized and efficient sec force, had to have a lot of power to back him up. So why was he toadying and brownnosing to this jumped-up little prick in the pretty jacket?

"Shall I tell you who our new guests are, Adam?" the baron asked with a shrinking hesitancy that sat oddly with his statuesque bulk.

"Yeah," Traven replied with a dismissive wave of the hand.

It crossed Ryan's mind that it would be a good feeling to have the cartilage in the man's throat crunching between his fingers.

"The ladies are Miss Wroth and Dr. Wyeth." The word "doctor" produced a flicker of interest from the little man. "Old one's called Doc Tanner. Kid's name is Dean. Son of Ryan Cawdor. Other one's J. B. Dix. Heard of 'em, Adam?"

"No." A considered pause. "Well, I might have heard the name of Ryan Cawdor. Some place. Some time. Brushed a few flies from around a frontier pesthole, up in the Darks. That it?"

"Something like that," Ryan said.

Strangling would be good, or maybe to press the muzzle of the SIG-Sauer into Traven's prissy mouth hard enough to splinter his front teeth and hard enough for the foresight to draw blood from the lips. And watch the arrogant bastard's eyes go blank and scared.

"Where they come from?"

"All over," Ryan replied before Larry Zapp could start his reminiscences about the old days with the Trader.

"Staying long, Cawdor? Nice ville. Look around. Take the kid on the rides. Baron Boss Larry'll show his ville. Won't you, Boss Larry?"

"Sure. Be glad to do that."

The man spun around, as delicate as a dancer, the lights shimmering off the shards of a mirror on his jacket.

"There. Happiness on every hand. I'll go back to my posse."

Boss Larry pulled his two silent supporters forward a few stumbling steps. "Adam?" he said plaintively. "Adam?"

"What is it, Lard Ass?"

"You know."

"I do? Oh, sure I do. You want me to fix up a little of this and a little of that, don't you?"

Larry Zapp's face split into a sunny beam. "That'd be real good, Adam. Thanks. Thanks a lot."

Ryan was standing beside Kelly, the sec man, and heard the faint hissed intake of breath. He glanced sideways, but the man's face was completely blank.

Traven stopped his spinning dervish dance, and stared intently at Ryan. "Yes, I've heard of you. Hear that flowers die as you pass by. Old women moan and little children weep. Your breath is ice and your piss is acid steam."

"I'd say that was all triple-crap," said the one-eyed man.

Traven nodded slowly. "You would, huh? Just so you don't stay here too long, outlander. Boss Larry has his own path to walk."

He rocked back on his high-heeled boots and strode toward the elevators. He left behind him a lake of discomfort.

Dean, finally sheathing his knife, went to stand beside his father, and looked up into his face. "All right?" he said.

"Sure."

Boss Larry had slapped his two servants again, steering them toward his reinforced chair.

"Why doesn't he speak to them?" J.B. asked Kelly.

"No point. Deaf and mute. That way they can't betray his secrets. Probably have had them blinded if he could have."

"Take them and feed them, and find them rooms," Zapp ordered as he sank into his seat. "And tell me when you've done it. Mebbe I'll see them later and show them around the rides."

He pushed himself petulantly in the revolving chair so that he was once more staring out across the Florida swamps.

"Time to go, people," Kelly said, gesturing to the six friends with the blaster.

"You don't need that, do you?" Mildred asked.

"My .45? Suppose not, lady. I mean, Doctor. No."

"So, would it be within the realms of the most

distant possibility that we might be allowed to retrieve our own firearms?'' Doc queried. ''It would really be most awfully kind of you.''

''Sure. Sucking death! Why not? Why should I care when Adam's posse run this ville? Help yourselves, people.''

''Thanks. But who is—''

Kelly wagged a warning finger at the one-eyed man. ''Best thing to do with your lips, Ryan, is to keep them sealed tighter than a duck's ass. That way you can pass a day or two here and have some pleasure. And move on, all alive and well.''

''Still a lot of questions hanging in the air,'' J.B. said, as they filed out to the central section of the tower, where the elevator doors stood open and sec men waited in front of each one.

''Same answer to most, and you just met him,'' Kelly replied.

NOT FAR FROM CENTERPOINT they were taken to what had once been a large hostelry, called the Gator Motel. It had been cruciform in shape, with its lobby at the midpoint of the four arms. But there had been a fire, long years ago, which had destroyed three-quarters of the building.

Now only the Gator Wing remained.

''How many rooms you want?'' asked the stocky noncom. ''Six, five, four, three, two or one. Makes no difference to me.''

Ryan glanced at the others. Mildred took an almost

imperceptible half step closer to J.B. Dean looked at his father.

"One single room for Doc. Double for J.B. and Mildred. Double for me and Krysty." He hesitated. "And a single adjoining for my son."

"Done. There'll be some of my men around the Gator all the time. Best you don't wander. Might run into some of the posse. Once Boss Larry's had his happy fix, he might call around and you can go on the rides. Until then, stay here."

"BEEN IN WORSE PRISONS," Krysty said, lying stretched out on the queen-size bed, feet crossed, staring at the star-painted ceiling.

Ryan had washed his face and shaved, using the disposable razor that was in a plastic mug at the side of the basin. The water was hot and only faintly tinted. He'd read that water in the old pre-nuke days had been clear in the center of big villes as it was in a mountaintop stream.

A rapping sounded on the bolted door between their room and Dean's. "I'll get it." Krysty swung off the bed.

The boy had also washed, and had gelled his hair to his scalp, making him look older and oddly sinister. Ryan went over and patted his son on the shoulder, hesitating a moment.

"Fireblast! What's that smell?"

Dean blushed. "Called Prince Mayakovsky Splash On. Said on the bottle to use plenty, so I did. Is it awful, Dad?'' He glanced at Krysty. ''What do you think?''

She sniffed cautiously. ''I think mebbe I'd use a tad less next time. But it'll wear off fast. Hungry, Dean?''

''Sure. Time for second food?''

Ryan glanced at his chron. ''Yeah, I'll order up for us.''

''Dad, can I ask a question? Know you think I ask too many.''

''Long as it's the right time, I don't mind. What is it?''

''The baron... All around are signs of triple-power, jack and sec men.''

''Right.''

''The guy...Adam Traven. How come he orders Boss Larry around like he does? Got him running scared.''

Ryan finished wiping his face on the fluffy white towel. ''Good question, son. Mebbe we'll find an answer. Until we do—'' he shrugged ''—who knows?''

Chapter Twenty-Two

A brief, flurried thunderstorm had blown in from the east while the companions were eating. Dean had dropped his paper plate of fried chicken and run to the smeared window. He pressed his face against the glass, watching the blinding daggers of lightning as they tore open the slate gray clouds, bringing a burst of torrential rain that laid the dust and cleared away the stifling humidity.

Ryan and Mildred had come in during the storm, followed shortly after by Doc Tanner. The old man had been drinking brandy, supplied by the sec men, and was in an unusually expansive mood.

"The pounding of the hammer of Thor upon the anvil of…of someone or other, whose name I have conveniently forgotten. I remember a particularly bitter attack of sheet lightning in the fall of 1895. We had been traversing a bare mountainside on our way to Hidden Lake, up in Montana. The very rocks sang with the concatenation of thunder and lightning. The ozone in the air made one's poor addled brain spin."

Dean looked at Doc, puzzled. "You said 'eighteen,' Doc."

"What was that, my fine young comrade?"

"You said you saw a storm in 1895, Doc. How can that be?"

"The tale is long, my boy. If you care to come to my room, I shall have another sip at the rather good cognac and I will reveal to you the mystery of my own being. Come." He stood, making an imperious gesture.

Dean glanced at Ryan, who nodded his approval. "Sure, son. Don't worry. Won't go off anywhere without you."

The boy went out with Doc, the old man's cane rapping smartly on the threadbare carpet in the corridor beyond.

The door hadn't closed properly, and Krysty moved toward it, hesitating a moment. "Someone coming," she said.

It was Kelly.

The noncom glanced around the room, seeing the remains of their meal. "Everyone eaten?" he asked.

"Sure, thanks."

The sec man had a sprinklig of rain across his shoulders, damping his short-cropped hair. "Hell of a storm out there."

"We saw it," Mildred said.

"Passed the old man and your boy along the passage. Once Boss Larry gives the word, you can take him on some of the rides. Be a double-buzz."

"When?"

"Traven wants you all out of here. Doesn't like any other outlanders stepping on his turf. *His* turf! So take what comes, Ryan, and then move on."

"Got no reason to stay."

J.B. had been fieldstripping his new scattergun, checking it for any signs of damp. He looked up at Kelly. "Want to tell us what's going down here?"

The man glanced at the door, then went to lean against it, making the rusted lock finally click shut. He looked at the curtains hanging over the picture window. He moved to stand by it, staring out across the misty field of green.

"Don't know why I should trust you people any more than Adam's posse."

"We're not evil. They are." Krysty's voice hung flat in the room between them.

The sec man nodded slowly. "Could be that's the up and down of it. Used to be a hell of a good ville once."

He launched into the story of the Garden of Eden and the serpent that had come crawling, unbidden into it.

Accompanied by two younger men and six younger girls, Adam Traven had appeared in Greenglades about three months ago. He'd come from the north, possibly, Kelly thought, by boat. He'd brought a supply of a scarce known drug. Known on the streets as dreem, it was a fine powder, tinted a faint pink, that could be either smoked or snorted. It gave a fast rush, like speed, coke or jolt, then eased the user into a mild and languorous lethargy.

"Like being awake and asleep at the same time," Kelly told them.

It also heightened all sensual experiences. Eating

became almost orgasmic, music hardly bearable in its insinuating beauty. Sex was a stretched splinter of time that rang with an infinite resonance through the linked chambers of yesterday and tomorrow.

Kelly described it with a cynical grin. "That's how Traven said it was. I tried some, and he was partly right. But you could see through it."

"How do you mean?" Ryan asked.

"Like you're wearing a mask. But you *know* that you're wearing it. Like watching things through a mist. Like seeing the gun fired, but it's not your finger on the trigger. Just not real. But Boss Larry doesn't see it like that."

The fat baron had become hooked on the drug, and the only supplier was Adam Traven.

"Wasn't just the drug." Kelly looked as though he were going to spit on the carpet, then he remembered where he was and changed his mind. "The girls. Not women! Girls. Oldest can't be more than fifteen. Tops. And they worship the ground Traven walks. Do anything for him. Boss Larry's hooked on them and what they do."

"Traven pimps?" Mildred asked.

"Kind of. More like a puppet master, pulling on the strings. He uses the girls himself. And the boys, I guess. But like he's sitting in a corner watching himself do what he does."

"Control freak," Mildred said. "What we used to call people like that. Manipulators. Dominators. Get their kicks from forcing others to obey them. Sick bastards, most."

Kelly nodded. He related how he and a few of the senior sec men had been thinking about taking care of Traven. But he wouldn't elaborate on that.

"So we figure that the safest step is the one not taken."

"You could chill him. Him and his gang. Posse, or whatever he calls it." Ryan looked past the sec man, out the misted window. "Why not?"

Kelly sniffed. "Reasons. Maybe you'll see some yourself, if you're here long enough."

"But we won't be here long enough." Krysty looked over at Kelly. "You keep plenty hidden, don't you?"

"You a doomie? Some sort of mutie seer? Boss Larry doesn't care much for muties. Nor norms, come to that. So—"

"Don't need to be a doomie to be able to tell when a man isn't spilling it all on the floor."

"How many in the ville?" J.B. asked. "Baron controls more than just this old park."

Kelly finally turned from the window. "Got to be moving, people." He hesitated at the door, his hand on the corroded metal of the handle. "Sure it's bigger. Sea to shining sea. Boss Larry's writ runs clear to the sea on the east. Into the swamps as far as a man with a blaster can control. But there's Cajuns that way. Not even Boss Larry's been able to remove them all from the game."

"You mean kill them?" Mildred said. "I always hated the way that wars use images from sport. 'Remove him from the game.' Jesus in the lilies! You mean kill, then say it.''

Kelly's fingers dropped from the door handle to the butt of his blaster, and his eyes narrowed in anger. ''I don't have to take that sort of softheart crap from you or anyone!'' he snarled. ''Faster you people get back to the outlands, the better for us all.''

The door slammed so hard behind him that it made the air quiver in the big bedroom.

A HALF HOUR LATER the door swung open and Doc Tanner walked in, his arm across the shoulders of young Dean Cawdor. The boy looked vaguely puzzled, as if the old man had shown him a wonderful card trick, then told him how it was done. And then done the same trick in a totally different and inexplicable way.

''Dad?''

''What is it?''

''Doc's lying to me, isn't he?''

''Now, just wait a minute, young fellow,'' Doc spluttered.

Ryan glowered at the boy. ''One thing you want to learn and learn now, is that you take care about calling anyone a liar. Call it a stranger, and you might end up trying to push your guts back inside the hole in your belly. Call it a friend, and you can finish up losing that friend.''

''But he ain't...isn't two hundred years old, is he?'' The boy looked around at the others for confirmation of his own doubts. ''Mildred?''

"Doc has his faults, Dean, and there are plenty of them. But telling lies never has been one of them. No."

"Nobody's two hundred years old!"

"I tried to make all of this simple for the lad," Doc protested. "Some ways I'm only in my thirties. Another way—it is true—you could estimate that I'm not just three score and ten. I'm something around ten score. But the trawling makes all sorts of things kind of muddled."

"I'd love to time travel." Dean sighed.

"Can't recommend it, son," Doc said, his sigh echoing the boy's.

"I could go back and see the first time you ever met my mother, Rona, couldn't I, Dad?"

The thought of having his son witness the first animal coupling with Sharona Carson brought Ryan closer to blushing than he'd been for more than thirty years.

"Could. But they gave up on the tests. Too many horrors."

"What sort of horrors?"

Doc patted him on the arm. "Believe me, Dean, it is better you never know."

IT WAS THE MIDDLE of the afternoon when they received another message. One of the sec men, with only two silver stripes on his arm, rapped on the door. "Baron Boss Larry wants to see you all."

"When?" Ryan asked, standing up from the bed.

"Now. Come on, outlander. Now!"

Called the Zephyr Rainbow's End Retirement Complex."

"They pay him for everything."

.....

"How many windows are there?" Dean asked.

"We've seen a lot together.

Chapter Twenty-Three

The ground smelled green and damp from the recent rain. They saw still pools of water coated with a layer of dark mud, and the leaves of the trees and shrubs dripped into the long grass. Their boots sucked at the sodden earth.

Ryan and J.B. had discussed what to do about the blasters that had been returned to them, finally agreeing that they'd leave the Smith & Wesson 12-gauge and the Steyr rifle behind in their rooms.

Now the companions walked along the paths, following Kelly. The noncom had a couple of his men with him, but they were only for show.

They passed an eatery with a group of about thirty people standing outside. As they got closer, Ryan saw that the strangers were all in their late fifties and sixties. One or two of the women looked as if they might even be in their seventies.

Kelly had also spotted them, and he slowed his pace to come alongside Ryan and Krysty.

"Oldies," he said.

"Where did they come from?" Ryan asked.

"Outside the park. There's a kind of condo development between here and the start of the swamps.

Called the Zapp's Rainbow's End Retirement Complex.''

"They pay him for protection?"

"Yeah. Just a small part of the jack that flows in. And then flows out again."

"How many wrinkles are there?" Dean asked. "Never seen a lot together."

"Around a hundred. They're getting frightened. That's a deputation over there."

"Frightened?" Krysty looked at the sec man. "What do they have to be frightened about if they got all that sec-men power?"

Kelly stopped before they got too close to the eatery. The group of old-timers had turned to look in their direction, conversation freezing.

"They're frightened because five of them have been chilled in the last three weeks. Chilled!" He laughed. "Butchered. Better word. Hacked apart and words daubed on the walls in blood. Jack and jewels taken. Nobody saw anything. Nobody heard anything. Boss Larry blames the swampies."

"You don't?" Mildred asked.

"My ma didn't raise me to answer stupid questions, lady."

"Mr. Kelly! Yoo-hoo! Can we speak to you for a moment?"

The sec man sighed ruefully and glued a false smile into place. "Why, Mrs. Owen. Didn't see you there. Hope the rain didn't catch you all out."

Mrs. Owen was a pocket version of Boss Larry, though she probably didn't weigh more than three hundred pounds. The pink flounced trouser suit was straining at the seams to keep it all under control and only just winning the battle. Her hair was tinted a startling shade of electric blue, which matched her eye makeup. As she sashayed toward them, face powder crumbled from the lines in her cheeks and chin like a miniature blizzard.

"Where is the baron?" she shrilled. "He's late for our meeting."

"Been working hard on some sec plans," Kelly replied, "hoping to solve the problems you got down at Rainbow's End."

One of the other guards, standing just beyond Doc, whispered something to the old man and sniggered. Doc raised an eyebrow and said nothing. Kelly caught the exchange and glowered at the sec man. "Lucky I didn't hear that," he said quietly. "If I'd heard it, then Boss Larry would have heard it."

Mrs. Owen seemed mollified by the noncom's hasty answer. She raised a tortoiseshell lorgnette to her beady eyes and twinkled at the group, paying particular attention to Doc. "Why, who are these strangers, Mr. Kelly? Such a rare sight here."

"Guests of the boss. Going to take them on some of the rides."

Mrs. Owen had been clutching a hand across her capacious bosom. Now she moved it, revealing a fine necklace of chunky amber beads, the largest one tipped with a silver cross. It was a very striking piece of jewelry.

"I believe that I've met this handsome gentleman

before, haven't I? She addressed the question to Doc, who dropped a low, formal bow, one hand across his heart, the other striking an angle with the swordstick.

"Madam, I think not. I'm certain that even a failing memory like mine could scarcely have edited you from my mind. The loss is mine."

Mildred said something that might have been "Randy old lecher."

"I came originally from the Tecumseh Valley. My late husband was a builder of bridges there."

"Indeed, and now you've burned those bridges to retire here to the glades."

"Why, yes. Yes."

Kelly had been tapping his foot with shrinking patience. "Want us to go on and leave you here with Mrs. Owen and her friends, Doc?"

"No." The word was delivered at surprising volume and without a moment's hesitation. "No, thank you, my dear fellow. I must keep with my companions." He bowed again. "Fare you well, charming lady. Perhaps our paths will cross again."

"Oh, I hope so," she simpered. "And do tell the baron we're still hoping for a meeting. Mr. Kelly, won't you?"

"Sure."

They went on.

BARON BOSS LARRY ZAPP finally made an appearance. A flatbed truck of impenetrable pedigree approached, the engine coughing and spluttering, gray smoke gushing from a broken exhaust.

On the back was a pile of what looked like old mattresses from the motel, stacked together to provide a horizontal throne for the ruler of Greenglades ville.

"He's stoned shitless," Dean hissed, grabbing at his father's sleeve. "How's he goin' to take us on the rides?"

Kelly heard him. "Boss doesn't go himself. You go and I go, and he sort of hangs around and asks us what it was like. They don't make any rides the right size for the boss."

Zapp opened an elephantine eye. It rolled in the socket, finally managing to focus on Ryan's face.

"You nearly battered me to death, you one-eyed son of a bitch," he said, his voice as mild as warm milk. "You and John Dix."

"You're right," Ryan agreed. "But you had it coming, Larry."

The great head nodded, like a gargantuan Buddha. "True. Sad but true. Kelly here is going to take you on one or two of the rides. My dear companion in sensual excess, Adam Traven, will be riding with you as well as a few of his posse."

He stopped speaking. Not because he'd actually finished, but because his brain had closed down some of the lines of communication. The only sound was the rumbling of the truck's beat-up engine, filling the air with its labored stench.

"That's it?" J.B. said. "Audience with the baron over?"

"Shit," Kelly said. "That dreem's fucking his

head into the middle of next week. Come on, people, let's go and have us some fun.''

The noncom made ''fun'' sound like something you did facedown in a pigsty.

RYAN STOOD IN LINE, looking up at the skeleton of rusting steel that was painted a dusty yellow. The sign said Pharaoh's Curse. He reached into the pocket of his coat, his fingers touching the frail, crumpled piece of paper from the redoubt. For a moment he considered throwing it away, then he looked around, seeing how clean everything looked. Suddenly his attention was distracted.

Someone had switched on a machine, and a crackling voice came looping through the mild afternoon air from a number of speakers, which were disguised as plastic pyramids.

''Welcome to the house of funky King Tut, last of the royal daddies. And his mummy, Nefertiti. Are you ready to face his ride of death. Mighty Osiris and Anubis wait to snatch your souls and ride the race into eternal darkness. If you are...''

There was a flat hissing sound. Kelly looked up. ''Sucking death! Tape's broken again. Keeps on happening on a lot of the rides.''

Dean had reached out and touched Ryan's hand, holding on for a moment. ''It really dangerous?'' he asked. ''Said a ride of death and—''

''No,'' Mildred said. ''Just a load of showmen's hype, turning the pitch and bringing in the marks. It was ever thus, Dean.''

"Company." J.B.'s quiet voice made Ryan turn around.

Adam Traven was walking toward them, accompanied by a raggle-taggle group that Ryan assumed must be his posse.

There were eight of them, though at a first glance it was difficult to determine what the sexual mix was. There were four with short hair and four with long hair. But none of the cropheads looked particularly masculine.

"Hi there, Kelly. The outlanders having their treats before they go back into the wilderness?"

"Boss said to take them on some rides." The noncom's voice was curiously flat, as though he were trying to subordinate his dislike of Traven and not doing a very good job of it.

"Good. Mebbe one of two of my little family might care to join you."

He danced around, feet tapping, jacket whirling, the splinters of mirrored glass catching the watery sun. None of his posse showed any response. Now that they were closer, Ryan was able to pick out the two men among them.

Both wore tight pants in thin cotton material that accentuated their maleness. But both were slim, with long fair hair that tumbled over their submissive faces. They wore jackets sewn together from bright scraps of old material, like antique patchwork.

All but two of the girls also wore tight pants, some with long coats over them. Two had very short pants cut high, the stretched material vanishing into the taut cleft of their buttocks. They also had on high-heeled boots with platform soles.

"Tenderloin hookers," Doc said, a comment that only Mildred understood, and she nodded her agreement.

One of the girls moved to hang on Traven's arm, swaying gently backward and forward. "Can I go ride with the outlanders?" she asked in a thin clear voice.

"Sure, Sky. Anyone else? No? Wouldn't mind myself. Show your son the excitements of this place, Ryan Cawdor. But me and Lard Ass got some more talking to do, and we got to plan us a visit, as well."

For some unaccountable reason, the word "visit" seemed to strike a chord with the bored group, and they all looked up at their leader, simultaneous adoring smiles lighting their tight, pinched faces, as though he'd pressed a button for them.

The girl called Sky hopped up and down. "Can we all come, Adam? Can we?"

"On the visit? Sure. But we'll all talk about it tonight."

"We going on the ride?" Dean asked eagerly. "Come on."

Ryan glanced from his son to Traven. And saw there an expression that chilled his heart, raising the hackles at his nape. The little man's eyes had been locked to Dean's face with something that came close to hunger.

"So can I go, Adam?" Sky kissed Traven on the cheek, distracting him. He blinked, taking his eyes off the ten-year-old boy.

The girl was close to Krysty's five feet eleven inches, and she had short reddish hair. She was the only member of the posse in a skirt. It was loose cotton and swirled around her knees in a bright batik pattern of mauve and citrus. Her eyes were a very pale green, unusually close together. Above the skirt Sky was wearing a long-sleeved blouse with pearl buttons, cream colored, tucked in. Her legs were bare, and she had low-heeled sandals on her feet, thonged up over her ankles.

As far as Ryan could see, she wasn't carrying any kind of weapon.

She looked at the line, waiting to climb the steps toward the start of Pharaoh's Curse. "Hey, you got an odd number. Who do I ride with?"

Kelly turned to Ryan. "I'll sit with the boy," he said.

Doc smiled broadly, showing his excellent set of gleaming teeth. "I believe that the opportunity to chaperone such a delicate flower of the Everglades is going to fall to yours truly. I'm Dr. Theophilus Tanner, but you may call me 'Doc.' Everyone else does, my dear."

"Sure," she replied. "Whatever you say. I'm Sky. Got no other name now."

"Now?" Krysty asked, curious.

"Used to have some other names, but Adam called me Sky and that's what I am now."

Traven waved a hand and beckoned his little flock tighter around him. "See you later, Sky," he said. "Have a nice day."

They walked off, the sparkling mirrored jacket catching the eye as Traven moved along the path toward the center of the ville.

Sky bounded toward the start of the ride, dragging Doc behind her. Dean went next, eyes alight with excitement, Mildred and J.B. following him more slowly. Krysty smiled and began to climb after them, with Ryan at her heels. But Kelly caught him by the arm and stopped him.

"A word, outlander," the sec man said quickly and quietly. "I seen Traven a lot. Know him. Keep your boy from him and get away from here as quick as you can."

"I saw his face. But—"

Kelly was very close, so that Ryan could feel his breath on his skin. "Bad things happen here since that little prick arrived. I told you. Boss won't lift a finger, Ryan. Just watch the boy. Watch him close."

HIS MIND RACING, Ryan climbed the steel steps, following the stocky figure of the sec man, joining the others on the platform that was lined with mock hieroglyphics.

Dean was waiting for him, grinning. "Come on, Dad," he said. "Let's go."

Chapter Twenty-Four

Despite the loose connections, the showers of bright rust and the rattling and vibrating, Ryan enjoyed one of the most amazing afternoons of his entire life.

As they waited on a narrow platform with painted instructions to Stand In Line and Only Two To A Car, they heard a grinding of gears and a whirring rumble of oiled chains. Then the line of linked capsules came lurching into sight.

Each was painted to look like the sarcophagus of an Egyptian mummy, with tiny antic figures and dog-headed gods.

"Goodness!" Doc exclaimed in misty-eyed awe. "Look at the god-headed dogs."

Nobody took any notice of him.

There was a barely audible warning about keeping arms inside the cars, which was overlaid with some strange Eastern music of reed pipes and a slack-skinned drum.

Ryan climbed in, adjusting the holster on his SIG-Sauer, patting the thin-gauge metal of the carriage with his hand. Krysty sat beside him, pushing her hair back off her face. A heavy restraining bar, its padding leaking in white nodules, pulled down over their shoulders and locked into place.

"If Traven or Larry Zapp wanted to take us out, this'd be a good time and place," Ryan muttered.

Dean and Kelly took the second car, with Mildred and J.B. behind them. Doc and Sky squeezed into the fourth and last Egyptian carriage, the girl giggling at something the old man had said to her.

"Don't know what you mean, Doc, but you sure speak funny. You aren't like some of the other wrinklies that—" She stopped as though she'd been on the verge of saying something she shouldn't have.

The moment passed as the recorded voice of a man dead a hundred years warned, "Enjoy your corkscrew journey into the past of old Nile. And say 'Hi' to Cleopatra for us."

There was a terrifying jolt as the little train began to move along the twin rails.

"I read about things like this," Krysty said, having to raise her voice above the noise of the ride. "Never thought I'd ever get to go on one."

"Me neither... Fireblast!"

They gave a lurch to the right and then the left as the cars climbed up a steep rise. On either side there were panels, some of them torn and splintered, that had once portrayed extraordinary scenes from the imagined life of old Egypt. Most of them seemed to have shown ladies with enormous breasts and men with large swords.

"Moral there, lover," Krysty said, the words jerked from her by the vibration of the whole teetering structure.

Ryan gritted his teeth as their car paused on the brink of the hill, inching forward.

"Oh, Gaia!" Krysty gasped, gripping Ryan's hand in both hers.

Ryan closed his one eye, wincing at the sight, his last sentient thought a flaming anger that he'd been so easily trapped by Zapp. He'd actually sat in his own execution vehicle and locked himself snugly in.

As they bottomed out and roared up the next slope, he had a moment to realize that the drop hadn't been more than a hundred feet and they'd been completely safe all the way.

Behind him he could hear the whooping of his son and Kelly stringing out a monotonous recital of florid curses.

There was a yell from farther back that he suspected might have been Doc Tanner, but the noise of the roller coaster overwhelmed everything.

They rushed through the warm air, faster and faster. The cars dipped and rose, the g-forces quadrupling and quartering within fifteen seconds. Some of the time it felt to Ryan as if his head weighed a ton.

"Why...call...corkscrew?" Krysty yelled, her fingers digging painfully into his arm.

"Don't know," he managed, the two words jarred from his midriff.

A moment later he knew.

It was the nearest thing Ryan had ever experienced to making a jump through a gateway. His brain flopped loosely around inside his skull, and the snack meal he'd eaten an hour or so earlier came rising before him like the ghosts of dead enemies. He managed to clamp his mouth tightly shut, swallowing hard. Pressure clawed at his ears, and his eye felt swollen in its socket.

They went around twice through three hundred and sixty degrees, then they were back the right way, powering along through another set of tight curves and dips and rises.

The hydraulic hiss of the train's braking system was magic to Ryan.

He lifted off the upholstered safety bar and climbed back onto the platform. Krysty, smiling, got out after him.

"Around the world and home again, lover," she said. He noticed that the sentient crimson hair had curled itself into a ball at the back of her neck.

"I wouldn't ride that triple-bastard again for all the jack in Deathlands," he said, hoping he wasn't actually going to throw up.

It was a relief to see from the heightened pallor of J.B.'s face that the Armorer hadn't relished his first encounter with an antique roller coaster, either.

Mildred was grinning all over her face as she got out. "Boy, did that bring back some wonderful memories," she whooped.

Doc was being helped out by Sky, struggling to keep a glassy smile in place.

"Interesting," he said. "The double corkscrew is something that I will recall for many long winter evenings."

Kelly got out, chewing gum, looking utterly unchanged by the ride. Dean didn't move, sitting in his seat, eyes as big as pinwheels, head moving a little from side to side, as if he were listening to the entrancing melodies of the piper from the gates of dawn.

Ryan stooped over his son. "You feeling all right, Dean?" he asked.

"Oh, yeah. Again, Dad. Again, *please!*"

The second time wasn't quite as bad as the first. Only Dean and Ryan took a car, with Mildred on her own in the rear carriage.

She took a rain check on the third trip around Pharaoh's Curse, and father and son rode it alone. It was just about as bad as the first time.

With extreme prejudice, Ryan kept the boy company for a fourth—and last—ride.

ALTOGETHER KELLY TOOK them onto five rides, all different in their effects. One had diminutive electric-powered miniwags painted in bright colors. All you did was go around and around a slightly banked circuit less than two hundred yards in circumference.

"At least it doesn't send your stomach on a journey of exploration to your back teeth," J.B. commented, recovering a little self-possession.

Paraglide Paradise was the most fun, even though the machinery seemed remarkably hesitant to function and J.B. kept telling them how frayed some of the main support cables were.

"Rusted clean through," he called to Ryan, who was pressed with Dean and Krysty in one of the metal baskets.

"Where?"

"Just above you."

Ryan chose not to look where the Armorer was pointing, just below the tattered parachute.

J.B. and Mildred were standing close together in a second carrier, while Doc was whispering intently into Sky's ear in a third one. The girl, who only looked about fifteen, kept giggling and shaking her shoulders.

"Hope Doc knows what he's doing there," Krysty said. "Could find himself out of his depth."

Kelly stayed on the ground, operating the controls that hoisted the three metal baskets high into the air over the park. Once they reached the top, they remained there for several seconds.

It gave Ryan the opportunity to recce the park and the surrounding land.

He could see the central tower where they'd been given their royal audience with Larry Zapp. Near its entrance was a group of people who looked like the oldies from the Rainbow's End Retirement Complex. Away to the east, leading off a winding blacktop, he saw a number of small buildings, with the hollow remains of several swimming pools nearby. Ryan guessed that they might be the secure compound of homes for the wrinklies.

There was nothing beyond it but the limitless expanse of gently waving green that was the swamps. Here and there he could see the glint of sunshine on water, and in a few places, far off, there were rising pillars of smoke from cooking fires, where the Cajuns lived.

"Over…" he began, swallowing his words with a gasp of shock as Kelly threw the control lever that released the dangling capsules.

The first forty feet or so were in plummeting free-fall. After that a checking mechanism came into effect, slowing the descent.

Cables creaked and groaned, and the carriage came to a final shuddering halt just above the ground.

"Liked that," Dean said. "Can we go on it again? Please?"

Kelly caught Ryan's eye. "One thing you have to remember," he said. "Boss Larry used to be a techno genius. Greatest I ever heard of. He found all this and made it work. Back in Centerpoint there's all kinds of radio and vid devices. Boss made them run."

Doc came over in time to hear the end of the conversation, with Sky hanging on his arm, a stoned smile on her lips. "I notice that you seem to be employing the past tense in your description, Mr. Kelly."

"What?"

"You tell us how it was. How it used to be. What the baron *was* like. How are things now?"

The sec man took in a slow, hissing breath. "There was a wife. Before my time. Before anyone's time. Some say she was a whore, near Dallas. Boss used to cut through the years to the very night it happened. Fight with a crazy out the swamps. Woman took a knife meant for Boss Larry."

J.B. and the others were all standing around now. The Armorer gazed up at Paraglide Paradise. "Things started to slip, huh?"

"Could say that. But he was still sort of hanging on the edge until..." The noncom looked meaningfully at the girl, Sky, who was whistling to herself and staring out toward the dominating silhouette of Camelot Castle, a tottering Gothic ruin with minarets and crenellated towers with slitted windows. She was oblivious to Kelly's unspoken message.

"So we best be careful what we ride, in case it all comes down around our ears," Mildred said. "Glad you didn't tell me that when we were swooping up and down on the Curse of the Mummy's Tomb, or whatever it was called."

"We'll go around the castle and maybe try one other ride. The big loop's one of the safest. Or the Helter Skelter."

DEAN DIDN'T THINK very much of the rambling ruin of Camelot Castle, though some of the rescued holo-vids were impressive enough.

As they walked through the lonely, echoing corridors, with floors of crumbling plastic and rotting arches over the roof, the alcoves on either side were pits of midnight shadow.

Kelly held up a hand. "Keep close. Parts of the floor aren't too safe, so don't wander away."

Ahead of them they heard a whisper of sound, like the last fall leaves being gathered in by Harlequin's broom.

"Something wicked this way comes," Doc breathed, making Sky squeal in fright.

The first alcove became fitfully illuminated as they neared it, showing a tall man in full armor, who proclaimed that he was Sir Gawain and welcomed them to the castle of Camelot, home of chivalry and shrine of the Round Table and the Holy Grail.

A second hologram figure was a woman in a long dress who twirled as she spoke. Sadly the sound had totally gone and her lips moved and smiled in total silence.

"Must be Guinevere," Doc suggested, but only Mildred nodded.

After a few minutes Dean began to get restless. "Boring," he said. "Can't we go on one more ride?"

Kelly looked around at him. "Sure. There's Helter Skelter working. We nearly finished. Haven't been in here for an age. Boss Larry likes it. Comes with his muties some evenings."

Only one more alcove remained.

The first of the group tripped the floor contact that set the hologram into operation, a ball of shimmering light that slowly resolved itself into the head and shoulders of a man—a man who was immensely fat, with long silver hair. As he moved a hand in regal greeting, rings glittered on every finger. He wore a tiny golden crown perched on the top of his head, looking like a wedding ring on a side of beef.

"Boss Larry," Dean said.

Kelly was equally surprised. "Yeah. This wasn't

here last time I came through. I told you the guy's a techno brain.''

''I am Arthur the king, baron of Greenglades and lord of England. Arthos the Bear. Uther Pendragon. Monarch of all he surveys. And ruler of...ruler of fucking nothing.''

The recorded voice slurred and faded.

But the 3-D imagine remained, gazing blankly out at them. Kelly coughed. ''Guess that's it, people.''

But Larry Zapp hadn't finished.

''Enjoy your time in this magic park.''

The image leaned forward, blurring, making Dean take an uneasy step back.

''Clap hands if you...if you want to be happy. I wished to carry the sword into the sunset and light a light this day that shall— Once she'd gone I stopped caring.'' A tear shone on the face of the ghostly monarch. ''I am Arthur, last of the line. The last.''

The hologram finally faded away, and the corridor became dark and silent.

Doc broke the stillness. ''On the mere, the wailing died away,'' he said very quietly.

It was a relief for all of them to get outside again into the sunshine.

Chapter Twenty-Five

The Helter Skelter was a tall tower painted in flowing, hallucinogenic stripes of brilliant colors. It had been decorated more recently than any of the other rides in the park.

"Climb up inside, and when you reach the top you just sit down and slide the polished chute. Who wants to go first?" Kelly looked around the group for a volunteer.

"Looks boring," Dean offered, catching a glare from his father, adding quickly, "but I'll give it a go first."

"I went on things like this," Mildred said. "I'll keep you company."

The sun was behind the clouds, and the shallow-sided bed of the chute gleamed dully like pewter.

Doc was shaking his head. "I fear that these old limbs are beyond such frivolity, my dear Sky. You go, and I shall remain here below and wave encouragingly."

"Ryan?" Krysty said.

"No."

Kelly glanced at his wrist chron. "Better get moving, people."

Dean went first, with Mildred at his heels, then Sky

and Krysty last. Ryan positioned himself at the bottom of the ride, looking upward into the dull sky. The Helter Skelter loomed over him, its fluorescent colors bringing back a moment of dizziness. He could just see Dean, waving a small fist to him as the boy sat on the top of the ride, ready to push off.

"Here I come, Dad!" The voice was small and faraway. Ryan waved a hand.

Mildred was also in sight, pressing a hand to her temple, making Ryan wonder if she was suffering from one of her occasional migraine headaches.

The sun came out, slicing across the park, bringing every detail of the ride into clinical detail. The bottom of the chute now shone like silver, and near the last curve Ryan suddenly noticed other pinpoints of diamond light. He leaned forward, vaguely aware of his son's yelping voice speeding nearer to him.

What could gleam so brightly, looking like tiny slivers of jagged, razored steel?

"Whooooo!" Dean was only one single turn away from the last stretch.

"Stop! Stop there! Hold the sides!" Ryan managed to keep his voice clear and sharp, avoiding a note of panic, which might have freaked the boy.

Fortunately ten years of surviving in Deathlands had given Dean excellent reflexes.

He grabbed at the edges of the run, bracing himself with his new boots, the soles squeaking at the fierce pressure.

Behind him the others had all heard Ryan's warning shout, everyone managing to stop without sliding into anyone else.

J.B. shook his head. "Old can tops and broken fragments of knives and chisels. Section of a crosscut saw. All drilled into the base of the chute. Someone really wanted to do some hurt."

Kelly, face pale, glanced up the Helter Skelter, to where the sun caught the reddish hair of Sky.

"Best they come down slowly, and we'll help them all off. Safer than trying to climb way back up the slide."

Dean was first away, swinging himself agilely into his father's arms, running around to look at the metal splinters, all angled toward anyone riding down.

"I'd have gone... Had my legs open and... Some sick bastards in this ville, Dad."

"Can't argue with you," Ryan said.

DOC WAS THE LAST to come into Ryan and Krysty's bedroom for supper.

"Sorry I'm a trifle tardy, my friends. I was somewhat detained."

Mildred was sitting at the round table near the front door to the suite, spooning at a thick fish gumbo. "Detained, Doc? How's the little girl?"

"Who?"

The black woman laughed. "Come on, Doc. One way of looking at it is that you're old enough to be her great-great-great-great—"

"Nonsense! Absolute hogwash and taradiddle, Dr.

Wyeth. Admittedly Sky is somewhat younger than I am. But age is no deterrent."

"You're joking us, Doc?" J.B. said, breaking a fresh-baked sourdough roll in half and reaching for the butter.

"No. I think not. The young lady is far from happy with being a member of Adam Traven's posse. As the diminutive psychopath calls it."

"You saying that Sky wants to come join us, Doc?" Krysty smiled. "You think she'd fit in?"

"And why not, pray?"

"Jak rode plenty of good miles with us, and he was about as far out of the ob slit as you can get." Ryan laughed. "But we're going to be away soon...probably tomorrow, Doc. Where's the girl now?"

"She is a young lady, Ryan, and I would be obliged if you could all remember that salient fact."

"Sorry. Where is she?"

"Said that Traven insisted that everyone in his group was together at night. Sky also told me some things about the way that he dominates the young people. It is, I am reluctant to admit, like the description you used, Mildred. The man appears to be the worst kind of bullying control-freak."

Ryan wiped his mouth with a threadbare linen napkin. He looked with some reluctance at the pile of uneaten crab claws, but decided he'd reached his capacity.

"Doc. One thing. Since Jak went, I think all of us have sort of been looking for someone to replace him.

That's wrong. Jak Lauren's safe with Christina Ballinger in New Mexico now. I hope. Life moves on. But if Sky wants to join with us and there's no problem, then there's no problem."

"That is spoken like a gentleman and a scholar, my dear Ryan. Now, those crab claws appear quite delicious. Or perhaps the deviled whitebait. Maybe even both. Is that a caper sauce with the grilled sole? I vow that I have rarely encountered a baron who took such care over the inner man."

LATER THE PARTY SPLIT UP into its current components. Doc returned to his own room and watched some vids of a television series that Boss Larry piped through. Ryan and Krysty tried to watch it, but it seemed a plot of such staggering complexity that they gave up on it.

"It wasn't the giant and the dwarf," Krysty said, lying back on the huge bed. "Nor the damned fine coffee and the cherry pie. It was the woman who was dead, then Japanese, then alive again."

Mildred and J.B. had also made their excuses and retired to their suite along the corridor.

Dean had gone to bed early, then got up and shyly asked if he could come in with Ryan and Krysty.

"Tell me stories about all the dirt bastards you chilled, Dad."

Ryan shook his head. "Too many and it's too late, son. Man remembers all his enemies, and he never locks himself into the present or the future."

"You remember *some* enemies."

"Two. Cort Strasser. Skull-faced sec boss of a frontier ville. Ran into him two more times. Now he's gone to rot forever. Other was a Russkie."

"You knew a Russkie!"

"Twice. Man called Zimyanin. Tell you that story sometime, Dean. Bald bastard, nearly chilled me. Last time I saw him was through a gateway door and some great…great golden shape was closing on him. Probably dead now."

"Tell me…" The boy's voice was pleading, but he kept yawning, head nodding.

Krysty patted him on the arm. "Sandman time, Dean. Come on."

"Sandman? Who's that? That another enemy like Skullhead and the Russkie?"

Ryan squeezed the small hand in his, and the boy meandered across the room, through into his adjoining room, and closed the door softly behind him.

He whispered a good-night through the gap.

The door opened a moment later. "Dad?"

"What is it?"

"Pharaoh's Curse was about the best ace on the line I ever had in all my life. Thanks."

"Glad you liked it. Don't think I'll forget it in a hurry."

"Yeah. G'night, Dad. G'night, Krysty."

This time the door remained closed.

A little later Ryan and Krysty held each other tightly in the great bed and made gentle, tender love. And then slept a quiet and dreamless sleep.

KELLY ARRIVED soon after dawn.

"Boss Larry'd like to see you, Ryan. In an hour."

"Just me?"

"Yeah. Just you."

Krysty rolled on her back and stretched, clawing at the cool morning air. "Did that group of oldies get to see him yesterday?"

"Mrs. Owen and friends?"

"One with that lovely amber necklace. Silver cross on the end of it. One that Doc sent all a flutter."

"No. They waited, but Boss Larry was too stoned."

Ryan got up and began to dress, oblivious to the presence of the sec man, pulling on his pants and lacing his boots. He reached for his coat.

"You dropped something," Kelly said, leaning against the front door of the room. "Bit of paper. Down by the leg of the bed. There."

"Thanks." Ryan stooped and picked it up, seeing that it was the odd coded message. Bright lances of sunlight came through a gap in the curtains, and for the first time he could read part of the scribbled message.

"R.5. S NMex nr Tex," it read. Then some numbers. He slipped it back in his pocket, intending to talk to J.B. about it.

"I'm ready," he announced.

Kelly nodded. "Traven and his posse stayed in the park last night," he said.

"Yeah. So?"

"Nothing. Let's go see the boss."

KELLY TOOK HIM to the vast shadowy lobby of Centerpoint, where several sec men were standing around, most showing signs of tiredness. Their body language revealed they were about to come off duty and be replaced by the next shift.

"Good time to hit them," Ryan said.

Kelly nodded. "Training's slipped in the last couple of weeks. Traven's subverted a number of them. Younger men. That's what worries me, Ryan. Seriously worries me. Been a couple of executions for treason in the last week. Hadn't been more than a handful of traitors in the last four or five years."

"Can't you take him out?"

"Traven?"

"Sure." Ryan looked at the elevator, where a shifting light showed that there was a car moving toward the lobby. "Doesn't carry a blaster, does he?"

"Could've chilled him when he arrived. Too late now."

"Never too late."

Kelly shook his head, unsmiling. "Wrong, friend. Too late when you're in the big hole and the wet earth's landing on the back of your neck. That's too late. Here's the elevator. Go on up. Press 'Roof.' Boss is up there waiting for you."

Ryan took a step toward the open steel doors, then hesitated. "Something else?" he asked.

"Keep your boy close," Kelly said quickly. "Now,

get going. Boss Larry doesn't take kindly to being kept waiting."

The doors slid shut, and Ryan pressed the recessed button with the word Roof alongside it in raised black letters. There was the faint hum of the machinery clicking into gear, and the elevator began to rise smoothly.

Already he was starting to sweat. Ryan had never been a lover of intense humidity. The dry heat of the southern deserts didn't bother him, but this sweltering moistness was uncomfortable.

With a slight jar the elevator halted, and he stepped out into the revolving room at the top of the tower.

It was dark and silent, with only one guard leaning sleepily against a wall. He straightened as Ryan appeared in front of him.

"Yeah? Oh, you're the outlander Boss Larry wanted to see. He's in his workroom."

"Where's that?"

"Up there," the man replied with a wave of his hand in the general direction of the back of the vast room.

Ryan's temper had never been of the best, but as he grew older he generally managed to control it, to recognize the first crimson flaring of the fire and extinguish it.

Not this time.

Without a moment's pause he stepped in close to the sec man and locked both hands into the lapels of his jacket. He braced his wrists inward and lifted at the same time, taking the man's toes clear off the floor.

"Asked you where," Ryan said quietly, watching the man's face begin to swell and turn purple.

The only reply was a rattling, choking sound. Ryan released some of the pressure and let the man down gently.

"Show you." As Ryan let him go, the guard rubbed his neck and stooped to pick up his beret, which had fallen off in the brief struggle. "Didn't have to show me the fuckin' black sleep."

"Try doing your job properly."

"Yeah, sure. Come on." He muttered to himself, "Do the job and you don't know who you're working for. Boss or that Traven and his posse. Yeah, sure."

They reached another elevator, concealed in a decorative column at the center of the slowly moving room.

"Boss is up there."

Ryan nodded. "Thanks."

The man looked at him for a moment, then turned on his heel and trudged back to his post, fingering the butt of his Government Model Colt.

There was only one button, showing an arrow pointing upward. Ryan pressed it, and the doors opened almost immediately. He stepped in, sniffing at the powerful scent of sweat that filled the car.

He guessed that the workroom was hidden in the very top of the tower. The elevator didn't seem to go up more than fifteen or twenty feet, then it stopped and the doors slid open.

"Come in, Ryan Cawdor," said the familiar voice. "I wanted to tell you that dear Adam has told me to have you chilled."

Chapter Twenty-Six

"I like starting the day with some good news, Larry. What else did the little prick have to say?"

Boss Larry Zapp was sitting in a huge canvas-and-leather chair by a long bench, which was covered with a mountain of electrical hardware. Ryan had never seen so much stuff—circuit boards, wires, plugs, sockets, chips, monitors and tangles of dusty equipment that threatened to topple and overwhelm even the giant figure of the baron.

And the rest of the workroom was the same.

Laser-vid screens sat in one corner, oscilloscopes in another. Comp recorders jumbled clear to the dusty ceiling. Another bench with shelves on top of it was lined with thousands of mags and books, all in total disorder. Ryan noticed, at a second glance, that the two shaven-headed mutes were sitting on each side of the shelves, like a pair of carved, life-size bookends.

Boss Larry didn't reply. His breath wheezed in and out, and he looked at the small piece of techno gear in his pudgy fingers.

Ryan waited.

"If that's all you got to tell me, Larry, I'll be going. Can't waste a nice morning up here."

"He means it, Ryan." There was a weight of despair in the words.

The one-eyed man stepped a little closer, wrinkling his nose as he tried to identify a strange, sickly odor in the room. Then he saw the scraps of crumpled, blackened silver foil on the bench, all showing traces of a fine pink powder.

"You been dreeming, Boss," Ryan said. "Traven gives you dreem and then pulls your strings."

The leonine head nodded slowly, the disarrayed silver hair covering the face. "Oh, yes, Ryan. But you forget his lovely young friends. They don't care that I'm old, ill, terrified and fat. To them I'm as young and spry as they are. Such sweet children and they make me—" He paused, then shouted in a deafening bellow that made Ryan jump. "Make me happy!"

The two servants both turned their heads slowly toward the baron, as though even their vanished hearing had caught something of the roar of anguish.

At that moment Ryan realized a terrible truth: anything that Baron Larry Zapp had once been was gone, destroyed by the insidious application of dreem, combined with who knew what sexual excesses. The whirling little dervish with the pretty clothes was someone to reckon with, a figure of genuine, potent evil.

Ryan knew it was time to move on.

"Why tell me what Traven wants, Larry?" he asked.

"Thought you'd like to know."

"We'll go."

Again the movement of the head. "Not, Ryan. Not. Sec men are his now. Promises of— All the ways out are way-out now."

Ryan nodded. "I see."

The hidden workroom was quiet. Without windows to see from, Ryan was only just aware of the ponderous revolving of the tower.

"Your son."

Ryan wasn't sure he'd heard the soft whisper. "Dean?"

"Adam likes him, Ryan. Oh, yes. Precious. His precious, Ryan. Boy that young. Pretty. What he wants most."

That was the moment when Ryan Cawdor made the conscious decision that Adam Traven would have to be chilled. Regardless of the personal cost and the consequences.

"Who's going to do the chilling, Larry? You? Traven?"

"Don't know. Don't care. Don't—"

"Going now, Larry."

"Want a radio?"

"What?"

"Gift for you. Souvenir from Greenglades ville. Thank you and come again." His hands rummaged through the morass of gear in front of him, emerging triumphantly with a small black box with a plas-glass dial and silver controls. "Here. Found hundreds. Worked on them myself. Still few in Deathlands got radio gear. Pick them up and talk. Late at night. Can't see me when I talk. Listen in. Here."

Ryan took it, warm from the boss's hand. "How's it work? Range?"

"Easy. Buttons marked. Autosearch. Talk and listen. Tuner. Range?"

"Yeah."

For a moment Ryan was glimpsing something of the old Larry Zapp, a technical genius and hustler. Before the drugs pulped his brain.

"About three...maybe four thousand miles. Old days wouldn't have been anything. Airwaves jammed and crowded and packed and filled and— Now the skies are clear as a child's smile. Take it."

"Thanks." Ryan slipped it into his coat pocket, his fingers again brushing the torn piece of paper with its cryptic message.

"Sorry, Ryan." A gobbet of a tear glistened on the man's unshaven cheek.

"Never apologize, Larry. Trader used to say it was a sign of weakness."

"And good old Trader was right." Now he was busy again, pouring something from a vial onto a piece of metal foil and lighting a burner under it. He leaned over and inhaled the acrid fumes. "Ah, yes."

Ryan turned away, his mind racing as he tried to figure out a plan that would get them away from the murderous trap. Behind him he heard the noise of the elevator moving, gears humming, the thick cables vibrating. He eased his hand onto the butt of the SIG-Sauer and waited.

Boss Larry was slumped over his bench, oblivious to anything.

"Wondered if I might find you here," Traven said as he stepped out into the room with one of his young men and two of the girls. A brace of armed sec men were behind him, blasters already drawn.

"Just leaving."

The room was too dark for the mirrored jacket to look its best, but the diminutive figure was still impressive. "Don't think so, Ryan," he said. "Lard Ass been dribbling off at the mouth."

It was a statement, not a question. Ryan left his hand where it was, ready for a last whirlwind firefight. He looked at the faces of Traven's companions. The odd androgynous bisexuality, the narrow, flat eyes, totally without expression reminded Ryan of the dead eyes of the great white shark that he'd once seen.

There was nothing as overt as hostility, just a blankness, a pinched and corrupt disinterest.

"He said I'd be happier if you and your crew were some other place?"

This time it was a question.

"Yeah. We're going today."

"Where?"

"Some other place."

"Ah." Traven spread his hands like a haggling merchant. "Some other place. I think we should stop all this shit."

"Go ahead."

"I'm clever, Ryan Cawdor, taking this over. Don't need a blaster or a blade. Just this." He tapped his narrow forehead. "My posse does what I say. Give me all the pleasing I want. Now I want your son."

"Why?"

"Because I want him. Just that. I could get Larry to have you all executed. There's an easier way."

"Tell me."

"Walk. You, the black woman, the redhead, the gun freak and the old one. Walk out the gates into the daylight and leave the little boy. I truly want him very badly."

"My son."

"Sure." Traven threw back his head and laughed, a sound like a hacksaw slicing through a sheet of crystal. Almost as if he'd thrown a switch, his posse all laughed at the same moment.

"Need to talk about it, Traven," Ryan said.

"Sure, buy time. Can't spend it. Life costs in minutes and hours. Then your account runs out, and there's no more jack beating in your chest."

"Tell you my decision tomorrow morning."

Traven smiled. "Same time and same place." He half bowed. "And y'all have a nice day."

Ryan left the gloomy chamber, the only sound the muffled sobbing of Boss Larry Zapp.

KELLY WAS SITTING on a low wall around a display of ornamental cacti. He saw Ryan come out of Centerpoint and stood.

"What'd Traven want?"

"Larry, you mean?"

The sec man shook his head. "No. Boss is sinking real fast. You think he's mebbe waving, and you find out the poor fat bastard's drowning."

"Traven wants us all to leave."

"Your kid?"

"No. Wants Dean left behind."

Kelly nodded. "Thought so. You gonna run for it? Hard to get out, I tell you."

Ryan's policy in life wasn't to trust anyone too far. The exceptions were Krysty, J.B., Doc, Mildred and Jak Lauren. The stocky noncom wasn't one of the exceptions.

"Maybe."

"Sucking death! Here comes that redheaded beanpole from the posse."

Sky was running in slow motion, her arms spread wide, like the long wings of an albatross. She was wearing precisely the same clothes she'd had on the day before.

"Hey, Ryan." She ignored Kelly completely, as though the noncom were a dead man.

Ryan nodded to her. "You looking for Doc?"

He was rewarded with a bright smile. "How d'you guess? Course. Adam says we can go out tonight, and I want to tell Doc I'll see him real late. After dark snaking."

"What's that? Dark snaking?"

She touched her hand to his lips and held it there. In an uncomfortably arousing moment, Ryan realized that he could taste the young woman's body on her own fingers.

"Secret," she said. "Adam up in the tower with our fat friend?"

"With the baron? Yeah."

"See you later, Ryan. Bye." She headed toward the main entrance, floating like a multicolored bird riding an invisible thermal of warm air.

Kelly spit among the magnolias. "Bitch," he said with little passion.

"Yeah."

"You tell Doc from me he'd do better letting a swamp scorpion get in— Hell, he can find out for himself. I'm through with advice."

Without another word the sec man walked away from Ryan, vanishing around a bend in the winding path that led toward Paraglide Paradise.

RYAN TOLD Krysty everything, sitting beside her on the bed in their room. Dean was watching the television, locked into a crackling vid about some dead crazies in an isolated cabin. Every time Ryan glanced across at the screen, there seemed to be heads flying through the air, or empty eye sockets or severed hands coming through walls.

"We going to try and break out?"

Ryan closed his eye, feeling a sudden wave of exhaustion. The whole place sickened him, with its patina of swift and evil corruption. "They may be getting ragged around the edges, but Larry's still got one of the best sec forces I've seen. Not easy to get away."

"The gateway?"

"Might be our best chance. If it wasn't for—" he nodded toward the back of his son's head "—I'd think about hanging around a day or so and seeing what we could do about swatting the flies away from the ville. Needs doing.''

Without looking around, Dean spoke to his father. "Why does Traven want me? He an ass fucker?''

"You got good ears, son. Truth is, I don't know. That's what makes it creepy. Seems like Traven gets his kicks from dominating folk. His posse does what he tells them.''

"Let me go with him, and I can slit his throat and then we get away.''

Ryan smiled. "I reckon you could do it, Dean. But it's a triple-risk.''

"Rona used to say all living's a risk.''

"True, but this is something special. If there was some safe place I could take you, then we could do something about Traven.''

"I don't want to lose you.''

"I know. But—'' There was a long pause. "Dean, go tell the others to come in here. We all have to talk.''

Chapter Twenty-Seven

"Not our business," Mildred said.

Krysty agreed with her. "They don't know about the redoubt. Lost in the woods. We can get out of the ville that way."

"Don't much like someone throwing me my blaster and telling me to get out," J.B. said, busily polishing his glasses, "but the boy has to be made safe."

"Oh, incidentally, Larry gave me this radio. Worked on it himself." Ryan pulled it out of the pocket of his long coat, the crumpled scrap of paper falling onto the floor. Ryan stooped to pick it up.

"What is that?" Doc asked.

"Found it under that old cap just outside the gateway. Hardly read it. Need a strong light."

"Would you mind awfully if I attempted my poor eyes on it? Thank you, Ryan, my dear fellow. Most kind of you."

J.B. took the radio, holding it as though it were a nugget of pure gold from the mother lode. "This is fabulous. You reckon that poor brain-dead lump of dripping put this together?"

"Said so. His place is flowing over with all sorts of techno gear. Most I ever saw in one room. Said you can talk and listen over two or three thousand miles. But I figure there aren't many people in the whole of Deathlands who got this kind of equipment.''

The Armorer was fascinated.

He switched it on, flipping open a slot in the back. "Sol power," he said. "Larry's better than I thought. He really figures it's got that sort of range?'' He moved the tiny dial that controlled the frequency. There was nothing but a sibilant hissing and crackling. As J.B. eased it along, they suddenly heard a faint voice that swam into the room like the ghost of yesterday's dreams. Faint and immeasurably far off, it spoke what sounded like a Mexican dialect. It almost immediately faded back into the ether.

"Works," Mildred said. "How about that, Doc? Walkie-talkie with the rest of— You listening to me, Doc?''

There was no reply.

The old man had gone into the alcove where the washbasin and bathroom were concealed. He'd switched on the bright light over the tarnished mirror and was staring intently at the piece of paper.

"Doc?" Ryan called.

"What is it?''

"You found something?''

Doc turned, his face alight, eyes wide. "By the three Kennedys! Did I hear you asking me whether I had found something?''

"Yeah. What is it?''

"If my memory hasn't gone wandering off down

Alzheimer Avenue, I think this could be a gateway code. Someone risked a fearful wigging for this sort of security breach.''

"You mean the code to make jumps to particular places?'' J.B. switched off the little radio and threw it on the bed.

"Only one or two that I can decipher,'' Doc said hastily.

He laid the paper on the flat surface by the basin, angling it to catch the best of the light. ''Down this side are a sequence of numbers, each prefixed with the letter *R*.

They could all see that, huddled around: ''R.1., R.2.,'' and so on.

"I believe this may mean simply 'redoubt.' The digits may relate to some master code. The sequence of numbers at the end is, I believe, linked to the control panel that we have seen by every doorway.''

Krysty pointed to the scribbled writing. ''And that tells you where the redoubt is.''

"Since this is the very nub of the business, I'm desolated to say that only about three or four are even minimally legible.''

"LA SW.''

Dean read out the four letters. ''What's that mean, Doc?''

Krysty answered. ''Guess it's southwest Los Angeles, isn't it?''

"That was also my supposition. This one is a shorthand for northern Missouri close to the Iowa state line.''

"The one in Los Angeles is a last-train venture," Ryan said. "That part of California was one of the first places to go at sky-dark. Slid under the Pacific Ocean. Parts of Missouri and Mississippi got swallowed up by Big Muddy changing course."

"Third one I can make out seems to have been in Alaska. Could be the one we passed by when we encountered that Zimyanin fellow you spoke of the other day, Ryan? And this other one, number five."

"S NMex nr Tex."

Mildred looked at the others with dawning recognition. "One of the first places I jumped to. Southern New Mexico, not far from the border with what used to be Texas. And that—"

Ryan completed the sentence for her. "That's not far from the Ballinger spread, where Jak Lauren and Christina are living." He hesitated. "Where they *were* living, anyway."

"Only problem is that the redoubt blew up. Took the whole mountain with it."

Ryan had remembered that even before J.B. spoke. The place had been boobied with all sorts of self-destruct devices that they'd triggered trying to escape. The resultant explosion had come close to wasting them all and had blown away the whole of one flank of the hillside.

"Not the whole mountain," Ryan said thoughtfully. "We were stuck because that sec door dropped and cut us off from the gateway. It was way deep and on the farther side of the complex. Good chance it's still secure down there."

Krysty was standing by the mirror, brushing her long hair. "One thing we've never found out, lover, is what happens when you jump into a gateway that no longer exists. That's a thousand feet under the sea or pulped beneath trillions of tons of dirt. This could be the time to find out."

Dean had picked up on what they were discussing. "You going to take me to this Jak Lauren man?"

"Maybe, son. Question of safety."

"So why don't we all go?"

It was a good question.

For several long heartbeats nobody answered the young boy.

Finally Ryan said, "Trader used to say that there were some things that a person couldn't always just ride around."

"But I can stay and fight." Dean's voice broke, and Ryan realized that his son was on the edge of tears. "Don't send me away."

"I'm not *sending* you away." He knelt by Dean and put his arm gently on his shoulder. "I'm taking you to see if Jak can have you for a few days. No longer. If there's a problem there, we both come back here. It's not that I don't care, son. It's that I *do* care about you. Understand?"

"Suppose so."

"Soon as we've kicked Traven's skinny ass, we'll all be down to see you," Mildred told him.

"Promise?"

Doc laid his gnarled hand across the center of the boy's chest. "Regardless of what this raggle-taggle parcel of sturdy rogues might claim, Dean, you have the sworn oath of Dr. Theophilus Tanner that we shall see you again, very soon.''

''What an old jerk-off you are, Doc!'' Mildred grinned.

RYAN PASSED ON TO DOC the news that Sky might well be calling on him later that night, after the posse had been to what she'd referred to as ''dark snaking.''

''Means Dean and I have to get away before midnight. Don't want her creeping around and watching us break for it.''

''Surely. But what will we tell the sec men or Boss Larry?''

''Part truth. Me and the boy went for a late walk and didn't come back. With any luck they'll suss the Cajuns. That'll be my story if I make the return jump safely.''

Ryan had already discussed with Krysty what they should all do if he wasn't back in seventy-two hours.

''Chill anyone you have to and get out. If I can get hold of a communication device, I'll try and contact you some time on the radio. One hundred band.''

They'd sent Dean outside for a while so they could enjoy a brief moment together.

Krysty had been quiet and introspective. ''You know why, Ryan. Being away from you is like losing a part of myself. And I'm scared.''

''Scared of what?''

''Uncle Tyas McCann told me an old, old saying. Said it was Latin.''

"Where's that?"

"More than two thousand years ago, in Europe. Ruled most of the known world. Want to know this saying, lover?"

"Yeah." He was lying on the bed beside her, running his hand gently over her thighs.

"He said *'Timor mortis contrubat me.'* Know what it means?"

"Tell me."

"It means that the fear of death moves within me, lover."

RYAN AND DEAN LEFT the ville a couple of hours before midnight.

Chapter Twenty-Eight

There'd been a brief rain shower while they were eating supper. Now the night was filled with a heavy scent of vegetation, and water still dripped off the jagged edges of leaves. Beneath their boots the ground was moist and clinging.

To the east, against the concrete desolation of what had once been Miami, the sky showed the remains of a violent chem storm. Streaks of purple-and-pink lightning tore open the banks of low cloud, and the faint rumbling of thunder was discernible.

"You sure you can get back, Dad?" Dean whispered as they crouched together in the lake of black shadows outside their motel.

"Sure. Mildred tumbled to the bit on the bottom of the scrap of paper. The letters L and D. Just press those for the 'Last Destination.' Shrewd guess."

"But how do you *know* that's what that means? What if she's wrong?"

Ryan managed to sound a hundred percent confident. In fact, there'd been a long argument about whether the letters were indeed an L and a D.

Most of them were agreed on the first letter being an L, but the D was the subject of much more discussion. Krysty had held the paper sideways to the

light and announced that she thought it looked much
more like a *P*.

"What if the place is demolished like J.B. said it
might be?"

"If it is, then the gateway won't function and we
stay where we are. If we get to it and there's a problem, then there's a thirty-minute automatic reset on
all the mat-trans units. So we'd finish back here in
the ville a half hour after we made the jump. No problem, son."

"Yeah, but..."

Ryan lowered his head, managing to control his
anger. "You got any more questions? Then let's have
them now, Dean."

"Just... Will Jak Lauren like me, Dad?"

"He's only about fifteen. Maybe sixteen by now.
Never had anything you could call a childhood. Like
you, son."

Dean was silent. "I finished with the questions,
Dad."

"Then we can go."

THEY HID among some ornamental orchids as a sec
patrol passed them. Ryan thought he caught a mention
of Kelly's name, but he couldn't hear what was being
said about the noncom.

They didn't see anyone else before reaching the
cutoff into the impenetrable deeps of the positronic
jungle. The temperature was way into the high seventies, despite the lateness of the evening, and Ryan

was aware of sweat trickling down into the small of his back.

The moon reluctantly eased its way through a rift in the low clouds, helping father and son to pick their way toward the long-lost redoubt.

Ryan was relieved to have the light, aware of the pits of sucking mud that lay all around waiting to drag at an unwary footstep.

He heard the deep croaking of a frog, and something flew through the air from under his boots, landing with a splash in one of the gleaming pools.

Dean was at his heels when he suddenly slipped, falling with a squeak of shock into a cluster of waxen flowers with long tendrils.

"You all right, son?"

"Got fuck…wet knees. I'm— Hey the leaves are sort of grabbing at me."

"Don't be a stupe. Get up."

"It's holding me." The voice was louder, carrying a frayed edge of rising panic. They were still only a few hundred yards away from the patrolled regions of the ville.

In the thick undergrowth the moonlight was filtered and dissipated. Ryan dropped to his knees and felt with his hands, finding that Dean had fallen awkwardly, arms and legs spread. The bushes were mainly long vines, with tendrils thicker than a man's finger, strong and resilient. As Ryan touched his son, he had the illusion of the plants moving, coiling over Dean's leg, wrapping themselves around him.

"Pull me up, Dad!"

"Keep your voice down," Ryan snapped, getting his hands under his son's arms, bracing himself to lift.

As he heaved the boy up, he heard the clear sound of some of the vines snapping like whipcord, rustling around on the ground like a nest of young moccasin snakes.

"You all right?"

"Guess so. Were they alive?"

Now that they were both standing, it was easier to see. The boy's black denim jacket glistened with slimy green strings, some of them seeming to move and writhe. Ryan brushed them all off into the muddy earth.

"Never come across mutie plants like that. Could've been real bad. Step careful and follow me close. I'll go out at point."

There were no further alarms, though Ryan started several times, reaching for his blaster, at sudden movements and sounds in the swamps.

"Made it," Dean said, breathing a loud sigh of relief.

"So far, so good," Ryan agreed, opening the outer sec doors to the redoubt.

"We staying here or going straight on to make the jump?"

"Straight on. Quicker we can try and get to Jak's place, the better. Don't like leaving everyone here to the sick mercies of Traven."

The entrance doors closed solidly behind them, and they moved fast through the various sections of the complex until they reached the tumbled steel door in the rotted frame that opened up to the gateway itself.

Ryan's combat boots echoed dully off the metal slats of the stairs down. The memory of the giant mutie rat was fresh in his memory, and he carried the SIG-Sauer drawn and ready.

The passage was completely silent, the air still overwhelmingly moist, though it did seem a little fresher than a couple of days ago.

They reached the main doors into the mat-trans section without incident.

"Can I do the code?"

"Yeah. Remember it?"

"Three, five and two."

"Do it."

There was the usual breath-checking moment when nothing seemed to be happening. But the century-old mechanism was still functioning, and the double sec doors rose ponderously.

The cameras still swayed back and forth, the red light gleaming on each of them. When father and son reached the other doors, Ryan heaved up on the green control lever and opened the way into the main control room of the gateway.

The Atlanta Braves baseball cap lay where Dean had dropped it on the muddied floor of the small anteroom.

"It'll be okay, Dad?"

"Sure. Let's see if we were wrong or right about this little piece of paper." Ryan had copied onto a postcard the bits of information and code that the companions more or less had agreed on.

The fifth notation—if they were right—referred to a redoubt that was situated in southern New Mexico, not far from Texas, in a military complex that had been largely reduced to rubble by several explosions several weeks earlier.

"You go in."

"You're coming?" Again Ryan heard that tiny scrap of threatened panic at the idea that he might be left in this alien chamber on his own.

"Sure. Got to punch in these numbers."

"Should I sit down?"

"Back against the wall. Legs out straight, or maybe knees up and your arms around them. Kind of tuck your head in. Main thing is to get comfortable, ready for the jump."

Dean walked in gingerly, avoiding the metal disks in the floor, and sat on the far side. He picked a spot where he could keep an eye on Ryan, who stood by the control panel.

The console felt slightly sticky to Ryan's finger as he punched in the long code. He glanced at the L and the D buttons, wondering if they really meant "Last Destination" as they hoped. If they did, then he'd be back in the blue-green walls without any serious difficulty.

Wouldn't he?

A second later he finished the sequence, paused, then joined Dean. He squatted by the boy and put his arm around the slight figure.

"Hang on, everybody," he said. "Here we go."

There was the growing swell of the humming noise, and the familiar mist began to gather near the roof of the chamber. The disks started to glow, brighter and brighter.

"Can I try and keep my eyes open for the jump, Dad?" the boy asked, his voice faint and receding down a limitless corridor.

"If you want to. But I don't…think…you'll be…"

The dark carnival revolved inside his skull, the whistling music of the calliope growing louder and ever more shrill.

Ryan felt his son starting to shudder, his whole body vibrating.

Someone out in the dazzling blackness was beginning to scream.

Chapter Twenty-Nine

The walls of the gateway chamber showed a pale filtered silver color, and Ryan remembered that was the right shade for the redoubt down in the wilderness of what had once been called New Mexico. At least the jump seemed to have taken them to the correct place.

He took several deep breaths, trying to fight down the inevitable nausea, closing his eye again, and felt a tight steel band clamped across the frontal lobe of his brain.

"Fireblast," he said. "Least we're still alive."

He looked down at his son.

Dean was unconscious, his mouth open. A faint smear of blood covered his lower lip, but he was breathing steadily and his pulse was strong. Ryan still had his arm around the boy and he shifted carefully, lowering him so that he could lie on the floor.

"I'll get some, Rona," Dean whispered.

But his eyes stayed closed.

Ryan stood, stretching like a great cat, muscles creaking with the strain. Out of habit he checked his weapons: the butcher's cleaver on his hip, safely in its sheath, and the slim-bladed flensing knife in the small of his back; the pistol in its holster and the new Steyr bolt-action rifle slung across his shoulders.

He couldn't remember much about the actual gateway. A terrifying illness had struck him in the redoubt beyond, taking his mind for a time and nearly taking his life.

The glowing disks in floor and ceiling had all cooled and returned to their usual dull sheen. The mist was gone from the air—air that felt noticeably drier than in Florida.

"Kept my eyes open all the time, Dad."

The small voice made him turn around. Dean was struggling to sit up.

"Lie still for a bit. Otherwise you'll throw up. How do you feel?"

"Sick. But I kept... No, I don't think I did. But I *tried*, Dad."

"Never managed it myself. Seems part of the mechanics of the jump that you have to pass out. Something to do with all the bits of your body and mind being scrambled up and then brought back together again. That's what an old friend called Rick told me once. Don't understand it."

"I dreamed about Rona."

"Nice dream?"

The boy sat up, wincing, and put a hand to his head. "I know she was crying. We were in some big stone ville. Lots of people. And she was crying. Can't remember why."

"Fit to fight?"

"Sure." The boy stood, then wobbling knees folded in on themselves. Ryan was just in time to catch the lad and save him from falling.

"Wait a while longer, Dean. There's no hurry to get moving."

"Will it be the same time here?"

"Night?" He looked at his son. "You know, I don't think any of us have ever really thought much about that. I think it is. Often we don't find exactly where we are until we get outside the redoubt. That sometimes takes days."

Dean tried again, this time managing to stand unaided. His face was frost pale, and his eyes didn't look too secure in their sockets. But he was upright.

"Will there be a place we can rest and eat?"

"Doubt it. The fact that the mat-trans unit is still here and functioning is a real double ace on the line for us."

"Jak Lauren? Will he—" Ryan lifted a warning finger. Dean managed a wan smile. "Sorry. Too many questions. I'm ready, as long as we don't go too fast." Ryan pushed at the door, and immediately outside he checked the control panel, making sure that it also carried the *L* and the *D* buttons.

"Get your blaster out," he said.

"Why?"

"There's a lot of golden dust around the floor. Don't remember that from last time. Could mean someone else has been using the gateway, or that it's open to the outside. Either way it's dangerous."

"If Krysty was here she'd feel if there was danger, wouldn't she?"

Ryan nodded, his finger on the trigger of the P-226 9 mm pistol. "Most times. But not always."

The boy drew his Smith & Wesson 425, eyes narrowing. "I'm ready for them, Dad."

"Trader used to reckon that the man who survived was the man who was ready...even when he wasn't ready. Get it?"

"Think so." Dean sounded doubtful.

They exited the small room, then the main control section for the gateway, into the passage beyond.

Ryan stopped. "Shit," he muttered.

He remembered that Krysty sometimes quoted a saying of her mother's that good luck and bad luck were often tangled together. You might fall down and break a leg, yet just avoid going over a thousand-foot cliff.

The autodestruct devices that had been laid throughout the complex had done most of their work with devastating efficiency. Ryan and his companions had been the reluctant witnesses of that.

The good luck was that the gateway hadn't been damaged. The bad luck was what he saw at the end of the passage—sky, a circle of vinyl black, sprinkled with a myriad stars.

"Keep back while I take a look. Could be undercut and dangerous."

He moved forward very cautiously. All the lights were out in the corridor, and his feet slid through a thick bed of sand and pebbles. By the time he came close to the brink of the opening, Ryan was already aware of a sighing wind in the night and the sense of a vast space beckoning him on.

"I'm coming back," he called.

"What is it?"

"Don't like it. Can't see a hand in front of my face, and I have a feeling there's a big chasm out there. Tackle it better in the light. Right now we'll get some sleep."

"We could try it, or we waste a lot of time, don't we?"

"No. We'll need sleep. Need to be alert for the walk across open desert to Jak's place."

"How do you know he's still there?"

It was a fair question, one that Ryan had been repeatedly pushing away into a locked room at the back of his mind. In Deathlands nothing was certain. And the Southwest was an unusually hostile environment for survival.

"Dad?" Dean's voice came from the pool of light that spilled out from the open doors of the mat-trans control area.

"I'm here. It could be that something's happened to Jak and his woman. But you have to take risks in life, or you're deader than a spent round. Find out in the morning."

For safety they went back inside the chamber, curling up together on the floor. Ryan had his blaster in his hand all the time.

"DAD!"

Ryan came awake immediately, instantly aware of where he was.

"What?"

"Look."

A small bird was perched in the doorway, head on one side, looking curiously at the two figures on the floor. It had a bright crimson beak and a splash of gold on its head.

As Ryan sat up, it turned and flew away, the whirring of its tiny wings vanishing into the morning.

Dean went out for a piss, calling his father from the passage. "There's footmarks here."

"Mine?"

"Yeah. And others. Different patterns of boots in the sand. A lot of them, Dad."

That wasn't good news.

Ryan joined the boy, nodding his head in agreement. "Yeah. Looks like a dozen of them. Not too recent. See the way the blown dirt's drifted in on some of the boot-marks."

"Hey, look out there! You can see for a million miles."

In daylight the end of the passage was now clear. The side of the mountain that had contained the redoubt had been sliced open as the plas-ex exploited a major geological fault. Half of the hill had vanished as though a gigantic machete had carved through it.

Moving carefully, father and son made their way to the edge of the gulf.

Ahead the whole countryside lay open before them like a scorched paradise.

It was still only a little after dawn, and that flank of the mountain was still in darkness. Far below, the floor of the desert was littered with patches of shadow from frost-riven boulders.

A maze of narrow arroyos seamed the land, and farther away there was already enough heat to cause the distant ranges of hills to shimmer. It might not have been a million miles, but Ryan's guess was that it was possible to see more than a hundred.

"Can't see nobody. Nothing. No houses. No ville. Nothing."

At the bottom of the slope Ryan could just make out the rusted remains of the battered comm dish that had sheltered them from the blowout. He leaned out and was able, to his relief, to spot a narrow, winding track.

It wandered to the right, then cut sharply in a series of break-back turns, eventually reaching the flatter land below. It wasn't possible to tell whether it was man or animal that had originally broken the trail. Now boot prints appeared along it, as well as the spoor of a number of medium-sized animals.

It took them nearly half an hour to negotiate the steep twists and reach level ground. Dean wiped sweat off his face, staring up above them.

"Must've been double-thrilling."

Ryan was breathing hard from the exertion. The temperature was already up into the eighties, but it was baking, dry heat. "What?"

"When you all escaped the mountain blowing up like that."

"Thrilling? One of the closest times I ever came to shitting my pants."

"Really?" Dean smiled at his father.

But Ryan wasn't amused. "Not a joke, Dean. That

dish over there was the only thing that saved our lives. There were stones blizzarding down all around us. Some as big as implode grens. Some bigger than a war wag.''

The desert was almost empty of life. They spotted a blur of movement as a tiny orange lizard skittered and jinked between the rocks.

''Which way?''

Ryan pointed toward the south west. ''That way. Should be there by noon unless something goes against us.''

It was less than fifteen minutes later when he saw the telltale puffs of dust rising from the far side of a ridge, not more than a half mile away.

Dean caught the movement and stopped. ''What's making that?'' he said.

Before Ryan could reply, the answer revealed itself. A pack of twenty or more mutie coyotes loped over the top of the hill toward them.

Chapter Thirty

The pack was running silently, concentrating their ferocious energy on the hunt. These coyotes were larger than any that Ryan had seen before, and they were also much more heavily muscled.

They were moving at an easy lope, aiming a little in front of Ryan and his son.

Dean drew his pistol, but Ryan motioned for him to put it away.

"Waste of time. If they get within about forty or fifty paces, you can chill some. No, it's worth trying the new long gun."

He unslung the Steyr military sniping rifle from his shoulder, working the bolt to put a 7.62 mm round under the pin. The Starlight nightscope and the laser image intensifier wouldn't be a whole lot of help on such a bright, sunlit morning.

The problem was going to be selecting a target from among the shifting, moving pack and focusing in on it.

"Shouldn't we keep going? Run for it?" Dean was looking all around as though he expected to see a rescue party appearing on the skyline.

"They'd have us in less than ten minutes." Ryan knelt, wishing there'd been a handy boulder to rest the SSG-70. "If I can knock over two or three, the others might lose interest."

"Much farther to the spread?"

"When we came here last time I didn't know there was anybody for miles, so I didn't pay that much attention. Never thought I'd be coming back here with— Fireblast!"

"What's... Oh, yeah."

He saw what had annoyed his father. The pack of coyotes had disappeared into a dried creekbed, making a shot impossible. It would also bring the pack that much closer before Ryan could draw a bead on one.

There was no sound and nothing to see except for the occasional smear of dust from the arroyo. Ryan held the rifle cradled against his cheek, looking where he expected the animals to come into vision again.

"There!" Dean said excitedly.

Without a word Ryan moved the sights a little to the left, picking the lead animal and squeezing the trigger. There was surprisingly little recoil, and the flat crack was quickly swallowed up by the vastness of the desert.

"Missed," Dean said, unable to conceal his disappointment.

"See where it went?"

"I think a bit short. Difficult to see in all the dust."

Ryan fired twice more, succeeding with the third shot in bringing down the hulking coyote in a snapping tangle of legs.

The rest of the dogs halted and stood around,

watching as the leader died, kicking and snarling in the bloodied sand.

"Move," Ryan ordered, standing up. "While they're thinking about what to do."

He and Dean covered another mile or so, circling around the threat. The coyotes watched them, heads lowered, close together. It almost seemed as if they were holding a committee meeting.

"Coming again."

Dean was grinning broadly, as though he and his father were taking part in an exciting game. It occurred to Ryan that the boy genuinely didn't realize that they were in serious danger, that a large hunting group like this would chase and chase until they wore down their prey.

Now the targets were even more difficult, coming after them head-on only showing Ryan the front part of their heads. Nonetheless, he tried four more shots, killing one of the coyotes outright and sending it leaping high in the air, biting at its own back legs. Two more of the animals were wounded, but it hardly slowed the pack at all.

"How much ammo you got?"

"One in and one spare. Twenty rounds altogether. Not fucking enough. Didn't think I'd need any more than twenty."

He'd already fired seven. Two coyotes were dead, two more injured, limping along at the rear, and about sixteen still coming.

"That's…" Dean began, stopping as he realized he was stating the obvious.

"Yeah."

Ryan had only one plan, and even that wasn't terrific—move toward where he thought Jak Lauren's homestead should be, stopping every now and again when the hunting dogs came close enough to pick one or two off and hope that eventually the slavering animals would give up the chase.

The morning grew hotter, with a haze distorting everything. And the survivors of the coyote pack grew more cunning.

They split up into three groups, taking advantage of the broken ground. One group actually managed to circle its way so far to the north that it suddenly appeared out of a draw, less than a hundred yards in front of the man and boy. But the animals paid the price for their own cleverness. Ryan fired three times and killed two of the dogs outright, breaking a leg of a third animal.

"How much ammo you brought for your blaster?" he panted as they kept walking briskly toward the south west.

"No spares. Got ten in the mag."

"Save them till I tell you."

THE BOY WAS BUSHED. His face was pale, and he was so dehydrated that he'd stopped perspiring. They'd brought water with them, but Dean admitted that he'd drunk most of his before they'd even left the redoubt.

According to Ryan's wrist chron they'd been hunted by the coyotes for more than two hours. Eleven of the original pack were still in the chase, and he was down to his last four rounds of ammunition.

The outlook wasn't good.

If he and Dean tried to hole up and wait, there was always a serious risk of more of the big mutie animals joining the pack. At the moment there was a better-than-even chance that he could chill enough, using Dean's .22 as well, to drive them away.

But how long would that take?

"Too long," he muttered through cracked lips.

The sky was unrelievedly blue, and the temperature was way up over the hundred-degree mark. Without any water they'd become delirious in a couple of hours, in a coma an hour or so later and dead fairly soon after that. If the coyotes didn't get them first.

There was one other alternative that had crept over the horizon into his mind. He could stay behind and attempt to delay the animals while Dean went on alone to try to find Jak Lauren and bring help.

But that left an awful lot of incalculables to be faced. Almost too many.

"Rest, son. Then you take the pistol and make for the house. Can't be far now."

The boy looked up at him. "Dad?"

"Yeah."

"Two—" he swallowed hard "—two things. One is that I'm too fucked to go far. Second is that if I felt fine I wouldn't leave you." He grinned weakly. "So, what're you gonna do about that, Dad?"

"Slap your ass redder than a fried chili. But not now."

"Sure."

The remaining animals were hunkered down on their bellies about two hundred yards off, barely visible through the trembling air. Ryan could make out that the pack looked tired, jaws gaping as if they were laughing. But he knew that the moment he and his son rose and began walking again, the coyotes would be up and after them. Eternally patient.

It was still hours until the hottest part of the day.

Dean actually slipped into an exhausted sleep. Ryan lay beside him, watching the skulking mutie animals as they occasionally advanced a few feet. If they came ten or fifteen yards closer, he'd try to take out another with the Steyr.

Apart from tiredness and the pressure of the heat, Ryan felt only a bitter and futile surge of anger.

His life had been filled brimful with danger and adventure. Now, unless they had an extralarge slice of luck, he was going to die a squalid and pointless death in the middle of nowhere, butchered by a mongrel bunch of coyotes. And he hadn't said a proper goodbye to Krysty.

It was no way to go.

"Sorry if this is the end, Dad," said a quiet voice at his side. A hand touched his.

"I'm sorry, as well, Dean. But we all have to go sometime."

"Least we found each other. Could've been we'd both died and never knew each other. Least there's that, isn't there?"

"It's not over till it's over, son. We got ammo and

we got knives. They want us, they're going to pay a shit-high blood price.''

"Reckon I could go a bit farther.''

Ryan stood and looked around. "Sort of a rise over that way.'' He hesitated. "It does look a bit like the ridge we crossed before we looked down on the Ballinger spread, where Jak lives.''

Dean got to his feet, the movement provoking obvious interest in the pack of hunters.

Ryan watched them. "Dean, go about twenty yards toward the hill, then stagger and fall down. Might bring them on and I can pick off two or three more. Worth it. Must come a point where the bastards are going to give up.''

"Sure. Here I go.''

Ryan felt a wave of pride at the ten-year-old's indomitable courage. Out on his feet, dried to a husk, the boy was ready to go out in the open and chance his survival on his father's shooting.

Ryan dropped down again, lying prone, resting the barrel of the Steyr in the dirt. Dean walked southward, stumbling and falling once. The boy was so exhausted that Ryan couldn't be sure whether he was faking or not.

"Go now, son!'' he called quietly.

With a piercing, throat-rasping scream, Dean threw up his arms and crashed down in the sand, thrashing around for a half minute and then lying still.

Ryan kept motionless, resting his cheek against the walnut stock of the rifle. There was no point in squinting through the scope until the coyotes made their move.

It wasn't long coming.

The pressure of the heat and the chase, combined with the slaughter of several of their pack, had brought the powerful dogs to a raging edge of foaming excitement.

They began to move in a strange circling motion, snapping at one another as though they were psyching themselves up for a charge. Between them and the boy was a pattern of deep draws, but Ryan had made sure there was plenty of flat ground near Dean to give him time and space for the shooting.

A thought crossed his mind that Jak or Christina could have heard the sound of shooting if their homestead was fairly close. But the eternity of the desert easily swallowed up noise.

The coyotes suddenly disappeared.

Ryan stayed where he was, concentrating through the blinding heat, feeling a raw pain in his lost eye from the salt sweat. The pack could only be after the boy, and that meant they'd have to come out in the open before closing in for the kill.

Dean lay utterly still, a light wind ruffling his hair.

There was a hint of dust from one of the concealed arroyos to the right of the boy, showing where the dogs were moving.

Ryan laid his index finger on the trigger of the rifle, took in a long, slow breath and waited.

The brutish muzzle of the first of the coyotes slid into sight, scenting the air.

"Not yet," the man whispered. "Come on, you bastards. Come on."

One by one they emerged, until ten of them stood there, huddled in the pack, heads turning as though they still suspected a trap.

Then, as if by some unspoken command, they started to trot toward the recumbent figure lying less than a hundred yards from them.

One more breath taken in and held.

Trying to keep as calm as if he were in the butts at a redoubt practice range, Ryan opened fire on the cluster of animals.

Four spaced shots resulted in three clear kills and a fourth coyote down with its hind legs dragging.

Dean was up, as well, leveling his pistol in both hands. Ryan dropped the rifle and picked up the SIG-Sauer, ready for a death-or-glory charge against the surviving animals—when his reflexes gave him a belated warning of danger.

The massive dog loomed over him, already in midspring, jaws gaping and saliva dangling in ropes from its questing teeth.

Ryan had no time to do anything except try to roll away, punching at the animal with his blaster. There was no chance of a shot and less opportunity of drawing his panga.

The instant the powerful mutie creature struck him, Ryan knew he was in deep trouble.

He was pinned on his back, scrabbling in loose dirt and stones, the P-226 discarded. One hand was locked in the shaggy coat at the side of the coyote's neck, the other beneath the underslung lower jaw, fighting to keep the slavering fangs from his face. Rank, stinking breath festered in his nose and mouth, and the blood-mad eyes were inches from his own.

The coyote was heavier than he'd expected, weighing in around one hundred and twenty pounds. Its hind legs kicked at his groin, and it took a tremendous effort for Ryan to roll to one side to protect himself.

Dimly Ryan thought he heard the sound of a burst of gunfire, the noise booming like a small cannon. Not like Dean's target .22.

But he had his own survival to worry about. His right hand and arm were bent back, weakening his leverage, allowing the coyote to fight its way closer to him.

He felt rather than heard a solid thunk, as if something had struck the coyote. The animal jerked upward, head straining toward the sky. For the first time it howled, a sharp yelp of pain torn from its chest.

Its legs kicked, then it went limp. As Ryan struggled to push its corpse off, he noticed the taped hilt of a throwing knife, protruding just below the coyote's left ear.

And he knew.

The voice merely confirmed it. "Like old days, Ryan. Saving ass for you."

"Hi, Jak."

Chapter Thirty-One

Dean finally fell asleep on the old sofa with the faded Navaho blanket on its back. Christina Lauren tucked a woolen blanket over the boy, smiling at Ryan and her husband.

"Not much doubt about who the father is," she said, rejoining them at the table.

"So they tell me. Yeah, course. I'll put him to bed after we've finished talking."

Jak poured himself another mug of black coffee from the blue enamel pot. "Not much more to say."

Jak hadn't changed much, but to Ryan's keen eye, the teenager seemed a few years older, more mature, more solid. His hair was still a flaring white, like a bright sun off snow in the Cascades, his eyes like molten rubies, and he still wore the huge satin-finish Magnum on his hip.

Christina seemed to have changed more.

Her early life had been sheer misery, turned into a drudge by her crazed father and psychotic brothers. She'd been accustomed to being quiet and subservient, knowing the price she'd pay in bruises and kicks if she stepped out of line. Now she had blossomed.

Then her hair had been a dull brown, tied back in a stringy knot. Her eyes had seemed a pallid and watery blue. Now she had shoulder-length hair, a luxuriant autumnal russet, and her eyes were a strong and steady blue.

Christina was still disabled, halting with a built-up boot on her left foot. But it didn't drag her down. Now she swung around the house with an effortless grace and ease.

Ryan remembered her as homely, which was the kindest word he'd have used back then. A long, rawboned face made her seem older than her twenty-odd years.

Now he'd have been forced back onto the overused word *beautiful* to describe Jak Lauren's wife.

Despite there being more than a dozen years between their ages, the difference had shrunk to virtually nothing.

IT WAS TRUE what Jak had said. There really wasn't much more to say.

After they'd driven off the handful of surviving coyotes, one of which had come within five yards of Dean Cawdor, Ryan and Jak had embraced, hugging each other with the unashamed delight of old and good friends. Then the boy had been introduced, but the rest of the news had been saved until after they'd gotten back to the spread.

The farm had been in excellent shape. There were now more cattle, with a half dozen quarter horses and thirty pigs, a wired compound for chickens and a hundred sheep roaming around the spread.

"Sheep most difficult. Some vanish. Local wandering tribe. Went and spoke. No more trouble."

Jak grinned and Christina nodded approvingly. Ryan knew the young man well enough to wonder what form his "speaking" had taken. Jak Lauren was about the finest natural killer that Ryan had ever met, and not a person to cross.

Dean had been disappointed that Jak had never met Sharona Carson. He was always desperate for someone who'd known his mother from the old days.

The supper had been excellent, with some of the freshest food that Ryan had ever tasted. Jak and Christina shared the cooking chores, bringing dishes to the table until it almost groaned beneath the weight of food.

"It's not every day we get visitors, Ryan," Christina said, smiling. "Specially not someone who means as much to both of us as you do."

Over the chicken and creamed corn, the woman sat with her chin in her hands, listening as Ryan, prompted occasionally by his son, explained the reason behind his journey.

"You want him back with you?" she asked, her face blanking out her pleasure. "That what you came for?"

"No. No, it isn't, Christina."

"If wanted me, I'd come," Jak said quietly, avoiding his wife's eyes. "Have to. Blood debt running deep."

Ryan shook his head, feeling the tension beginning to boil beneath the social surface. "No, that's not it, truly. Just to keep the boy safe. Shouldn't be more than three or four days. Week at the outside. Now I got the code, we can come visiting you when we want. I didn't think the gateway would still work, after that blowout."

Christina glanced across at Jak as she collected the plates. "There's..." She let the sentence trail off, obviously changing her mind. "Got apple and blueberry pie. With good cream. You got a gap left, Dean?"

"Yeah." Seeing his father's face, he added, "Please, Christina. Thank you."

The woman went into the kitchen, and Ryan leaned forward. "What's the problem, Jak?"

"You see tracks?"

"Ah." Ryan sipped at his mug of coffee. "Yeah, I did."

"Been up there. Someone using it. Someone comes and goes. Someone got code like you."

"Mercenaries?"

Jak shook his head. "Not heard of much bad trouble. One or two... Heard Indians lost children. Not many. Some."

"Slavers?"

"Maybe. Chris is... See, she's—"

"Pregnant."

Jak sat back so suddenly he spilled his drink on the white cloth. "How did...?"

Ryan grinned. "Something about a woman when she's carrying a child, Jak. Sort of glows."

"I do, don't I?" Despite her limp, Christina was capable of moving silently around the house. Now she stood in the doorway, arms folded, holding a cloth. "And I'd be real grateful for a hand with these dishes. Anyone game?"

AFTERWARD, WITH DEAN tucked safely into bed, Jak took Ryan out to his workroom, leaving Christina sitting contentedly by a small fire, working on some lace.

"Got wind generator and water pump. Old man Ballinger triple-sick demon but picked land well. Traders come by and pay good for meat and eggs. We deal locals too."

The light clicked on, and Ryan nodded appreciatively at the neat row of tools on the walls, three long bows and two crossbows, as well as a whole rack of honed knives.

"You've done real well, kid," he said, deliberately teasing the albino teenager.

"Thanks. Don't mind calling 'kid' now, Ryan. Like Jak better."

"Sure. You happy here with Christina?"

"Very happy."

"Sort of thing Krysty always wants. Well, guess we both do. Settle down someplace where there's good land and sweet water. Some— Hey, that's a shortwave radio trans, isn't it?"

"Yeah. Got real good range but hardly anyone ever listens or talks."

"Cover the hundred?"

"Sure. Traded it month ago. There's a teacher in ville near sea talks. Woman, sounds stupe, by Four

Corners. Says she'll come see us one day. Freaky radio trans. Some days works and some not. You got one?''

"Yeah. Keep it on hundred. We can talk to each other sometime."

Jak nodded. "Wants some ammo for Steyr?"

"Couple of ten-clips be good. Got some?"

"Here." There were boxes of several kinds of ammunition, mostly full-metal jacket, with some caseless and even the makings for a cap-and-ball revolver.

Ryan shoved the mags into one of his pockets. "When I get back to the ville I'll try calling in a day or so. Let you know how it's going and when we might be down here."

"Best go in. Christina doesn't like me being out here too long. Want another coffee?"

Ryan shook his head. "No. Bed seems the best idea I can think of. Mebbe show me around the spread in the morning?"

"Sure," the teenager replied, turning off the lights and locking the heavy door behind him.

DEAN WAS SLEEPING soundly when Ryan entered the bedroom. As he got undressed, he thought how much Krysty would love the place and the calmer, safer way of life.

His last sentient thought was to wonder if all was well back in Greenglades. Not much was likely to go wrong in the night.

Chapter Thirty-Two

Doc Tanner generally slept well. Every now and again his rest would be disturbed by gibbering phantoms of the night, specters who came to him from the swirling blackness, with faces and forms that were almost familiar yet whose appearance and touch brought only a sickly loathing and a sweating terror.

The worst dreams were when all his various pasts became blurred and mingled. He'd see Strasser, with a gloating smile, having sex with his beloved wife, Emily. Or his little children, wearing Victorian clothes, being chased along a shadowy corridor by beckoning stickies.

Gradually the nightmares were becoming less frequent.

He'd waited up in his room, on the off chance that the girl, Sky, might keep her word and come to him. There'd been a flickering vid of the TV in his room, but the quality was so poor he gave it up. There was a Bible in one of the drawers on the bureau, and he thumbed through it until he felt his eyelids begin to droop.

The overhead light clicked on, its brightness dragging him slowly back to consciousness. But someone operated the dimmer switch, and the bedroom became a cozy, half-lit world.

"Sorry," whispered a woman's voice. "Didn't mean to wake you. Not like that."

He half sat up. "You have been out with your chums tonight, doing that snaking thing?"

"Dark snaking." She giggled. "Sure. Best yet."

There was just enough illumination in the room for him to make out the girl's figure. She was still wearing the same blouse and skirt, but he noticed that her legs were streaked with what looked like drying mud. In the stillness he could catch the feral, exciting scent of her body, and he felt himself beginning to stir with arousal.

Sky saw him watching her and started to twirl, her skirt swelling out, rising above her knees, showing the whiteness of her thighs. Faster. Higher. Doc was aware that his pulse was speeding, and there was a tightness across his chest.

"Caution," he muttered to himself. "You must go gently into this good night."

It wasn't easy to tell, but the flaring skirt spun out around the narrow hips and Doc was *nearly* sure that Sky wasn't wearing any underclothes.

The giggling and spinning stopped.

"Dizzy, dizzy… Traven gave us biggies for snaking. Said all we had to do was dreem. So, we dreemed, and now I got you, Doc."

Doc shuffled sideways to make room for the girl on the enormous bed. By the time he'd turned around again, Sky had peeled off her clothes and was unlacing her thonged sandals, balancing awkwardly on the side of the table.

"There," she said with the pride of a child performing a difficult trick.

"Bravo, my dear."

She was stark naked, silhouetted against the dim glow of the light. Not quite naked, Doc noticed, as she had some kind of necklace around her slender throat.

"It was sooo good," she hissed, stepping closer to him, lifting her feet exaggeratedly high, arms spread as though she were flying.

"You move like the lady of the dance, wherever you may be," Doc said, finding that the pressure on his chest had eased, but his voice had become unaccountably hoarse.

The bed moved as she jumped into it, pulling the sheet and blankets up over her. Doc felt the burning heat of her body as she wriggled closer to him, a hand touching his shoulder.

"You're cold, Doc. Sky better play some games to warm him up."

He felt her lips touch him on the neck, then inch lower, through the grizzled hairs on his chest.

Lower.

"By the three Kennedys!" The exclamation was torn from him as his hips jerked and his hands grabbed at the back of the young woman's head.

The bedclothes fluttered and Sky reappeared, licking her lips, grinning at the old man.

"Warmed up?" she whispered.

"I think that is a more than adequate summation of my physical condition, my dear. Much more than adequate."

"You talk such big words."

"I have frequently been reproached for that failing and— What are you doing, my dear?"

"Climbing aboard, Doc."

"I fear that my reserve batteries will not yet permit my being able to— Oh, I see that I am wrong and that…"

She was astride, heels digging into his thighs, guiding him inside with her long, strong fingers. Doc sighed at the sensation of warm depths surrounding him, sucking him in.

"You can pinch my tits, if you want. Hard as you like."

He reached up, staring at her as she loomed over his naked body in the half light. Sky rocked backward and forward, like a jockey urging a horse over rising ground. Now that he was closer he could make out the necklace more clearly. It was made from a string of chunky amber beads. The largest of them, dangling in the valley between the woman's breasts, had a silver crucifix swinging from it.

It stirred something in the old man's memory, and he reached up to touch it, fingers caressing the amber, finding it sticky.

"Sticky?" he said wonderingly.

"What? Come on, Doc, get your hands on these."

In the cavern of the bedroom, whatever was smeared all over the necklace was almost black. Doc brought his fingers to his own lips, hesitating and reluctant, tasting blood.

"Mrs. Owen's amber necklace," he whispered, feeling himself shrinking inside the thrusting girl.

She felt his waning enthusiasm and stopped moving. "What's up, Doc?" she asked.

He remembered now. Mrs. Owen was the old woman who lived in the retirement complex just outside the theme park. She was scared of attacks and murders.

"Tonight," he stammered, holding his hands out wide to avoid touching Sky.

"What?" She sounded irritated now.

"Dark snaking. This necklace. I recognize it, you know. And there's blood upon it!" There was revulsion in his voice. "Oh, the horror!"

"Fuck," Sky said in a little girl's voice. "What a pity, Doc."

And she punched him in the face.

It was a brutal, roundhouse swing that he barely saw coming. He managed to shift his head to one side, so that her fist struck him on the temple. Pain exploded in his skull, and he nearly lost consciousness.

By the time he'd recovered his senses, Sky had wriggled higher so that she was squatting on his chest, her knees pinning his arms to the mattress. Her thighs were spread obscenely wide, inches from his face. But the sight filled him only with disgust. Bile rose in his throat, and he began to struggle.

She slapped him again across the cheek, making

his teeth rattle. "Waste of time, you triple-stupe old bastard."

He considered yelling, but his room was a little distance down the corridor from the others. Yet Ryan had said that you had to try anything.

Doc opened his mouth to shout.

"Goodbye, Doc," Sky whispered, her long, strong fingers clamping around his throat, cutting off the yell.

He kicked out convulsively, but there was only the ghastly realization that the young woman was actually stronger than him.

And that she was going to strangle him.

Shame at the humiliation was more potent than the actual threat to his life, and he wriggled and heaved, arching his back. But she dug her heels into him, laughing as her fingers tightened, slowly throttling him.

"Traven tells us what to do, and we all do it. He's the leader, the boss, the baron. Dark snaking's best. Better than all the fucking in the whole Deathlands, Doc."

The words came out in gritted bursts, as she squeezed and then relaxed her hold for a moment, making his dying agony deliciously prolonged.

"Got necklace tonight. Mrs. Owen was squealing like when you slice the balls off of a pig. Throat opened at a touch."

As she relaxed for a second, Doc managed to croak the single word "Bitch!"

Sky leaned farther over him, dribbling warm spittle

into his open mouth, laughing delightedly as she did so.

"Best end it now," she whispered.

Darkness was swimming into Doc's brain as the young woman braced herself, her body right over him, breasts brushing his forehead, her thighs clamping near his cheeks.

She threw her own head back, eyes closing with anticipation of the shuddering moment of death for her victim.

Doc's mouth was open, and his mind was aware, just, that her muscular thigh was against his lips. With his last reserves of strength, he clamped his jaws shut, biting as hard as he could.

He tasted blood, his ears filling with a shrill scream of shocked agony. The grip relaxed on his throat, and he sucked in a precious gulp of air.

Doc Tanner wasn't a trained fighting man, like J.B. or Ryan, with lethally heightened combat reflexes. But he knew instinctively that death had only taken a short step backward.

He managed to rear up in a wrestler's bridge, loosening Sky's hold, shifting her sideways off his chest. As she began to fall away, he finally opened his teeth, spitting and coughing out shreds of skin.

The woman rolled off, hands searching out the torn flesh, still screaming. Doc sat up, struggling for breath through his bruised throat.

"You shithead fucker!"

In her rage and pain, Sky had totally forgotten to defend herself, and Doc unhesitatingly struck her a clubbing blow across the side of the jaw, sending her toppling limply onto the floor.

He flopped down on the bed, massaging his neck, swallowing hard. A gobbet of blood trickled from the corner of his mouth, and he stood to check the damage in the mirror.

As Doc walked across the room, Sky came to convulsive life, seizing him by the ankle and nearly pulling him down on top of her.

"You're mine, fucker," she panted, grabbing toward his dangling genitals.

Doc's clothes and his ebony cane were on a chair nearby, and he heaved himself toward it. His fingers closed around the silver lion's head and twisted and pulled, freeing the slender steel blade from the swordstick.

He yelled as Sky's clawing nails raked a bloody furrow down his legs. Holding his weapon like a matador about to administer the killing blow, Doc lunged at the woman's throat.

Sky's reflexes were snake swift, and she lifted her left hand to parry the thrust. But she only deflected it from her neck, the point glancing off her fingers, striking her in the left eye. Doc felt the sword grate against the bony cup of the socket. Clear liquid, mingled with a trace of pink blood, spurted down her cheek.

She screamed, high and shrill, grasping at the slim blade. Doc wrenched it clear, seeing more blood gush from the inside of the woman's palm. Sky let go of him and fell to the floor, pressing her wounded hands against her blinded eye.

The old man hesitated, poised like a classical sculpture, sword raised.

"So very young," he said.

And thrust down, the blade driving through the center of the girl's chest, between the breasts.

With death clutching at her, Sky's murderous hatred fueled one last attempt. She pushed herself off the carpet of the room, trying to haul herself along the blood-slick steel, hands reaching for Doc.

But the extra effort was too much, and the young woman slumped back again. Dark liquid gushed from her body, and she lay still.

Doc was about to get washed and dressed when he heard steps in the passage and a rap on the door of the bedroom.

"Doc! You in there?"

"Yes, my dear Krysty. I'm here. Allow me a moment to make myself decent and I will admit you."

He hastily pulled his pants on, slipped his arms into the sleeves of his shirt and opened the door.

Krysty was wearing only dark blue pants and her shirt, holding her stubby Smith & Wesson blaster. She looked past him into the dimly lit room.

"I heard... No, I *felt* big problems. You all right, Doc?"

"I'm well, but..." He gestured to the corpse of the young woman, lying naked on the floor.

"Oh, Gaia! What...?"

He touched his neck, showing the livid bruises.

"Nearly chilled me, the minx. See the necklace she is wearing? It is smeared with fresh blood."

Krysty entered the room and closed the door gently behind her, then stooped over Sky's body. "It was the woman Mrs. Owen. Her necklace. So they…"

Doc sat on the bed, suddenly looking worn and very old. "Traven makes them hunt, steal and kill for him."

Krysty laid a hand on his shoulder, feeling him trembling. "You did all right, Doc."

He shook his head vehemently. "No! No, I did not do all right."

"But if she—"

"Oh, my heart sickens me, Krysty. This poor child was spawned in a gutter and has known nothing in her short and wretched life but violence and dark madness. And she now lies dead."

Krysty shook her head. "Crap, Doc! Did the vicious gaudy slut a favor and saved your own skin."

They both stood in silence, looking down at the dead girl—who opened her eyes, staring blankly ahead. Her mouth moved.

"Owls fly backward from the light," Sky said, her voice soft and gentle.

"She's…" Doc, stammered covering his eyes with his hands.

Krysty knelt and felt at the throat for a pulse. "No, Doc. Really gone this time."

"That's good."

The woman stood again, face serious. "All we have to do now is find a way of hiding the corpse."

Chapter Thirty-Three

To Ryan's incalculable relief, the Last Destination code buttons worked and he found himself recovering consciousness back in the humid, fetid air of Green-glades ville.

He stood and took a few deep breaths to counter the inevitable nausea.

Somehow the brilliant beauty of the New Mexico morning that he'd just left behind seemed an eternity away.

While Jak and Christina had prepared breakfast for them all, Ryan had taken Dean for a stroll down to the creek.

It had been a magnificent dawn, with the sky a serene blue from horizon to horizon. There were clusters of small flowers along the banks of the stream, yellow and silver. Finches darted among the bushes, hunting insects. The air was brimming with the freshness of juniper and piñon pine.

"What do you think about staying here, son?" Ryan had asked the boy.

"Boring."

"Jak and Christina'll find you plenty to do. Help them out."

"Sure. I sort of like them but..."

"But what?"

"Jak knew you years didn't he?"

"I guess so."

"Wish he was me. I mean, I wish I was him. I'd been him... Oh, you know, Dad."

Ryan had understood.

The farewells had been brief.

Jak had walked most of the way to the redoubt with him, leading a spirited pinto pony behind him. "Be back at the spread in no time," he said.

There'd been a quick clasp of the hand and a smile for old times shared.

"Watch these tracks," Ryan had warned the teenager. "Could be someone found a mat-trans and is making jumps. And use the radio on one hundred if you need to make contact with us."

"Limit of range."

"We'll try. Look after the boy."

"Like he was own, Ryan."

ONCE HE WAS OUTSIDE the redoubt, the sec doors locked safely shut behind him, Ryan found the damp heat almost unbearable. The sky was overcast, and he kept hearing the rumble of thunder somewhere over beyond the Cajun swamps. There was a flurry of rain, great lumpy drops that pattered on the broad leaves of the bushes all around.

The ground squelched beneath his combat boots, and the pools of water seemed larger. Underlying the sound of the far-off storm, Ryan could hear the croaking of frogs.

He paused, considering carefully what he was going to do and say once he'd penetrated the dozens of yards of undergrowth and returned to the civilization of the ville.

The others would already have reported the story they'd planned in advance: Ryan and the boy had gone for a late walk toward the swamps. Krysty had heard the sounds of a scuffle and a shout for help, but there'd been nothing to see.

Ryan would explain about the Cajuns, tall, lean, bearded figures, ragged clothes, stinking of fish and wood smoke, looming from the darkness in small dugout canoes. They'd taken him and the boy, but Ryan had managed to fight his way free during the night and struggle back.

So now he had better do something about making his disappearance convincing. He'd left the Steyr rifle inside the redoubt. He couldn't bear to be parted from the SIG-Sauer and was ready to explain how he'd stolen it back from the guard when he'd made his getaway.

Knowing that the swamps were full of gators, Ryan wasn't keen on going swimming. But he couldn't turn up looking neat and tidy.

The sound of the frogs was louder, closer, almost deafening.

He glanced around, hesitating in front of a large wallow of mud, which was at least fifteen feet across, with no indication as to how deep it was. Perhaps if he knelt down in the grass and smeared a handful or two of the slimy dirt over his clothes it would lend credence to his story.

Something brushed against Ryan's lower leg, and he looked down. It was one of the bayou frogs. But generations of nuke-induced breeding mutations had changed it.

Its body was an iridescent, almost luminous blue, pale and vivid, glistening with a sheen of moisture. There was a daub of pollen yellow on the end of its nose, and crimson-and-yellow patches along its ribs and down the back of the immensely muscular thighs. A bright pink stripe started along the jawline, beneath the huge, bulbous eye, running along the body toward the base of the spine.

It was clinging to Ryan's pants by big orange suckers on the end of each toe. Its body was at least fifteen inches in length. Taking the legs into account, the frog was more then two feet long, weighing about the same as a medium-sized chicken.

"Get off," Ryan said amiably, glaring down at the boggling creature.

The frog opened its mouth and croaked loudly.

And he saw its teeth.

No frog that Ryan had ever encountered had teeth like that, and he immediately reached for the hilt of his panga.

The creature had a double row of fangs, with canines and incisors like those of a wolf. Ryan was staring straight down its throat, and he thought for a moment he could detect little sacs of poison, like those at the back of a rattler's hollowed needle-teeth.

Even as he was drawing the panga, another of the mutie frogs jumped onto his other leg, and a third and a fourth, weighing him down.

"Fireblast!" he spit, cutting down at his attackers with the eighteen-inch blade, seeing out of the corner of his good eye that there were dozens more frogs circling him.

Dozens?

Hundreds!

Ryan jumped away from them, landing in the middle of the pool of mud, part of him wondering how deep it was going to prove.

The answer was less then three feet.

He sprawled into it, going under, nearly dropping the panga. There was a moment that was as close to panic as Ryan Cawdor ever got, while he flailed and kicked with arms and legs, recovering his balance. He found himself on hands and knees on the other side of the stinking black pool.

He used his free hand to wipe the noxious ooze from his eyes, fingering a gobbet out from behind the patch covering the empty socket.

The frogs had gone, except for one poor twitching headless corpse, lying on the other side of the mud patch.

Ryan spit, trying to clear his mouth of the rotten slime. He touched his cheek where he must have cracked it on a buried log in the swamp.

There was one consolation. The stinking condition of his clothing would lend credence to his story.

"YOU THINK I MADE all this up? About the kidnapping?" As soon as Ryan had neared the ville, he'd been picked up by a sec patrol.

"Yeah. You stashed the kid someplace safe—though I'm struggling to even guess where that might be—and you came back because... Because why? Chill Traven and save Boss Larry?"

"You can think that, if you want to, Kelly, but you can't expect me to say anything about it."

The sec man looked around, as though he feared there was a shadow at his shoulder.

"Step like you're on eggshells, Cawdor. Wait and see, is my advice. There's things moving here that might change the whole picture. No more than a day. Two at the outside. And the darkness at noon could be lifting." He winked. "We aren't all jumping when the microprick hops by."

"I'm going back to the motel now."

"Sure. Oh, one thing. Sky's disappeared. Traven isn't a happy man about that. Wants questions asked. Mainly to Doc Tanner. Could be the old guy's been lifted for terrogating by now."

Ryan sighed. "Not good news that. Doc's had some triple-shit times with sec men in the past. Doesn't stand up too well. I'll see you, Kelly."

HE REACHED THE GATOR WING of the hotel almost simultaneously with three sec men, led by one of Traven's young men.

"Heard you had Cajun trouble," said the youth, whose name Ryan didn't know.

"Heard right. Got to clean up."

"Seen Sky?"

"No. Kelly said she was missing."

The blank face stared into his. "Kelly? He said she was missing? We got an ace on the line for Kelly, we have."

They stood in the corridor outside Doc's room in an uneasy tableau.

"Look, I need a wash. You coming in?"

"Yeah. Take Doc for a talk."

"Wait and I'll come with you."

He received the same curious, pinched gaze. "No. You all stay here."

He knocked on the door with ringed fingers. Krysty opened it so fast it was obvious she'd been aware of them outside. But she hadn't expected to see Ryan, covered from head to toe in stinking mud, clotted into patches as it dried.

"What?"

"Want to search for Sky and take old man for some questions."

"Ryan, where have…? And where's Dean?"

"Tell you after I've washed."

The room became crowded. Doc sat on one end of the bed, looking tired and drained. J.B. leaned against a wall by the blank screen of the TV, his fingers rapping on the butt of the Uzi. Mildred was in one of the chairs, her own blaster lying casually in her lap.

They all looked up in surprise at Ryan.

"Tell you later. Cajuns jumped me and the boy. Still got him. I escaped in the swamp. Details after a bath. They want Doc to go to ask him about Sky. Seems the girl's gone missing.''

There was something wrong.

Triple-wrong.

All of Ryan's reflexes warned him there was a grave threat hanging in the air. It was as if everyone wanted to tell him something, but the presence of the sec men and Traven's boy held them back. If he needed any other warning, it was in J.B.'s and Mildred's readiness with their blasters.

He looked across at Krysty, whose whole body language radiated extreme tension.

"I'm going to wash up," he said, heading toward the bathroom.

"I think..." Krysty began, her green eyes boring into him.

"Better check if Sky's hiding in there," one of the guards suggested.

All of them had the 8-shot Colts in holsters, but none was drawn. If there was a sudden firefight, then the odds would lie strongly with J.B., Mildred and the others. But getting out of the ville alive would be another matter.

"I'll look," Ryan said. "Going in anyway."

He pushed the door open and peered in. The shower curtain was drawn across the bath.

"Nobody's in here. And you take care, Doc. See you soon."

"I will, Ryan. Many... Yes, care."

He pushed the door shut and slid across the small brass bolt. The idea of getting himself cleaned up from the clinging filth was wonderful and momentarily overwhelmed the strangeness that he'd seen and felt in the others outside.

Ryan shucked off the clothes and tugged back the shower curtain.

And found he wasn't alone.

Chapter Thirty-Four

Sky was dead. Her body was wrapped in a stained sheet off one of the beds, bundled up so that only her short, ginger hair and waxen face showed. One eye had popped from its socket and hung by a thread of gristle over the cheek.

Ryan stooped and touched the sheet, finding it soaking wet. Closer to the corpse his nostrils could catch the sweet-sour stench of incipient decay. The skin on her face, below the mutilated eye, was cold and taut. He tried to move the body but found that it was relatively stiff with rigor mortis.

The room was warm and the weather around even warmer. It looked as if the girl had been killed some time the night before last, while he and Dean were still on their way toward New Mexico.

"Who?" he said quietly.

Looking more carefully, teasing down the top of the folded sheet, he saw the entry wound of a knife, a very slender blade.

Then he knew.

"Oh, Doc," he said, sighing.

He heard the sec men and Traven's creature leave accompanied by Doc. A few moments later there was a soft knock on the door of the bathroom.

It was Krysty. "They're gone."

"Heard them."

"It's the girl, Sky."

"I know. Doc did it."

"Yeah."

"Give me a hand with her."

"Why?"

"So I can have a bath. Then we can talk."

THEY SAT closely huddled together while Ryan told them briefly of his jump to Jak's place and his action-filled return.

He held out the compact radio. "I'll give him a try on this. See if it works."

But first they explained what had happened in his absence and how there happened to be a corpse in the bathroom.

J.B. finished the story. "Couldn't move her yesterday. Sec men all over the place."

"You could all've tried the jump to Jak's place," Ryan suggested.

"You had the only code, lover," Krysty pointed out. "So it meant making a blind jump or risking a bloody firefight here."

"Think Doc'll stand up?"

Mildred looked at him. "You know the answer to that one, Ryan."

"Yeah. Mebbe."

Krysty was lying on the bed, worrying at a ragged edge of fingernail. "Reckon we should spring Doc and run for it?"

Ryan ran his finger through his hair, checking how dry it was. "If I'd been back a half hour sooner, we could have left the girl in the bath and jumped out of the ville. Could probably have gotten away bloodless and free."

"Now?" J.B. said.

Ryan rubbed his chin, realizing he could do with a shave. "No," he said. "Not now."

HE TRIED THE RADIO a half hour later standing outside the window of his room, not wanting any of the sec men or Traven's spies to watch him. He angled the integral aerial toward the west, aiming it roughly in the direction of New Mexico. Working as accurately as he could, Ryan turned the fine needle to the one hundred mark. There was a digital screen with a liquid-crystal display, but it was malfunctioning, repeatedly showing only a straight row of sixes.

Once he had it as close to the one hundred as possible, he switched it to Send.

"Come in, Jak. This is Ryan calling from Florida. Come in, Jak."

He switched to Receive.

Ryan heard very faint crackling, the kind of static that he'd been used to hearing on the internal comm sets on the war wags.

The unit had a volume control, and so he turned it up to the maximum level. The crackling simply grew much louder.

He turned the needle to Send again.

"Jak! Come in, Jak! You there? Christina, you

hearing me? Jak, Dean, you there? Calling anyone down there. This is Ryan Cawdor calling out on the one hundred wave band to anyone there. Jak, come in.''

Switching across again, he heard only the hissing and whispering of the atmospheric ether.

Ryan shook his head. J.B. leaned out of the nearby window. "Any luck?"

"No."

"Didn't think there would be."

"Me neither. Thought that—"

"...ing...fai...very...can't hear what...ain...peat again."

"Jak!" J.B. exclaimed. "Dark night! That sounds like the kid."

Ryan tried transmitting again, the ribbed mike close to his mouth. "Jak, that you? We heard something then, Jak. Faint and broken. That you, over?"

This time there was nothing but static, not even the most distant and ghostly echo of a human voice.

Ryan switched the set off and slipped it back into his coat pocket.

"Try again later," he said.

HIDING SKY'S STIFFENED corpse proved easier than Ryan had feared. Several of the unoccupied rooms in the motel had their doors open. While Mildred and Krysty kept watch, J.B. and Ryan carried the body, in its dripping shroud, along the passage and into one of the rooms. The one-eyed man had already noticed that the ceilings of the suites were only plastic tiles, some of them ill fitting and damaged.

"Get her up there," he suggested. "Chances are we should be away from the ville before anyone tracks her down."

"She won't be growing any sweeter," Mildred pointed out. "Not with the heat and humidity. Another day or so, and you'll be able to smell her from clean across the other side of the park."

Ryan had seen enough chills to know that the doctor was correct.

Already, despite their efforts to keep her cool, Sky was showing unmistakable signs of deterioration. The flesh around the wounds was corrupting, and her skin was starting to discolor. The soft tissues of her body were rotting, and the smell of decay floated around her like an obscene perfume.

The corpse seemed to have a bizarre life of its own, slipping and sliding as the two men fought to stuff it into the roof void above the abandoned bedroom. Twice the dead girl somehow contrived to slither clean out of the makeshift shrouds, landing in Ryan's arms, as slippery as a netted salmon.

But at last it was done, the body jammed into a corner, a length of torn blanket holding it tight to an angled joist. The ceiling tiles were replaced and the room tidied to remove any sign of what had been done.

The two old friends paused in the doorway, looking around for a last check.

"You think of death, Ryan?" J.B. asked.

"Times like this, you mean? Bloody-hearted little bitch goes six deep and—" He shook his head. "Krysty has some old saying about no man being an island and that every death touches everyone."

"You figure that?"

Ryan pulled the door of room 237 closed. "No. Anyone near gets chilled, and you feel the touch. Not someone like this. No. Doesn't touch me at all."

The girl's clothes had been carefully sliced up and flushed down the toilet. So had the bloodstained bedding.

It was as though Sky had never been.

THE RAPPING ON THE WINDOW made them all jump.

"It's Kelly," Krysty announced. "Looks like he's seen a ghost."

Ryan was first across the room to slide back the heavy glass panel. "What is it?"

The sec man was breathing hard, as though he'd just completed a crippling triathlon. Sweat streaked his face, soaking the collar of his uniform.

"Gotta go. Shit in fans. Traven's fed dreem to the old man. Stoned him from the inside of his skull outward."

"Hurt him?"

"Nope. Not whipped or cut or anything like that. Look, I gotta go. Traven wants you, Ryan. Wants you and wants to know where the boy's hidden."

"You said there was a plan, Kelly."

The noncom managed something that was nearly a sickly grin.

"Yeah. There was. Now there isn't."

Ryan heard the sound of someone shouting, then the shrill blast of a whistle. Kelly looked away to his left.

"Like I said. Gotta go."

"Good luck."

He nodded. "Sure."

Kelly vanished. A few moments later Ryan could hear more shouts and a single shot from a blaster.

"Government Model Colt .45," J.B. said, at his shoulder.

Less than ten minutes later there was the sound of boots in the corridor outside the room, and half a dozen sec men, faces tight with excitement, burst in, accompanied by one of Traven's faceless, pretty little girls.

"He wants you," she said, pointing at Ryan like a shaman indicating a victim for a human sacrifice.

"Why not?" he replied.

Chapter Thirty-Five

Ryan walked alongside the young woman, watching her out of the corner of his eye. Though she was shorter and fatter than Sky, there was still a strange resemblance.

"How're you called?" he asked.

"Rainbow."

"Pretty name."

"Go fuck yourself, you stinking heap of rotting shit."

It quite seriously crossed Ryan's mind to draw the SIG-Sauer and put a 9 mm round through the side of Rainbow's head. But it would do nothing to help Doc, so he simply bit his lip and walked on in silence.

Centerpoint dominated the park, dwarfing even the spidery framework of Paraglide Paradise. Ryan noticed that there was unusual activity, with several groups of Boss Larry's sec force moving nervously along the winding maze of swept paths.

"What's going on?" he asked, turning to the young guard at his elbow.

The man ignored him, keeping his brutish face turned resolutely to the front.

Just before they reached the baron's headquarters,

Ryan heard another brief fusillade of shots, coming from the swamp.

"Hunting?" he asked. But once again he got no answer from anyone.

Noticeably it was Rainbow who was in charge of the patrol, holding up her hand with its bitten nails to bring them to a halt.

"Wait here," she snapped, then turned to look at Ryan. "You come in with me."

"What was the firing?"

"Just clearing out some rat holes," she replied, favoring him with a gap-toothed smile.

Another of the posse of pubescent females was in the lobby and she beckoned Rainbow over, whispering something in her ear, bringing a widened smile.

They both went to join Ryan near the bank of elevators.

"Up the top," Rainbow instructed.

"You coming?"

"No."

"Shame."

"Fuck you, too."

RYAN BREATHED SLOW and easy as the cage slid toward the top of the tower. The only important thing to do, now that Dean was safe, was to rescue Doc from Traven and then get the hell out of Greenglades ville.

When he reached the revolving top of the building, the doors slid open.

Ryan stepped out, hand on the butt of the blaster.

His senses were prickling, anticipating a sudden and violent attack.

The lobby area was deserted, but he could hear laughter from the big room inside. The laughter had that pitch of hectic cruelty that was heard in the voices of children merrily pulling wings off flies.

The semidarkness stank of putrefying food, smoked dreem and sex.

Ryan catfooted his way past the dividing rail that separated the two slowly moving sections of the tower. He paused, still invisible in the shadows.

Traven's voice was resonant and measured, as though he were reciting some incantation. "As I order it, so must it be. As I ask, so shall you answer. As I speak, so shall you listen. As I smile, so shall you laugh. As I frown, so shall you weep. And as I chill, so shall you die."

Then came a ragged chorus from his young posse of acolytes.

"As speaks Adam Traven, man's son, so shall it be."

Ryan was reassured by the coldness of the metal butt of his SIG-Sauer. There was something infinitely frightening about this liturgy of blind obedience and the implicit binding of their souls to the diminutive madman.

The horror was deepened when he caught the croaking voice of Boss Larry, the words slurred and heavy with the drug.

"He's a friend. Loyal friend. Been with me longer than anyone in the ville."

Traven's whispering voice was inaudible.

Boss Larry spoke again. "Promise?"

"Here and now."

The baron laughed. "Then I will. Just go ahead and do it, but don't bother me."

Again Traven spoke, his words just reaching Ryan's straining ears.

"After that I'll ask the old man more. How they got here, jumping in from no place. He'll tell me. Where the kid is. What's happened to pretty little Sky. Lots of questions. And then lots of answers."

Ryan started as he heard Doc Tanner's voice come booming in, sounding tired and strained but still in control.

"I shall see you rotting in the lowest circle of Purgatorio before I give you one mite of information, you loathsome vermin."

Ryan chose that moment to step out from the blackness into the half light.

His eye had adjusted to the dimness, and he was able to take in the whole of the squalid tableau with one raking glance.

The two mutes, standing together by the farthest window, arms around each other, stared blankly out across the swamps; half a dozen sec men stood lounging on some of the plush maroon banquettes along the walls; Boss Larry was sprawled in his chair, illuminated by a stray beam of dusty sunlight. His legs were apart, trousers open and pulled over his fleshy thighs. Two members of the posse, one male and one female, knelt on the carpet in front of him, doing everything they could to try to rouse some life in the baron.

Larry Zapp's eyes were squeezed shut, mouth hanging open. He looked incredibly stoned, old and tired.

And watching over all, master of the revels, lord of misrule, was the antic jester himself.

Traven.

He rocked backward and forward on the heels of his maroon boots, the sharks' heads gleaming pale on the toes. He was dressed almost identically to their first meeting—patched jeans and the ruffled white shirt, over all the black leather jacket with the fringes and the pattern of sewn shards of mirror.

He still wore the fingerless black gloves, and in his right hand he was holding the chromed 9 mm Beretta 95.

The diminutive figure was standing with his back to Ryan, but that didn't stop him being aware of the one-eyed man's presence.

"Just who I wanted to see," he drawled. "Come in, come in."

"I'm in already. What do you want? Hi, Doc."

The old man had been standing, ramrod stiff, away to the right, his dark figure blending into the draperies. He waved a hand to Ryan. "Greetings, my dear fellow. Is all well?"

"No problems, Doc. Just come to collect you."

"Jolly good. Then I'll be on my way, Mr. Traven. Like to say it's been delightful meeting you. Like to say that, but couldn't, as I fear that it would be a massive falsehood.''

Boss Larry was blinking in their direction. ''You that son of a bitch Ryan? Yeah, y'are. Can't talk t'you now. Real busy.''

From what Ryan could see it was the young boy and girl who were real busy with the baron. Still to scant effect.

Traven stood, poised on his toes like a dancer, head on one side. His face was in shadow, his mouth hidden by his mustache. But Ryan could swear that the man was smiling at him.

''Don't go, yet, Doc. Not yet.''

This was it.

Ryan had seen moments like this before in other places with other evil people like Adam Traven.

The old man looked at him, bushy eyebrows raised in an unspoken question.

''Traven holds some high cards, Doc,'' Ryan replied, ''so he gets to open the bidding.''

''Correct. First off we play questions. Where is Dean and where is Sky?''

''Won't say and don't know.''

Traven suddenly stood totally still, his silence drawing every eye. Except for Boss Larry, lost in his own struggling world. Even the two deaf-mutes sensed something and turned around.

''Time's wasting, Ryan Cawdor. I'll offer you a deal.''

''Go on.''

''You all go free to where you want.''

"And?"

"And I won't pursue you. Or the boy. If Sky wants to leave with you, then that is her affair."

"Doc?"

"Yes, including Doc. All go free. It's such a wonderful feeling to set someone free, Ryan. To tell them to go and run about in the summer meadow with the sun to freedom on their backs."

"How much?"

"Did I mention a price?" His hands spread wide, his shoulders shrugging.

"Time's wasting."

"You come dark snaking with us."

"When?"

"This night."

"Where?"

"Wrinkly heaven. The retirement complex."

"Why?"

"Want you to come."

"Don't like cold murder."

"It's funning, isn't it, Mirror?"

A tall girl, sitting up on the floor watching Boss Larry, smiled silently up at her leader.

"No."

"Then Doc stays here, you all get chilled and I'll find your son if I have to look under every wet, green boulder in Deathlands."

"How about him?" Ryan pointed to Boss Larry, who had fallen asleep. The boy and girl had moved away, leaving him exposed, his shrunken cock like a tiny pink snail crawling up the vastness of his belly.

''What happens to him will happen regardless of whether you live or whether you die, Ryan. I'm bored with him, and his days are nearly done. But you are more of a challenge. More of a man.''

''All right, Traven. I'll come out tonight with you and your posse. Just me, or J.B. as well?''

Traven laughed quietly and wagged a finger. ''Stupid I'm not. You can be handled, but not a pair of you. No, just you.''

Ryan stood and thought about it. He and the others had firepower, but Traven had Doc. To try to escape from the revolving room by elevator was about the same as kissing the barrel of a 10-gauge.

''You got a deal.''

''No firearms, Ryan. Make me nervous. Me and the posse might have a blaster or two, but not you. Understand?''

Ryan nodded. ''Oh, yeah, Traven. I understand.''

Chapter Thirty-Six

Before leaving the tower, Ryan clasped hands with
Doc Tanner. The old man, his face screwed up with
worry, whispered to him. "I believe the little bastard
intends to try to murder you."

"Believe he does, Doc. If that happens, do what
you think best."

"I will. The best of luck, dear fellow."

As Ryan moved toward the elevator, one of the
deaf-mute servants materialized from a lake of shadows and touched him on the arm, beckoning. Glancing around to see that Traven had collected his brood
about him on the far side of the room, Ryan followed
the shaven-headed figure.

As he drew closer to the lolling Gargantua in the
padded chair, Ryan became aware of a strange scent.
It wafted around Larry Zapp, enveloping him, like the
miasma from a freshly opened coffin. It was the unmistakable stench of death.

The baron's heart still beat, his lungs still labored
to provide breath, but he was rotting away.

A plump, ringed finger waved toward Ryan.
"Closer. Closer."

"What?"

"Go back a fucking long way...you and me, Ryan. Larry and Ryan. Long ways back."

"Get on with it."

"Just...can't help it, Ryan." The voice was breaking like a rotted branch.

"Sure."

"Doc. Taking dreem. Girls and boys." The huge head trembled from side to side, and tears coursed over the vast furrows of the cheeks. "And Kelly. Poor Kelly."

Ryan leaned closer. "What about him?"

"Who?"

He nearly slapped the baron across the face. "Kelly. What's wrong with him?"

Zapp sighed like a beached whale at tide turn. "Couldn't help it. Traven asks and Traven gets. That's new rules. Kelly tried to—"

He stopped as the slight, mincing figure of Adam Traven danced into view.

"Not gone yet, Ryan?"

"No. Going now."

"I heard the name of Kelly. You and your friends can come to see it. Noon. Paraglide Paradise. A high riser, Kelly."

Ryan turned and walked toward the elevators, following by the doomed whisper of Boss Larry Zapp. "Couldn't help it, Ryan. Sorry."

BACK IN THE MOTEL ROOM there was little discussion.

"But don't you think that Traven is planning to

kill you, Ryan?'' Mildred asked, the most innocent of the four.

"Sure he is. Then he'll take out the rest of you. No doubt."

"Why not attack and rescue Doc, then make a jump down to New Mexico and join Jak and his wife? Is it very difficult?"

Ryan was sitting on the edge of the bed, tapping his toes on the floor. "Difficult? Traven's got most of the sec men on his side. Well armed and trained. And he's holding Doc up on top of the tower."

"Thought Kelly might be planning something," J.B. said.

"Sounds like he got caught with his dick in the door," Ryan replied. "We have to go to Paraglide Paradise at noon."

"Why?" Krysty asked.

"Find out when we get there. But it isn't going to be good."

Mildred persisted. "How is going with Traven and his gang going to be a better chance?"

Ryan shrugged. "Who knows? Get outside, and you can do some damage with people who aren't trained in night combat. Close combat with blades. I don't know, Mildred, and that's the damned truth."

TEN MINUTES BEFORE NOON they heard the now-familiar sound of combat boots in the corridor and a fist rapping on the door of the room. Mildred and J.B. had retired to their own suite for an hour or so, but now they were all back together.

Ryan had also tried the radio again, picking up nothing but a confused mumble of hissing and crackling. For a half second he thought he heard a voice, but so far away and faint that it was worse than useless to them.

It was Rainbow again.

"Show time," she said.

But there was a difference. They were "asked" by the chubby girl to leave all their blasters behind in the room.

The paths of the ville were busier than they'd ever seen them. Some of the sec men seemed particularly edgy, with holsters open and hands playing with the butts of their Colts.

Rainbow strutted alongside Ryan, thumbs hooked into a wide snakeskin belt. "Going to see the reward for loyal service," she said.

Ryan ignored her.

He'd already noticed the young woman's eyes. Her pupils were dilated like those of a hunting cat, linked to a fast blink-rate. Sure signs of heavy drug use. The fact that Traven kept his posse doped out of their vacuous skulls was one of the few things that Ryan felt might give him a chance during the proposed dark snaking.

The winding walkways opened up into the area around Paraglide Paradise.

"Oh, Gaia!" Krysty breathed, half turning her head away.

Rainbow heard her and grinned delightedly. "More to come, Copperhead."

Ryan stared impassively at the scene of butchery, knowing that nothing he could do or say would make the least difference to what had happened.

Or to what was about to happen.

There were four bodies.

Maybe five.

Or only three.

One lay at a little distance from the others, presumably having fallen at a slightly different angle or velocity.

The others had landed more of less on top of one another, a jumble of dislocated and tangled arms and legs, skulls buried in chests and pelvises embracing ankles. Blood had drained away down the slope of the path, soaking into the edge of a large flower bed.

The bodies seemed to be all male, and from what remained of their clothes, had probably been sec men.

"Kelly?" Mildred whispered.

"Can't be sure. I figure—" Ryan stopped as the woman's question was answered.

The sturdy figure of the noncom, four silver stripes glistening on his left arm, appeared through the small silent crowd. He was bareheaded and had obviously been given a bad beating.

Both eyes were swollen nearly shut, hidden beneath purple bruises, capped with crusted blood. His nose had been broken, and there was more black blood around his cut lips. He walked with a limp, his wrists cuffed behind him.

Rainbow clapped her hands excitedly. "I missed

the others," she complained to Ryan. "Least I'll see Kelly flying."

J.B. caught Ryan's eye and allowed his hand to stray significantly toward the hilt of his own Tekna knife. But Ryan shook his head.

"No point," he said quietly.

Kelly, walking unsteadily between two young sec men, had nearly reached them.

It was obvious that he was almost blind, but he paused as he passed Ryan, looking up. Head on one side, he tried to peer out through the curtains of puffy flesh.

"Be seeing you," he mumbled past broken teeth.

Ryan nodded, biting his own lip to contain his raging anger. "Yeah." He dropped his voice so that only Kelly could hear him. "Be sending some of them after you."

The noncom almost succeeded in a grin. Then his keepers pulled him away into one of the metal cages beneath the flamboyant parachutes. The three men climbed in and, at a signal, began to ascend slowly into the air.

"I want to go back to the Gator Motel," Mildred said.

Rainbow looked at her. "Take more than one little itsy-bitsy, tenny-weeny steplet, bitch, and you get to flap your arms up there. With Kelly. You read my lips?"

Mildred narrowed her eyes, and J.B. laid a hand on her arm, restraining her. "It's fine, John," she said quietly. "Wouldn't foul my hands with…"

Ryan was looking to the side, at the top of the Centerpoint Tower. There was a balcony around the revolving outer wall, and he could see several figures standing there. The sunlight danced off what he guessed must be the mirrored jacket of Traven. A huge shapeless mass stood between two smaller figures.

"Looks like Traven's dragged Boss Larry out to watch his handiwork," he said to Krysty.

She glanced around. "Yeah. No sign of Doc up there."

"Keep him snug inside."

"His head still together?"

Ryan nodded. "Far as I could tell. Don't think they've tried him out with any dreem yet. If they did..." He allowed the sentence to drift away on the rising westerly with its scent of the swamps.

The faint shrilling of the moving wires ceased, and the cage, now a tiny speck above them, hung motionless in space. Ryan turned and saw Traven raise a puppetlike arm and drop it smartly.

Mildred looked down at her feet; Krysty closed her eyes; J.B. was staring fixedly at the blasters in the guards' holsters.

Ryan watched the execution from beginning to end, wanting to remember it so that he could recall it when the time came to try to settle up the account books with Adam Traven and his posse.

The two sec men were struggling to lift up Kelly, ready to drop him over the side. But he wasn't making things easy for them.

The cage was rocking, the supporting wires jangling against each other. Even from the ground, the waiting crowd could hear shouts and cursing.

"They got him now!" someone bellowed.

"Drop the bastard!"

Ryan had never met a popular sec man, and Kelly obviously wasn't any exception.

It looked as if the end were a second away. But the bound man kicked out and fell inside the cage, bringing one of his guards down with him. Someone cheered, but others started to boo and hiss.

"Go for it," J.B. mouthed, joining Ryan in watching the aerial conflict.

But with his hands cuffed, and one against two, Kelly couldn't hope to hang on for very long.

Moments later they again lifted him. One locked his arms around the helpless man, going on tiptoe to lift him. The other seized Kelly's shoulders and bent him back.

Back and over.

"Yaaaaay!" screamed an elderly man to Ryan's right, waving a beret in the air.

"Taken one with him," J.B. said.

The cage, swaying from side to side, held only one figure. Kelly had managed, at the final moment of beginning his deathly fall, to lock his legs around the waist of the smaller sec man, his own weight and momentum taking him over the safety rail.

There was a single scream. The dual figure became two as Kelly released his grip. It seemed as if the wailing man were trying to run on air, legs pumping, arms working.

Kelly dropped like a stone, motionless, his body tipping so that it eventually landed headfirst, about ten feet away from the sec man.

The sounds of the twin impacts were almost simultaneous, an odd mixture of the dry and the wet, the brittle snap of bones cracking and the soggy thump of impacting flesh.

Both men died instantly.

There had been a yell of delight from the spectators, turning into an "ooooh" of surprise.

"God rest his soul," Mildred whispered.

"Could be worse ways to go," J.B. said, putting his arm comfortingly around her. "It was fast, and he took an enemy with him. Could be worse."

RAINBOW HAD BEEN so eager to gloat over the pulped remains that Ryan and the others were allowed to make their own way back with only a pair of sec men for company.

They left them at the entrance to the motel. "Don't forget you got to go with the posse tonight," one of them reminded.

"Yeah. They said it'd be at midnight. Wear dark clothes."

The guards went off together, laughing at a shared joke.

"Midnight," J.B. echoed. "Dark clothes."

"I know." Ryan looked across to Centerpoint, where the circular balcony now stood empty. "I know."

Chapter Thirty-Seven

"Getting tired of farewells."

J.B. and Mildred had gone back to their own room, promising to come back before midnight to wish Ryan luck.

At first it had seemed as though Ryan and Krysty were going to make love, lying together in the bed, naked, embracing. But somehow the lust slipped away almost unnoticed, and what remained was love.

They held each other close, arms tight, snug as spoons in a drawer.

"We aren't apart for long," he protested.

"It isn't that, lover."

"Then what?"

"It's being separated and the constant fear that I'll never see you again."

"I always come back safe."

"Apart from the occasional knife or bullet wound. And the day'll come when you don't. When I sit and wait and keep looking at the door."

"It's the way it is."

Krysty pulled away from him, shuffling to the far side of the bed, leaving a huge aching gulf between them.

"That's such *shit!*"

"Krysty, I just—"

"There's that ice-hearted little bastard himself. Half a dozen of his posse crazies. Maybe some sec men along, as well."

"I don't reckon—"

"All right," she said, her voice tight with her anger, "mebbe there'll only be the seven of them, all with blasters. And you with your panga. Good odds, lover. Real good odds!"

"Seen worse."

Krysty sat up, the sheets falling away from her body. "You're like a little boy, Ryan. There's times I think Dean's got more sense than you. We could've gotten out of this ville, clean and away. But you wait. Wait until time slides by, and then it's too late."

"Can't leave Doc," he said, aware of the rightness of her anger and the weakness of his own moral position against it.

"Doc would've been dead a dozen times in the last couple of years if it hadn't been for you. We both know that. But there are plenty of those times that he needn't ever have been in danger in the first place."

"Yeah, I know that."

Krysty caught the note of apology. "I know you do. But this can't go on forever. Maybe tonight'll be the time you don't win through. Maybe tomorrow. Next week. Next month."

"Maybe never."

She slid back toward him. "You know that isn't true, lover. Because one day...one day it *will* happen to you. And then what do I do? I'm lost if you die, Ryan.''

"We'll find a place. Like Jak has.''

"Sure. I've seen it. You told me. Clean water and good earth. Fresh food and as near peace as you can find in Deathlands.''

"Want me to tell you again?''

"Yeah. And hold me, lover.''

Once again they cuddled close, and Ryan began to talk in a quiet, even voice about the spread in New Mexico, painting a picture for her of the beauty and serenity of the land.

After a few minutes he was aware of her breathing becoming slower and steady. He stopped talking and quickly joined Krysty in sleep.

RYAN HAD THE ABILITY to bring himself awake whenever he wanted to. He didn't even need to glance down at his wrist chron to check that the time was within a couple of minutes of midnight.

He rolled out of bed and silently got dressed, checking that both the panga and the slim-bladed flensing knife were in their respective sheaths. During the evening they'd discussed the possibility of trying to conceal a blaster, but all of their guns were too large to use as a hideaway.

He glanced over at the bed, where Krysty seemed to be fast asleep.

Rather than wait to be summoned, he decided that he'd go out of the motel and walk to Centerpoint.

They'd already found that Traven had placed sec men at the front and back of the building.

He took the pocket radio out of his coat and put it in a drawer. The faint noise woke Krysty.

"I'll come outside with you," she said.

"Sure?"

"Yeah. Only take me a minute to get dressed."

They went out of the room together.

Ryan hadn't noticed that he'd set the radio control onto Receive.

In the confines of the closet drawer, it suddenly came to tinny life.

"Jak calling Ryan Cawdor. Come in, Ryan. Jak calling Ryan. Urgent...repeat, urgent. Come in, Ryan. Are you there? Come in, Ryan."

After three or four minutes the radio fell silent again.

Chapter Thirty-Eight

Ryan was slightly surprised to find that there were no sec men accompanying them on their expedition to the Zapp's Rainbow's End Retirement Complex. Then he guessed that this was probably because Adam Traven didn't want any outside witnesses around to what was going to happen.

One of the young men searched Ryan, hands probing into the small of his back, under his arms and into his groin.

"Clean, Traven," he said. "One big knife and one small one."

The leader of the posse had changed his clothes. Now he wore black pants tucked into knee-high black boots with some kind of ribbed rubber sole. A black T-shirt with a Mex-looking picture on it of white skeletons. Over that he now had a jacket of midnight blue suede, fringed at the elbows and wrists. Small pieces of dark glass were sewn all over it, but they didn't reflect any of the moonlight that filled the ville.

On his head Adam Traven wore a black beret, pulled down over his right ear at a rakish angle. The pearl-handled Beretta was on his right hip, and a long bayonet on the left. Ryan had never seen a knife quite like it. It was much longer than the usual M-16 bayonet, and it had a silver swastika pattern on the ornate hilt.

His girls and boys were all decked out in the colors of darkness—five young women, three in tight black jeans, and the other pair in short black skirts, all five in boots similar to those of their leader. They all had on black sweaters and either berets or, in a couple of cases, dark maroon ski masks with embroidered eye holes.

Both men were dressed more like Traven, but without the flashy jacket. They had on long-sleeved black sweaters instead.

Apart from Traven's Beretta, the rest of the group of devoted apostles all carried the sec man's weapon, the Government Model, 8-shot Colt .45.

And each was wearing a knife, but not just any battered old hunting blade with a taped-up hilt.

They were top-quality weapons with graphite-titanium blades and finger-molded permagrips. All matching, like the blasters, all with their own scabbards.

"How good of you to come and join us on our dark snaking," Traven said.

"Cut the crap. Let's get on with it. Sooner we start, the sooner it's over."

"The sooner it's over," the little man echoed. "How very true. In so many ways, for so many, it *really* is nearly over."

Ryan ignored him. He stood quietly, drawing in deep breaths of the night air, relishing the coolness after the oppressive, damp heat of the Florida days.

"We going?" asked one of the girls in the masks. From the build Ryan suspected that it might be the one called Rainbow.

"Of course. Ryan, I do believe that I've forgotten to introduce you to all of our group. Wouldn't you like to know the names of your companions?"

For a moment Ryan remembered a stone-faced trading man he'd met about fifteen years ago, somewhere down near the border country on the Grandee. He'd had a dappled pony and someone off War Wag One had asked him what it was called. He'd replied that he didn't want to know the name of something he'd probably have to chill one day.

"Don't want to know their names," he said.

"No?"

"No."

"How far?" Ryan asked.

Traven was in the lead and he turned around. "Not far, Cawdor. The wrinklies' heaven has to be close to protection."

"Need protection," said one of the two men, his teeth showing white in the gloom as he grinned at his own joke.

Minutes later they reached the complex.

It was a compound of about fifty small, single-story homes—mostly painted white—which was surrounded by a high wall, topped with razored sec wire.

Guard towers loomed over each corner, but all showed signs of serious decay. Ladders were rusted, and one of the structures tilted ominously to the left.

Ryan also spotted the broken remnants of what had once been searchlight towers.

"Why'd they set this place up like a high-sec prison?" he asked.

Traven again halted their small procession. "Because that's what it once was. Florida was one of the great carnage capitals, and they built several small units like this for killers nearing the ends of their sentences. Boss Zapp happened along and saw the chances to bring in some serious jack. Collected the oldies and got them to pay long and well for his protection. Most are double-rich."

"How?"

"Whores, drugs and blasters. How does anyone get rich in Deathlands, Cawdor? What a real stupe question!"

A large sign was posted about fifty yards ahead of them, near a brightly lit guards' hut, and it read Zapp's Rainbow's End Retirement Complex.

From where they were standing, it was possible to see a couple of uniformed sec men sitting together, playing cards.

"You going to chill them?"

Rainbow giggled. "No need, outlander. We got better ways, don't we, Adam?"

"We do, little peach." He pointed to the right then hesitated, turning back to confront Ryan. "Just before we go in and start the dark snaking, remember that Doc dies quicker than a moth in a candle flame if you try and play clever."

"Sure."

THE GROUND WAS WETTER as they looped around to the west of the complex, the undergrowth thicker. A gnarled mangrove rose alongside the wall, with some of its branches crawling across the top of the weathered masonry. As soon as Ryan spotted it, he knew that this had to be the easy way into the compound.

The posse crept up and over with a practiced ease, Ryan going in at number four. The tree was slippery with moss, and he nearly fell.

On the far side they were in a surprisingly neat garden, with trimmed lawns and ornamental flower beds. A stone-rimmed pond was just to their left, and Ryan could see the water rippling as fish came to the surface.

The houses were on the farther side, presenting blank walls, with not a single light showing in any of the windows.

"Which one?" a young man whispered.

"One we've been saving," Traven replied, "for this special visit."

Ryan caught his eye. "Why do you do this, Traven? The chilling and the stealing? Or just to prove you can do it?"

"Reasons are for little people, Cawdor. Not for me."

At a wave of the hand from Traven, they all ran silently across the damp turf, flattening themselves against the nearest home.

Beyond the old folks' compound the first of the great swamps began, primeval wastelands that ran almost clear to the ocean on the other side of the Florida peninsula. Ryan could taste the salt and the ooze.

Traven was breathing faster, and his voice was a notch higher with excitement. "Everyone ready to go dark snaking?"

He was answered by a chorus of whispered agreement.

The little man turned to Ryan. "This is what we do, and this is the funning part. We go in one by one. Break a window and slip the latch. Tour around the place, creeping and crawling. Real quiet."

"Yeah, real quiet," someone echoed, giggling.

"What about the folks inside the house? You know who they are?"

Traven nodded, moving so close to Ryan that he could smell the feral hunting scent.

"Sure. Old couple who collect weapons. Got some real nice knives, they say. Got a couple of sons staying with them. One's around seventeen. Other a year older. Sleep at the back. Wrinklies sleep that room." He pointed to the far side of the door.

"What happens to them?" Ryan waited a moment, then answered his own question. "You chill them?" Another pause. "Yeah, you chill them."

"If the gods of chaos hadn't wanted them turned into bacon, he wouldn't have made them pigs," Traven replied.

"We going in or talking all night?" asked the taller of the young men.

"Going in. Check the windows and report back."

One of the boys went to the left, the other to the

right. Ryan passed the time by trying to size up the young women, deciding which he'd try to kill first.

THEY WERE GOOD AT IT. One had brought some sticky tape, which she crisscrossed over the glass. Another rapped it once with the butt of the Colt, creating a crack. A third pulled the tape away, bringing the splinters of glass with it.

The room beyond gaped at them, as dark and silent as a tomb.

Traven did a little capering dance, clicking his heels together. "Dark snaking time, boys and girls."

Chapter Thirty-Nine

Ryan noticed that Traven was so sure of his power that he didn't even bother to post anyone outside on watch.

Once they were all inside, the tension and excitement was heightened. He could hear everyone breathing faster, and all the blasters were drawn. The room smelled of stale cigarette smoke and the remains of a fried meal.

Traven held up three fingers and pointed to the left, then repeated the gesture toward the right, which left himself and one girl with Ryan in the living room.

"Sit down." Traven pointed with the glittering muzzle of his Beretta to a long sofa visible in the filtered moonlight that broke into the room.

Ryan did as he was told, leaning back against the floral cushions, looking calm and relaxed, though every fighting nerve in his body was honed and ready. The chilling would start any moment now. His assumption was that Traven had brought him along for his own perverted reasons, and that should mean keeping him alive until close to the end of the dark snaking.

But with a crazy like Traven, nothing was certain. Nothing.

Minutes drifted by.

Traven juggled his pistol, smiling to himself, occasionally humming a tune. He caught Ryan looking at him. "Wondering what's happening? Sure you are. This is real dark snaking. You move around in the blackness. Go in their rooms. Sniff the soap. Pick up their discarded clothes. Maybe try them on. Brush your hair in their mirror. Wave to them, all sleeping tender like babies. That's what they're doing now." There was a faint sound from the room to the right. "Ah, looks like our hosts are waking up."

Traven moved to the wall and switched on the lights.

The room was smaller and tattier than Ryan had supposed, with furniture that looked as if it mostly dated from before sky-dark. The two chairs were of similar design to the sofa, but one was in green vinyl, the other in blue velvet, patched and torn. One of the low tables had only three legs and was propped up on a couple of red bricks. There was a TV-vid, probably wired into the ville's output.

In a couple of cases on the far wall were a number of edged weapons. Ryan started to look at them, but his attention was distracted by a burst of noise from deeper in the building.

A man had raised his voice, questioning. Then came the thud of a blow and a different voice, louder and angry, followed by a woman's scream, which was cut off as abruptly as if someone had clamped a gloved fist over her mouth.

Traven laughed quietly.

Ryan stood, aware of the muzzle of the Beretta moving to keep him covered.

The posse came back in, hauling four people.

"Let me introduce you to Leo Johnson, his wife, Laura, and his sons, Jerry and Benjamin."

For the first time Ryan realized that the young men and women had all been carrying sec cuffs, locking plas-strips that snapped shut around the wrists of their victims.

The family was pushed down onto the sofa.

"Please don't hurt us," the old man moaned. He was wearing a T-shirt and loose pants, his white hair ruffled. There was a deep gash across his scalp that was leaking a trickle of blood.

"Don't beg the sick swampies. You know it don't do no good." Laura was in a long cotton robe, with bare feet and bony ankles showing beneath it. Her face was flushed with anger, and her lip was bleeding. She had no teeth.

One of the sons had been clubbed and was scarcely conscious. He was wearing just a pair of drawers. His brother was naked under his T-shirt and was crying quietly.

The shortest of the women stepped in and smashed the butt of her pistol into his face. There was the clear crack of teeth splitting, and blood jetted from his pulped lips.

"Give you something to cry for, you baby bastard," she snarled, turning to Traven and receiving a nod of praise from her leader.

"We don't have much jack," Leo Johnson said,

his teeth chattering so hard it was almost impossible to understand him.

"Never mind," Traven replied smiling reassuringly at him.

"What?"

"Jack isn't why we're here, Leo."

"No?"

"No, Leo."

Ryan noticed that the moon had vanished behind a bank of thick cloud.

"Swampies!" the old woman spit.

"Can I?" asked one of the young men in the posse.

"Soon. We aren't swampies, Laura."

"Then who are you?"

"Friends of the baron."

Minding his own business, Ryan had traced the electric lines around the room, seeing that there appeared to be some kind of junction box on the wall of the hallway.

"Baron Larry? You ain't no friends of him!" The woman tried to spit at Traven, but her mouth was too dry.

The little man smiled vaguely at her.

Ryan could almost taste the killing that was going to happen.

There was something about men of unusual evil, like Adam Traven, Cort Strasser and the Russian, Zimyanin, some flaw that made the hairs creep at the back of the neck. Strasser was dead. Zimyanin might be dead. Traven was still alive.

"Traven."

"What do you want, Cawdor?"

"Thought you were interested in the collection of swords and knives."

The little man minced across to peer at the glass cases of weapons, looking at them for all of ten seconds. "Fifth-rate shit," he pronounced.

Ryan had to admit that he was correct. The collection included a Civil War saber with a new hilt badly fitted; a half-decent Spanish cinquedea from the nineteenth century, but its precious stones had been replaced with cheap glass; a modern replica of a poniard and its matching rapier that looked rusty. One of the cases held three bayonets, all from the Second World War. Not one of them was worth the price of a good meal in a frontier gaudy.

"You knew that before we set out from the ville," Ryan accused.

"Sure."

It was only seconds away.

Ryan pretended that he had an itch in the small of his back, feeling for the little knife, checking one more time the location of the main electrical control box.

Rainbow was panting like a bitch in heat.

"Come on, Traven. Please let's start. Please, master, please."

The rings on the little man's fingers sparkled as he waved his hand with a negligent dismissal, like a monarch agreeing to some small request.

"You may start."

The Beretta was steady on Ryan's stomach, making

any move instant death. Traven's brown eyes fluttered beneath the long lashes, and he smiled at his prisoner.

"Witness to my power, Cawdor," he drawled.

Few men in Deathlands were more hardened to the sight of death than Ryan Cawdor. Yet even he was sickened and appalled by the joyous way the posse began its bloody butchery.

He had to keep his concentration focused on Traven and the blaster that menaced his life, so that he bore witness to the slaughter only by peripheral flashes of violence, glimpsed from the corner of his eye.

The overwhelming image was of blood, splashed in dynamic patterns across the ceiling and over the walls, so much blood on the floor that it made movements treacherous. All of the posse was soaked with the blood of the murdered Johnsons, laughing and screaming in delight, licking it off their own blades and deliberately smearing it in handfuls over one another's faces.

Everywhere Ryan looked there was blood.

Images frozen in his memory—Rainbow sitting astride the naked father, Leo Johnson, kissing him repeatedly on the face and mouth, while her sharp little blade pecked repeatedly into the side of his stomach and chest; the screaming, pain-contorted faces; two of the girls yelling to Traven to look as they slit open the belly of the older son, dragging out ropes of entrails and threading them around the dying boy's neck.

"We're the fucking best, Traven, aren't we? Best posse you ever had!"

The little man, beaming like a psycho Buddha, turned to watch his darlings at play. As he moved, his high-heeled boots slipped in a lake of spreading blood, making him stagger sideways.

"Now," Ryan breathed to himself.

He powered off his left foot, crouching as he ran toward the hall.

"Can't escape, Cawdor! And we got Doc to—"

Traven's voice broke off as he suddenly realized that the one-eyed man wasn't trying to escape.

Ryan was making for the electrical junction box, leaping toward it and kicking out with all of his savage strength.

There was a shuddering impact, and a shower of silver sparks floated to the floor.

The house was plunged into instant pitchy blackness, filled only with the noises of shock. And of dying.

Ryan landed with practiced silent agility, drawing the panga in his right hand, the flensing knife in his left.

Chapter Forty

Five homicidal young women, all carrying blasters and knives, two murderous young men, their blood-lust flaring, similarly armed; Adam Traven, their leader, cunning and lethally in love with violence. Against them was Ryan Cawdor. No blaster against eight. His weapons were two knives.

The odds were unfair, but Ryan had one over-whelming advantage over the members of the posse—he'd done this sort of thing many times before. They'd done the *chilling* before, creeping and crawling into the homes of the weak and the elderly, cuffing them and butchering them. None of them had ever fought back.

Ryan had memorized every detail of the room that had become a stinking shambles, knowing where every stick of furniture was, having a clear picture in his brain of the dimensions, down to the life-or-death inches.

He also knew that the young killers would be standing around like frightened sheep for several heart-stopping moments while they tried to work out what had happened in the house.

And what was happening.

Ryan moved among them like the living spirit of

death, slitting the throats of three before anyone realized he was back in the room. His night vision was good enough to be able to pick out their huddled silhouettes, like dark gray ghosts in a midnight world.

"He's here!" Rainbow screamed, inches from him, hearing one of her friends kicking and frothing in her own blood.

"Yes," Ryan whispered in her ear.

He drove the narrow blade of the skinning knife into her stomach, just below the navel, steadying her with his right hand on her shoulder while he pushed it inward and upward. He grunted with effort as he lifted Rainbow off her feet, ramming the knife under her ribs, tearing open her lower lungs.

It was an automatic reaction for Ryan to twist his wrist as he withdrew the blade, for maximum damage. But Rainbow's end had come, and it was an unnecessary postscript to her passing.

Inevitably someone was going to lose his nerve and start shooting.

It came from near the window, the flattened sound of the shots revealing it was one of the Government Model Colts. Three shots were fired and none went anywhere near Ryan.

But the muzzle-flash was enough for him to find the shooter and nearly decapitate him with a single slashing cut of the eighteen-inch panga.

By now there were something like sixty pints of blood sloshing around on the floor of what the Johnsons had once called, with a bitter and unconscious irony, their "living room."

Now Ryan paused, standing near a bureau, recovering his breath. He wiped both blades, the broad and the narrow on the leg of his pants.

He listened to the noises of the dying gradually fading away into stillness. Three were alive, and he was sure they all remained in the room—Traven, a boy and the last of the young women.

It crossed through Ryan's racing brain that he should try to locate one of the dropped blasters. To find one wouldn't notably strengthen his position. To fumble for one and fail would immeasurably weaken it.

"Traven?"

It was the last girl, kneeling at the farther end of the sofa. The single word enabled Ryan to visualize where she was, as clearly as a great flash of lightning.

There was no reply, but Ryan thought he detected a flutter of movement close by the broken window.

"Traven, I think they're... I think he's... You there, Traven?"

Ryan slithered through the darkness, ready to take her.

But at the very last moment she moved, suddenly and convulsively, toward him. They collided so hard that Ryan almost lost his footing and fell into the lake of spilled blood. The young woman shrieked and squeezed the trigger on her Colt .45, the bullet scorching the back of Ryan's left hand and nearly making him drop the flensing knife.

As he grappled with her, Ryan heard the noise of breaking glass and splintering wood, and a wordless cry in a voice that he thought was probably Adam Traven's.

The blood was so thick that he could feel it lapping around his boots. The girl tried to fire again, but he had her arms pinned to her sides.

"Bastard prick..." she panted.

For a moment it was a frontier standoff. He couldn't let go to stab her, and she couldn't shoot him. They swayed back and forth, feet slipping in the pooled blood.

"Spray the room!" Traven ordered.

"What about Redwing?" asked the other survivor from the posse.

"Just do it!" A note of panic soared high into the night.

Ryan managed to hook his foot around the young woman's ankle, pushing her over. He landed on top, digging his knee into her stomach, driving the air out in a sour whoosh of breath.

She went limp beneath him, and he rolled to one side, feeling for her neck, ready to slice open the jugular when the room filled with bullets.

Lead poured in through the broken window. Ryan didn't count the shots, but he heard the sudden noise of hammers clicking on empty chambers, which meant they'd both fired the full eight rounds.

Ryan had flattened himself, hearing the shots hiss above him, crashing into walls, display cases and furniture. He was showered with splinters of wood and glass.

"Reload?"

"No. Back to Centerpoint. Come on!" A desperate urgency colored Traven's words.

It took Ryan less than ten seconds to locate the killing spot at the side of the semiconscious girl's throat and open it with the whispering edge of the big panga. Another five seconds had him moving across the devastated room, stumbling over two corpses on the way, and picking his way quickly and carefully through the smashed window.

Ryan was always careful around broken glass. He'd been in the building, years ago, when a tail gunner on War Wag Two had slipped climbing in through just such a window. The shards had ripped open the femoral artery in the inside of the thigh, and he'd bled to death before anyone could reach him.

By the time Ryan was on his feet in the damp grass, adjusting to where he was in the darkness, he heard Traven a couple of hundred yards away, screaming to the sec guards, warning them of an armed intruder.

But Ryan had cut away to the left, picking his way with faultless accuracy to the gap in the defenses of the Rainbow's End Retirement Complex. He climbed into the branches of the tree, then ran toward the heart of the ville, following the trail of Traven and the young man.

His mind was filled with worry for the survival of Doc Tanner.

There were two big strikes against his old friend. One was that Ryan had failed in his attempt to chill Traven and all members of his murderous gang. The two survivors would reach Centerpoint before him.

And two, with just the two knives, he couldn't hope to do much against the squad of sec men who'd be confronting him.

Which meant only one option. There had been the faint possibility of going again into that sodden shambles and trying to find a couple of the dropped Colts. Even if Ryan had succeeded without getting chilled by the sec guards, he'd have had a maximum of sixteen spaced rounds for close range, little use for the firefight that he knew was coming.

"Gator Motel," he muttered.

THERE WAS A BRIEF rain shower as he ran, barely enough to dampen the paths and make them glisten. The moon had broken through the cloud, throwing his shadow ahead of him.

Ryan considered the risk of Traven and his last sidekick stopping to reload, then ambushing him from cover as he sprinted blindly past them. But that wasn't the way it went. Traven had heard six of his seven acolytes chopped down within two paces of him. If he was feeling anything, it would be terror. And an overwhelming desire to find somewhere solid, with reinforcements.

Ryan reached one of the main trails that would eventually lead him to the motel and generated more speed, knowing that it could only be a matter of moments before Traven roused Greenglades ville against him. Against them all.

The motel finally came into sight, shimmering in the moonlight. A young sec man was dozing in front of the main entrance. He heard Ryan's boots pounding on the gravel and sat up, reaching for the blaster at his belt.

Without even breaking stride, Ryan swung the panga and hacked clean through the guard's slender neck and sprinted on. At his back he heard the pattering of blood and the hollow thunk as the severed head hit the ground.

Krysty had felt him returning and was out in the corridor, his SIG-Sauer in her hand. Behind her, in the doorway, stood J.B., holding the Uzi. As Ryan slowed to a walk, struggling to control his breathing, he also spotted Mildred.

All three of them were fully dressed, ready to move, ready for action. J.B. had the Steyr rifle slung across his shoulders.

"How many you chill?" Krysty asked. "Gaia! You're awash with blood. You hurt?"

"Not hurt. Didn't take out enough of them. One of the boys and Traven himself got away."

"Where?" J.B. asked. "Centerpoint?"

"Yeah."

Mildred's face was set like stone. "They hurt Doc? If they have…"

"Not yet. Got to move. Now. Real quick. Before they get organized. Come on."

They'd only gone a few paces when Ryan skidded to a halt. "Who's got the radio?"

"In the drawer," Krysty replied. "I'll get it." She saw Ryan hesitate. "Go on, lover. I can easily catch up with you. Run faster than you."

When she took the small transceiver out of the drawer, it was switched on. And Jak was sending a message to Ryan.

Chapter Forty-One

Ryan took his rifle from J.B. and slipped it over his shoulder, though he already knew this wasn't likely to be a long-range firefight.

The three friends raced toward Centerpoint. There had been another brief shower, and the air tasted cooler and fresher. A shot was fired at them from somewhere beyond Paraglide Paradise, but it went harmlessly overhead. They didn't stop.

Ryan held up a hand as he saw the main lights of the entrance to Centerpoint ahead of them. He looked over his shoulder. "Where's...?" he began.

But Krysty was already close, running lightly toward them, the heels of her boots clicking on the tarmac path. She was carrying the radio in her right hand.

"Message from Jak," she said, barely out of breath from her run.

"What?"

"Couldn't catch it properly. Faint and all broken up by static."

Ryan was torn by the desire to try to listen to the radio and the certain knowledge that delay could prove fatal for all of them.

"Hear *anything?*" he asked.

"Kept calling for you, lover, and I'm sure I heard him say Dean's name, as well. Want to try to…?"

"No. No time." He looked around at the others. "Only one plan. Here it is.…"

A QUICK CALCULATION made it certain that Adam Traven couldn't have had more than about three minutes to make any effort to organize the defense of the tower. It was also reasonable to assume that he'd want to get up to the top as quickly as possible.

Which meant the sec men who were milling around the main doors to Centerpoint would be like decapitated chickens.

Using the sniper rifle, Ryan picked off four of them, each time with a clean head shot. The other half dozen scattered into the night.

"Nice shooting in poor light," Mildred said admiringly.

"Fish in a barrel with the Starlight scope," he replied, laying the SSG-70 on the ground.

J.B. glanced behind them. "Think he'll call in some help?"

"Doubt it. No time. Be after Doc, mebbe Boss Larry, too, now most of his plans are blown out the window."

Ryan led the way, through the double glass doors with the brass alligator handles, across the main lobby toward the bank of elevators.

"One's already up at the top," Mildred commented, pointing to the left-hand indicator.

"Be waiting for us," J.B. said thoughtfully.

There were five more cages, waiting silently, doors gaping open.

Ryan looked at his companions for a moment. "All right," he said, "let's do it."

HUNDREDS OF FEET above them, the vast room revolved slowly. Doc Tanner stood near one of the windows, forehead pressed against the cool glass, watching the dark world of Florida moving gently past him. He appeared to be lost in a mindless dream, but every one of his senses was on the alert. Since Traven and his panic-stricken cohort had burst from the elevator, Doc knew that life was measured in short minutes. Whatever happened, he was ready to go down with fists flying.

Farther to the left Boss Larry Zapp was seated on his throne. With an enormous struggle during the previous night, his two mutes had lifted it onto a platform of stacked tables, then helped the bloated figure to be seated.

Zapp had been inhaling such vast quantities of dreem that his face and the front of his maroon caftan were dusted pink. As far as Doc could see, the baron was barely conscious.

His two attendants, shaven headed and muscular, stood patiently, one on each side of the throne.

Near the elevators, crouched behind their blasters, were two of the youngest sec men in the ville. The appearance of Traven and the one survivor of the posse, both shouting and on the edge of terror, had freaked the guards, and their fingers twitched on the triggers of the Colts.

Traven's boy, almost gibbering with fear, was sitting slumped at one of the round tables, head in his hands. Doc had noticed, from the pungent odor, that the youth had fouled himself in fright.

Last was Adam Traven himself.

His small figure was in a whirl of constant movement, dancing and singing, his glass-sewn jacket flaring around him.

ONE OF THE SIX ELEVATORS rested on the top floor; the other five were in the lobby.

Traven heard the whirring of the main drive gears and spun around, his Beretta gleaming in the subdued glow of the wall lights. "Here they all come," he drawled. "The little piggies ready for supper. Which one they using?"

"All of them!" shouted one of the sec men. "They're all fuckin' comin' at us!"

The illuminated indicators above each of the five sets of double doors were all showing movement. At the same time, the doors of the cage that had been standing empty on the top floor hissed shut, and that elevator began to move downward.

"Can't be more than four of them. They'll have split up, one to a cage." A long pause. "Mebbe."

There were twenty-five floors between Lobby and Roof.

Doc Tanner turned slowly to watch the final act of

the drama. "High farce, I believe it used to be called," he said to himself.

He took a cautious half step to the right, considering trying to lose himself among the draperies and dusty banquettes, but Traven sensed the movement and screamed a warning.

"You got a couple of minutes left, you old prick! Wanna make them seconds?"

Doc lifted his hands and made an elegant, half-apologetic shrug.

The big drive wheels stopped turning, leaving five of the cars stopped on the twentieth floor. The sixth elevator had also stopped at that floor.

The boy sitting at the table started to moan, lifting his Government Colt and looking wildly around the room. "Traven!"

"What?"

"Let's chill them all and get out."

"Get out! Our wings are a little on the fucking short side for flying."

The elevators started to move again.

"Going down, all of them," called one of the sec men, turning to Traven for orders. "Just watch them. It'll be a trick."

Doc was close to Boss Larry, and he was startled when the monstrous figure opened its eyes and beckoned him with a jeweled finger.

"What?" he whispered.

"Some spurs come in the door, and some spurs come in the window." The voice was barely audible, but the layers of flesh peeled away and showed Doc an enigmatic, stoned smile.

Traven looked back suspiciously, but his attention was distracted by the peculiar behavior of the elevators. Now they were all moving at random, some up and some down.

Doc puzzled at the drugged man's comment. There was no way that Ryan and the others could get outside the tower and break in through the windows, and the elevators were the only way into the top floor.

"Unless..." Doc said quietly.

One of the cars reached the top, bringing a moment of suspense until the doors slid open.

There was a burst of fire as the sec-men both started shooting, bullets sparking off the metal interior of the elevator cage. The *empty* cage.

"Stupes!" Traven roared.

The doors slid shut again, and the car started to descend.

Farther along the row, another one arrived at the roof level, and again the door parted to show an empty box of dusty metal.

"Keep watching! They're pressing the control buttons to bring them up and then down again. But they'll come bursting out of one soon. Real soon!"

The youth at the table had stood, rocking unsteadily, eyes blank. Doc could almost hear the boy's brain churning emptily, like loose change in the pocket of a bored man.

All of the elevator indicators had stopped three floors below the revolving room.

"Here they come!" shouted the taller of the sec guards. "All at once."

With only the smallest interval between them, every one of the cars was moving upward.

The first one stopped, and the doors opened on nothing.

And the second one.

Everyone was staring intently at the entrance as the third one hissed to a halt.

And people started to die.

Chapter Forty-Two

Boss Larry Zapp had known what was going to happen. Even through his dreem-broken brain, he'd still known enough about the jewel in the crown of Greenglades ville to be certain Ryan would work it out.

If the elevators had ever broken down with a revolving restaurant filled with diners, there had to be a way of getting them all to safety.

Ryan led the other three out from behind the filthy velvet curtain that concealed the emergency exit.

Trained to stand and fight, the two young guards spun around and opened fire, falling to the floor riddled with bullets.

Simultaneously the two mute servants of Boss Larry, moving with a bizarre synchronicity, stepped in to attack the last surviving member of the posse. Adrenaline and terror racing through his body, the boy opened fire on them, blasting holes in their chests at point-blank range.

Mildred killed him.

One .38-caliber bullet from her Czech ZKR 551 target revolver drilled smack between his narrow, foxy eyes, cutting neatly through his brain and exiting from the back of his head, taking a fist-sized chunk of skull with it.

Five dead. Or down and dying.

Traven moved with the reflexes of a cornered rat.

Krysty fired twice with her stubby Smith & Wesson 640, both bullets taking chunks from a table as the little man dived beneath it.

"Where's he gone?" J.B. shouted

"There!" Ryan yelled, seeing a flicker of movement in the darkness.

Doc moved to one side, trying to see where Traven had gone, standing directly in front of the giant figure of the looming baron.

But their target had vanished, scuttling on hands and knees through the shadows.

Traven suddenly burst into sight almost at Doc's feet, grabbed the old man by the arm and jamming his Beretta into the side of his scrawny throat. Doc completely obscured Traven from the others' guns.

"Let me go." Traven's voice was soft and gentle, pleading. "Or this stinking prick goes down like a sack of shit."

"Mildred?" Ryan said quietly.

"No," she replied. "Can't see an inch to hit. Terrible light."

"Come on, quick," Traven pressed. "I don't have all night to wait."

Behind him there was unexpected movement.

Shoulder-length hair shining like spun silver, maroon caftan billowing around him like the bloody mainsail of a man-of-war, Boss Larry Zapp was standing up.

Mildred was beside Ryan, and he heard her whisper, with an almost religious awe, "Mountain's come to Mohammed."

Traven sensed the shadow that suddenly hung over him and he half turned, jaw dropping, eyes widening in horror.

"Don't move, you lard-ass bastard, or you get it, too."

Zapp's throaty voice broke the stillness. "Should've stopped this before it started. Stop it now."

"Gaia!" Krysty breathed.

Zapp simply leaned forward from his elevated throne until gravity took over. His fall seemed to defy all the accepted laws of science, and he toppled toward Traven with an infinite slowness.

The barrel of the Beretta moved from Doc's throat, and the hand released his arm. Traven stared up at his nemesis, paralyzed.

Ryan wanted to shout a warning to Doc, but his voice was constricted and frozen by the vision of doom.

Of all the people in the revolving room, Doc was the only person who didn't know what was happening. His back was to Boss Larry. All he knew was that the immediate threat had been removed. With a convulsive shudder, the old man pulled clear and dived toward the nearest table.

Traven never even tried to escape the tumbling figure.

If Ryan ever tried to remember the scene in later life, it always seemed to him to have happened in total silence. Boss Larry appeared to envelop Traven and flow around him. There was no sound of an impact. Just the little figure vanishing beneath the huge bulk of the baron.

There was a moment of paralysis, with everyone standing where they were, watching.

Ryan reacted fastest, holstering his blaster and moving forward.

That was when the shooting began.

Fired out in the open the Beretta 95 would make a satisfying crack. But at the top of Centerpoint, its eight shots were spaced and muffled, almost as if Traven were shooting the gun underwater with a baffle silencer attached.

Buried under Larry Zapp, the muzzle of the blaster pressed deep into the multiple slabs of flesh, the sound of the shooting was barely audible.

Nor did it have very much visible effect.

Larry's head was turned to one side, his cheeks seeming to melt into the carpet. His body twitched and rippled a couple of times, but it looked as if the eight bullets hadn't harmed him.

Ryan knelt on the floor. "How you doing, Larry? You sure caught the bastard."

"Did, didn't I?" A spasm crossed the face. "Still feel him moving some. You better send...last train west. Do it for me, Ryan."

"Sure. But you can do it yourself when we get you up and off of him."

"No. He shot me, Ryan. Sort of felt it...deep down inside. Done for me. Sorry about—"

His eyes became blank and still.

"Gone," Ryan said.

Doc rose to his full height and looked at the corpse of his savior. "I must confess that Mr. Zapp was lacking in certain areas of acceptable behavior, but he chose to depart this life in a most courageous and gentlemanly manner. And I salute him for that."

J.B. shook his head. "Could leave Traven stuck under there."

"Be poetic justice," Mildred agreed.

"No." Ryan shook his head. "Evil dog like Traven needs putting away. Let's get Boss Larry off him."

Traven was barely conscious, face suffused, mouth open as he'd fought against being suffocated by the dead baron's immense weight.

Ryan kicked him hard in the ribs with the steel toe of his combat boot. "Wake the fuck up," he snarled.

The eyes opened under the long, almost feminine lashes.

"Some you win," he said, "and some you don't. See you all in hell."

"Maybe," Ryan replied.

He shot him with extreme accuracy through both kneecaps, then through both elbows. As Traven thrashed and screamed, Ryan put three more rounds from P-226 into his belly.

"Should do it," J.B. observed, calmly reloading the Uzi.

Ryan nodded. "Yeah. Take him some time to get to hell, but he should make it in the end."

OUTSIDE, THE FIRST HINT of dawn was already in the sky, with a freshening wind coming from the direction of the Lantic coast.

The ville was deserted, with the old theme park rides standing skeletal and abandoned. The rest of the baron's sec men seemed to know that disaster had struck, and they were without a leader. Without a job. Now Greenglades would stand open until someone else came along with the strength and the firepower to snatch it and hold it.

But that was no concern of Ryan Cawdor's.

Chapter Forty-Three

Ryan stopped the group when it was within a couple of hundred yards of the hidden redoubt entrance.

"Let's just try that radio one more time before we make the jump."

Krysty had been carrying the small radio, and she handed it over. Ryan adjusted the set and switched it on, setting it to the one hundred wave band.

"Ryan calling Jak. Ryan calling Jak. You receiving me? Over."

The swampy area was quiet. There was the large lake of mud just to their right, with an occasional greasy bubble breaking from its surface.

"Come in, Jak. This is Ryan. Got a sort of message. Is there trouble, Jak? Over."

There was still nothing, except the whispering of the ghosts that inhabit the space between the cold stars.

"Fireblast! Come in, Jak! Come in, this is Ryan! What's the trouble, Jak? Over."

The radio remained stubbornly unresponsive. Ryan had a prickling, uneasy feeling. Jak wouldn't have been trying to contact him unless something had gone wrong. That was his gut feeling, and he couldn't shake it.

"One more try. Jak, come in. This is Ryan. We're making the jump in a few minutes. Come in, Jak. Over."

The radio crackled and mumbled. For one second Ryan heard a voice, but it was only a single word, clear as a bell.

"Lost."

"Was that the kid?" J.B. said. "Could've been Jak."

Ryan felt a surge of blazing anger, the futile rage of man faced with a recalcitrant machine. "Fuck you," he snarled, and heaved the radio out into the swamp, where it splashed into the sullen darkness of the deep slime.

"Nice one, lover," Krysty said. "Real clever move, that."

Ryan turned to look at her, a pulse beating in his forehead. She took a hesitant half step back at the sight of his face, but he fought the mood and controlled it. He sniffed and finally smiled. "You're right, lover. But it's done now."

"Then we might as well make the jump."

He nodded at her. "Sure."

THE WALLS WERE SILVERED glass and Ryan knew they were back in New Mexico. It hadn't been too bad a jump.

Outside the ruined redoubt the morning sun was breaking over the mountains to the east, throwing long shadows out across the desert.

They managed to pick their way down onto the

level ground without any difficulty, though Ryan was worried to see plentiful new tracks on the trail from the redoubt.

"Someone coming," Krysty said, busily tying her hair back off her neck with a black bandanna.

With the rising sun in his face, highlighting the dazzling white hair, it was impossible to mistake Jak Lauren.

He was riding a bay mare, spurring the horse on at a fast trot that turned into a dust-burning gallop when he spotted the little group of friends.

Krysty stared intently toward him as he closed the gap to a hundred yards. Her face set like pale marble, and she reached out to grip Ryan by the wrist. Hard enough to make him wince.

"Oh, no," she said, her voice soft and shocked.

Jak reined in the sweating horse, throwing himself from the saddle. "Heard your radio message. Hear mine?"

"No. What?"

The teenager's eyes blazed like chips of nuked ruby. "Dean."

"What?"

"Taken."

"When?"

"Yesterday afternoon. Christina shot one of gang. Questioned him."

"Still got him?" Ryan was unable to control the anxiety in his voice.

"Died," Jak said, as laconic as ever.

"Why didn't you ask him all—"

"Did. Gang of slavers. Way north. Used gateway. Took Dean."

Ryan suddenly thought of the Last Destination button. If this gang had jumped, then he could follow them. All wasn't lost.

"I'll go after them," he said. "Food and rest, then I'll go."

"One other thing found from wounded man. Before died."

"What?"

"Slaver's leader."

"Yeah?"

"Russian. Name...Zimyanin."

Follow Remo and Chiun on more of their extraordinary adventures....

Take
2 explosive books
plus a
mystery bonus
FREE

Mail to: Gold Eagle Reader Service
3010 Walden Ave.
P.O. Box 1394
Buffalo, NY 14240-1394

YEAH! Rush me 2 FREE Gold Eagle novels and my FREE mystery bonus.
Then send me 4 brand-new novels every other month as they come off
the presses. Bill me at the low price of just $16.80* for each shipment.
There is NO extra charge for postage and handling! There is no minimum
number of books I must buy. I can always cancel at any time simply by returning a shipment at your cost or by returning any shipping statement marked
"cancel." Even if I never buy another book from Gold Eagle, the 2 free books
and mystery bonus are mine to keep forever.   164 AEN CH7R

Name	(PLEASE PRINT)	
Address		Apt. No.
City	State	Zip

Signature (if under 18, parent or guardian must sign)

* Terms and prices subject to change without notice. Sales tax applicable in
N.Y. This offer is limited to one order per household and not valid to
present subscribers. Offer not available in Canada.

GE2-98

From the creator of

comes a new journey in a world with little hope...

OUTLANDERS

OUTLANDERS

#63814	EXILE TO HELL	$5.50 U.S. $6.50 CAN.	☐ ☐
#63815	DESTINY RUN	$5.50 U.S. $6.50 CAN.	☐ ☐
#63816	SAVAGE SUN	$5.50 U.S. $6.50 CAN.	☐ ☐

(limited quantities available on certain titles)

TOTAL AMOUNT	$
POSTAGE & HANDLING	$
($1.00 for one book, 50¢ for each additional)	
APPLICABLE TAXES*	$ _____
TOTAL PAYABLE	$ _____
(check or money order—please do not send cash)	

GOLD EAGLE

GOUTBACK1

Desperate times call for desperate measures. Don't miss out on the action in these titles!

STONY MAN™

#61910	FLASHBACK	$5.50 U.S.	☐
		$6.50 CAN.	☐
#61911	ASIAN STORM	$5.50 U.S.	☐
		$6.50 CAN.	☐
#61912	BLOOD STAR	$5.50 U.S.	☐
		$6.50 CAN.	☐
#61913	EYE OF THE RUBY	$5.50 U.S.	☐
		$6.50 CAN.	☐
#61914	VIRTUAL PERIL	$5.50 U.S.	☐
		$6.50 CAN.	☐

(limited quantities available on certain titles)

TOTAL AMOUNT	$
POSTAGE & HANDLING	$
($1.00 for one book, 50¢ for each additional)	
APPLICABLE TAXES*	$ _____
TOTAL PAYABLE	$ _____
(check or money order—please do not send cash)	

To order, complete this form and send it, along with a check or money order for the total above, payable to Gold Eagle Books, to: **In the U.S.:** 3010 Walden Avenue, P.O. Box 9077, Buffalo, NY 14269-9077; **In Canada:** P.O. Box 636, Fort Erie, Ontario, L2A 5X3.

Name: _____

Address: _____ City: _____

State/Prov.: _____ Zip/Postal Code: _____

*New York residents remit applicable sales taxes.
Canadian residents remit applicable GST and provincial taxes.

GOLD EAGLE®

GSMBACK1